SAVIOR OF REGRETS

a VERONA LEGACY story

SAVIOR OF REGRETS

A VERONA LEGACY STORY

L A COTTON

Published by Delesty Books

Edited by Andrea M. Long
Proofread by Sisters Get Lit.erary Author Services
Cover Artwork by Dily Iola Designs
Cover Designed by Lianne Cotton

CHAPTER 1

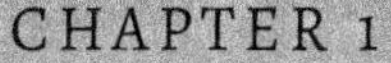

CAITLIN

His eyes followed me as I worked the floor, serving drinks and collecting up empties. They never left me, constantly reminding me that my life wasn't my own.

That he owned me.

God, I really hated this gig. The leering men and wandering hands. I didn't work the stage no more; Zander had put a stop to that after he almost killed a guy for getting too handsy with me. Back then, part of me had thought it was charming—him protecting my honor like that—but I soon learned that protection came at a cost.

One I had been unwilling to pay.

Zander DiMarco owned this place. It was one of his high-end strip clubs in and around Providence, its door only open to those with fat wallets and expensive tastes. I'd thought it would be a safe bet.

I was wrong.

"Caitlin," Shaun yelled over to me. "Table four drinks are up."

Nodding, I made my way over, trading my empty tray for the one full of glasses of whisky.

"It's the good stuff," he said with a wink. "So serve it with a smile."

I rolled my eyes, and he stuck his tongue between his teeth, making a tsking noise. "Lover boy can't take his eyes off you tonight."

"Don't call him that." A shudder raced through me.

"Is it so bad to have the boss's attention?"

I forced a false smile.

If only he knew.

Of course, everyone at DiMarco's knew to some extent. They saw the poorly covered bruises, heard me cry in the bathroom. But the number one rule of working here was not to ask questions you might not like the answer to.

And nobody, *nobody* questioned the boss.

I was Zander's favorite girl. Too good to work the stage, but not good enough to avoid floor duty. Because everyone had to pay their dues, even the boss's favorite.

Tray in hand, I headed for the table. One of the guys looked up and gave me a wolfish smile. "Well, hey there, pretty lady."

Oh good, a charmer.

Offering him a fake smile, I gently placed down their drinks. The other two guys barely acknowledged me, too entranced by Gisele as she worked the pole with her lithe, scantily clad body.

"Enjoy your drinks," I said. But the second I stepped away, Charmer's hand shot out and grabbed my wrist.

"What's the rush, sweetheart?"

"I'm sorry, but I have to—"

"Relax," he chuckled, "we're all here to have a good time. Right, Dominic?"

"Oh, I'm sure I could have a real good time with you, darling." Charmer's friend ran his eyes up and down my body, making me feel like a thousand spiders crawled under my skin. "How much for a private dance?" he grunted, pulling out his wallet.

"I'm just a server. You can speak to the boss about a private dance with any one of the dancers." I flicked my head to the stage.

"Thing is though, Red," he said, referring to my thick, auburn curls. "I don't want a dance off any of them. I want one off you."

My eyes darted to Shaun, hoping he would spot me and run interference before Zander realized something was wrong.

Gently yanking my arm out of Charmer's grip, I flashed them both a saccharine smile. "You enjoy the rest of your evening."

Just as I turned to leave, a hand slammed against the table, startling me. "Hang on a minute, you little bit—"

"Gentlemen," Zander appeared at the table at lightning speed. I should have felt relieved, but this never ended well—for anyone.

"Who the fuck are you?" the one called Dominic asked.

"I'm Zander DiMarco, the owner of this fine establishment." He ran a hand through his slicked-back hair before straightening his tie. "Now, what seems to be the problem?"

"Your girl here denied me a dance. My money not good enough for you, DiMarco?"

"Your money is plenty good enough, Cabrioles."

The guy's brows went up. "You know who I am?"

"Dominic Cabrioles." Zander's eyes narrowed. "Clocked you the second you walked into the joint. It's not often we have one of Lombardi's men in here. This is Marchetti territory," Zander added.

The guy snorted. "The Marchetti are a dying breed. Rumor has it Antonio is sick and that son of his has gone all soft since marrying the Capizola heir."

Everyone knew who the Marchetti were; the local crime family who ran most of Rhode Island. They hailed from Verona County but held power across the state. Their men came this way every couple of months to collect pizzo—protection money—and while Zander always paid up, he never did it with a smile.

Tensions between him and the Marchetti were even worse since there had been an incident a few weeks back. DiMarco's got trashed in a series of break-ins targeting Marchetti owned businesses and their associates.

But you didn't just cut ties with them.

"It's all a game," Zander said smoothly. "You just have to know how to play it."

There was something in his smirk. A wicked dark glint that made me bristle.

"I only like playing games if the prize is worthwhile," Dominic drawled, swirling his glass around. "And she..." He pointed at me. "Is a prize worth winning."

Zander stiffened, his entire posture tight with anger. But he managed to rein it in. "Caitlin is one of my best."

"I want to buy a dance. A private dance. I'll make it worth your while." He ran his finger over his thick leather wallet.

"Cait, go get us another round of drinks. It seems like me and my friends have things to discuss."

"Wha—"

"Now, Cait."

I hurried away, my heart in my throat. Surely, Zander wasn't seriously going to make me dance for him?

Bile sloshed in my stomach as I approached the bar.

"What's up?" Shaun asked.

"Table four needs another round please." My voice shook.

He studied me, leaning closer. "Something happen?"

"I... no, I'm fine." I smiled weakly. "Zander knows them. Or they know Zander."

"Just... be careful, Cait. Guys like that," he flicked his head toward them, "they always want something."

Wasn't that the truth.

He set about making their drinks and when they were done, I headed back toward the table on slow, shaky legs.

Zander reached for me, his hand slipping around my waist to steady my approach. "Thank you, Cait." He waited for me to place down the drinks. "Dominic, Jasper, and I were just discussing your... talent."

"Zander was telling us, you're quite the dancer."

"I..." Heat flooded my cheeks as I dipped my gaze.

"Don't hide." Zander's fingers dug into my waist. "I've

arranged a special viewing for my new friends. In the Purple Room."

The air left my lungs.

"I-I don't dance anymore." My eyes locked on his, silently pleading with him not to make me do this.

"Well, tonight you'll make an exception. Go and get ready. We'll be there in twenty."

"Zander, please." My voice cracked.

"Run along now, dolcezza. And change into something a little more… enticing." Zander slapped me on the butt, and I stumbled away from the table, hardly able to believe what was happening.

"Cait, what is it?" Mariella intercepted me as I burst into the back room.

"Zander… he…" I gasped, a big greedy lungful of air that did absolutely nothing to ease the fear taking over me. "He wants me to dance in the Purple Room."

"Oh, sweetie." She rested a hand on my shoulder. "It kind of comes with the territory."

It did. But not for me, not anymore.

Zander was too jealous. He'd almost killed a guy for touching me. I couldn't believe he'd just hand me over to that… that sleazeball.

"You know what happened the last time I danced for someone," I said to Mari.

"Maybe he's moving on."

"What is that supposed to mean?" It came out harsh.

"I'm just saying… perhaps you're not his favorite toy anymore and this is his way of letting you know it."

"Wow," I breathed. "Thanks a bunch."

"Shit, Cait, I don't mean it like that. You know I love

you, girl. But I thought you wanted out from under his shadow?"

"I do… but…" At least I knew what to expect with him. Zander was the devil in sheep's clothing, yes. But sometimes it was a case of better the devil you knew.

"It's one dance. Do it and you might win his favor. Don't do it and…" Her expression fell.

"Yeah, I know." I rolled my shoulders back and took a deep breath. "Can you help me get ready?"

"Sure thing." She laced her arm through mine. "Let's go see what we can do."

THE MUSIC THRUMMED THROUGH ME, amplifying the wild beat of my heart. It was dark, the mood lighting casting a deep purple hue around the small room. There was a long chaise and a wingback chair, a dark wood coffee table, and then the stage where I stood, my hand poised on the pole.

Mariella had given me one of her outfits to wear, a black lace bralette with matching booty shorts, and six-inch killer stiletto boots.

It was worlds away from the dainty and graceful outfits I used to wear dancing ballet.

I ran my hand up and down the pole, trying to expend some of the nervous energy coursing through me. But it only doubled when the door opened, a ring of light illuminating the profile of Dominic… and Zander?

They sat down. Zander in the chair, Dominic sprawled back on the chaise. Neither of them spoke as the music rose and a spotlight went on over my head. But I heard their intake of breath as I slowly circled the pole, letting muscle memory rise to the surface. It had been a while, months. I hadn't forgotten though, gripping the pole above my head and arching my back to gently dip down. Turning on the rise, I hooked a leg around the cool aluminum and spun myself around with ease, adrenaline drowning out everything else.

I loved to dance.

Loved the freedom that came with giving over to your body's movement. I reveled in how my muscles contracted and expanded to allow me to become one with the music.

The track shifted to something slower, more seductive as I danced my heart out, completely ignoring Zander's possessive stare, and Dominic's dark, hungry gaze. In that moment, it didn't matter that one of them owned me and one of them wanted to own me. Up there on that stage, I was free.

My eyes fluttered as I dipped and rolled, swayed and flew. Dancing wasn't just something you did; it was something you became. The music was my heartbeat, fueling me, pushing me. Breathing life into me.

I didn't dare look at Zander or Dominic. They were mere spectators. For these few moments, I held all the power here.

The closing notes of the song started to fade out and I came to a stop, my chest heaving, my breaths ragged. My muscles zinged and popped but I'd never felt better.

Until Zander stood, calling my name. "Come over

here," he demanded. "Come and give Mr. Cabrioles what he's owed."

Owed.

God, I hated that word.

I hated everything about it.

Gingerly, I moved to the steps leading down from the stage. Each one was like a shotgun to my heart, the adrenaline melting away. I didn't want this life. I never wanted this life. But sometimes bad things happened to good people.

"Dance for me, Red." Dominic shuffled on the chaise, letting his legs fall open. He patted his thigh, indicating I should sit on his lap.

"Go to him," Zander demanded.

Steeling myself, I approached him, refusing to acknowledge the obvious bulge in his trousers.

My stomach churned as I began to sway my hips, running my hands up and down my body. Throwing my head back, I dipped low, spreading my legs wide and then I glided back up. Dominic's eyes turned hooded, a wicked glint there. I risked glancing at Zander to gauge his reaction.

Dominic wasn't touching me… yet. But sexual energy radiated from him. Carnal lust and hunger swirling in the air around us.

I wanted to yell at Zander to stop this madness, to get on my knees and beg, but I wouldn't. Not now, not ever. Because my dignity was the only thing I had left. And no matter what Zander did to me, no matter how hard he pushed, I wouldn't give him the satisfaction of believing I needed him anymore than I already did.

"So fucking hot." Dominic's hand shot out and he grasped my hip, dragging me closer. I stumbled a little, my hands going to his shoulders to steady myself. I waited for Zander to lose his cool, to put an end to this game. But he didn't.

"I paid good money for this," he drawled, trailing his fingers over my bare skin. "Make it worth my while."

"Do as the man says," Zander said calmly. Too damn calmly.

What the hell was going on?

My palms were sticky, my heart a runaway train in my chest. I could smell the overbearing scent of his cologne, taste the bitter scent of liquor on his breath. His hands were too big, too wandering as he mapped the curves of my body.

"Ride me, Red." He smirked. "Show me what you can do."

Bile rushed up my throat as I tried to keep my distance. I didn't want to be here, doing this. My life wasn't supposed to turn out this way.

It wasn't supposed to—

Dominic cupped my ass and pulled me closer as he slid forward on the chaise, making all of him press up against all of me. I gulped, trying not to vomit all over him.

"Watch your fucking hands," Zander finally protested.

"Yeah, yeah, keep your hair on, DiMarco. I know the deal."

Deal...

My body began to tremble as I fought the urge to knee him in the balls and make a run for it. I'd stupidly thought this was all over when Zander took a shine to me.

But maybe Mari was right—maybe he was over me.

I didn't know how to feel about that.

I didn't love Zander, not even close. Most of the time, I hated every fiber of his being. And I was definitely scared of him. But at least I knew what to expect with him.

Dominic relaxed back against the chaise again and left me to my own devices. The air turned thick with tension as Zander tracked my every move. I didn't meet his heavy gaze. I couldn't. Just as I refused to make eye contact with Dominic.

After two more songs, Zander finally stood. "You had your money's worth, now get the fuck out."

Dominic chuckled, the epitome of cool, calm, and collected. "I'll give you whatever price you want if you let me fuck her, right here."

I froze, his offer echoing through my skull.

"You couldn't afford her." Zander laughed, but nothing about it sounded amused.

"Try me, DiMarco. I think you'll find I can be very—"

"Not tonight. But stop by again, and perhaps we can do business. Cait, go wait over by the bar." Zander dismissed me as if I was nothing.

Nobody.

Humiliation stained my cheeks as I went to the small bar in the corner of the room. A minute later the door opened. I glanced over just in time to see Dominic disappear into the stream of light.

When the door closed again, Zander was looking right at me. "Come here," he said, crooking a finger at me.

I went to him, hardly surprised when he curved his hand around the back of my neck and held me there. "You did well tonight, dolcezza. Maybe I should consider putting you on the roster again."

"I… I'd prefer not to dance."

"But you're so good at it." His eyes gave nothing away, which unnerved me. "He offered two thousand dollars to feel your tight little pussy wrapped around his cock, dolcezza." Zander leaned in, his warm breath fanning my cheek. "Something tells me he'll come back with a higher offer. Would you like that, Cait? Would you like him to pay all that money to fuck you?"

"You… you know I wouldn't."

"Right answer." Zander's fingers flexed around my neck, yanking my head back to leave me completely at his mercy. He ran his tongue along the seam of my lips before kissing me. Claiming me.

"You're mine, dolcezza. But maybe I'd be a fool if I didn't consider making a buck or two out of you. With Marchetti breathing down my neck, business is harder than ever."

Oh God.

He meant it.

Zander meant every word.

And something told me, if he sold me to Dominic for sex, it would just be the start of a long line of negotiations.

Negotiations that wouldn't end well for me.

CHAPTER 2

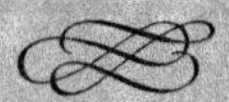

MATTEO

"What's up with you?" My sister nudged my sneaker with hers. "You're moping."

"Am not." I folded my arms over my chest, in a totally non-mopey kind of way.

"You so are." She rolled her eyes. "Is it because Enzo and Nora are in New York, and Nicco and Ari are… doing whatever newlyweds do?"

The humor in her voice made me lift my eyes and glower at her. "Go away, pulce."

"Aww, don't be like that, Matt. I'm only busting your balls."

"Hey. Language."

"Jeez, *Dad*." She poked her tongue out at me. "You know your problem?"

"No," I sighed, "but I'm sure you're going to enlighten me."

"You need to get laid."

"Arabella!" I shot forward, glaring at her. "I swear to God, if you don't—"

"Oh my God." She fell about the chair, laughing. "You should see yourself."

I loved my sister, something fierce, but she was a real pain in my ass sometimes. Even more so since our cousin Nicco got married. Part of me got it. We were young. Too fucking young to be wifed up. But what Nicco and Arianne had… it was something rare. It was that once-in-a-lifetime kind of love.

"Seriously though, Matt. There must be someone you like. Verona County is a big place, and it isn't like you don't get around."

"I just haven't met the right girl yet." I gave her a dismissive shrug, pulling out my cell phone and absently scrolling through my messages.

It was true—I hadn't found the right girl. There had only ever been one woman to catch my eye and she'd forgotten about me the second I walked out of her apartment after the best sex of my life.

Shit. It had been almost a year ago now, and I still couldn't get that night out of my head.

Scrubbing a hand down my face, I stood. "I'm going out."

"Out? But I thought we were going to hang out."

"Change of plans, pulce." I rubbed her head, and she swatted me away like a fly. "I need a drink."

Something strong.

~

L'Anello's was busy for a Sunday night, but then it was Valentine's Day. Guys were out to impress their girlfriends, and girls were out to try to score the man of their dreams.

Maybe this was a bad fucking idea.

"Matteo, what's up?" Billy, the bartender, headed in my direction. "No hot date tonight?"

"You know how it goes, Bill. Too many fish in the sea."

"A guy like you could have your pick of the bunch."

"If I didn't know better, I'd say you were trying to hit on me," I joked.

"In your dreams, my friend. I'm as straight as they come. Usual?"

"Yeah, make it a double."

"Sure thing."

I turned around and leaned back on the bar, scanning the room. A couple of familiar faces tipped their heads in greeting. Most of the clientele were couples, sitting close together, staring dreamily into their date's eyes.

A pang of jealousy cut through me.

I'd never had that.

Never really considered I could have it. Sure, my name was Matteo Bellatoni, but I was still a Marchetti by blood. My life, my loyalty, and my future belonged to the Family.

Finding a good woman to accept that, to accept everything that came with being a mafioso was no easy feat.

Except, my cousins—my best friends in the entire world—had both managed just that, leaving me to play fifth wheel to their relationships.

It sucked.

Big time.

But it wasn't like I could move on anyway. No, I was still hung up on the Irish beauty who had stolen my heart that night in Providence all those months ago.

"Get a fucking grip," I muttered to myself. I was a twenty-year-old guy for fuck's sake. I had the world at my feet. Good friends, good family, a job that would never see me go without.

"Double whisky on the rocks," Billy said, and I turned around, accepting the glass from him.

"Thanks." I knocked it back, downing it in one. "Hit me with another."

"Shit, man. It must be bad." He smirked and I flipped him off.

"Matteo, that you?" Jimmy, the owner of L'Anello's, strolled over to me, holding his hand out. We shook hands and he flagged down Billy to bring us another round of drinks.

"Alone?"

"Yeah, Nic's having dinner with Arianne, and Enzo is—"

"With his woman in New York. I remember now. Sucks to be us, right?" He clapped me on the back, and I faked a smile. Jimmy was a middle-aged, balding man with a missing tooth and crooked smile. My sex life wasn't exactly happening, but it wasn't that bad, not yet.

"Speak for yourself, Jimmy," I said. "For all you know I could be meeting a hot date here tonight."

"You can't kid a kidder, Matt." He took a sip of his drink, and tsked through the side of his mouth. "How about burning off some excess steam tonight?"

"Come on, man, you know I'm too pretty to get in the ring."

L'Anello's wasn't only a bar in downtown La Riva, it was a front for Verona County's underground fight ring. Before Nicco met Arianne, I'd watched him beat many opponents. They called him the Prince of Hearts, a play on his ruthlessness in the ring, but that all stopped when he fell in love. Enzo dabbled occasionally, but he didn't have the natural talent Nic possessed.

And me?

Well, I was a lover not a fighter.

"Try it on for size. You never know, you might like it."

"I doubt that, Jimmy. Maybe another time."

"Sure thing, Matt. Sure thing." He squeezed my shoulder before clapping me on the back again. "Enjoy your evening, kid."

I snorted at that.

'Kid' was a word the older men liked to use to remind us of our place in the hierarchy of things. But it was steeped in irony considering that as one of Nicco's most trusted men, I outranked nearly every man in here.

My father, Michele Bellatoni was Antonio Marchetti's second. And Nicco his third.

It hadn't always been that way. Enzo's dad had been Antonio's second, but he was gone now. And although the Family was still recovering from shock of Vincenzo Marchetti's betrayal, we were stronger than ever.

"Hey, Matteo," a sultry voice said, and I turned around to find Gina Fabiano smiling at me.

"Gina, you're looking beautiful." I leaned in and kissed her cheek. Left and then right. She placed a perfectly manicured hand on my shoulder and gazed at me through thick lashes. "It's good to see you."

"You too." I returned her smile.

Gina was the daughter of one of the Family's associates. Mario Fabiano owned a string of tailors across Verona County. He was Uncle Toni's first choice every time.

"I didn't realize you were back," I said.

Gina had been studying in Italy.

"Just for a few weeks. My Nonna is sick."

"I'm sorry to hear that."

"Thanks." She tucked her silky dark locks behind one ear. "Are you here alone?"

"I… yeah. Pretty pathetic, right?"

"I'm here with my cousin, her fiancé, and his friend. But between you and me, he's not my type." Gina brazenly checked me out, letting her gaze linger on my mouth.

"You should give the guy a chance," I said, not wanting to get involved.

"Or." She moved closer. "You could pretend to be my ex and we could get out of here."

"Listen, Gina, it's good to see you, it is. But I'm not—"

"Seriously? You're not interested?" She glanced down at herself as if the idea that I would turn her down was preposterous.

I knew most of the male population would agree. Enzo especially. He'd definitely have something to say about me turning down a girl like Gina Fabiano. But I wasn't feeling it. And truth be told, she wasn't my type.

Nowhere close.

"I came to have a quiet drink before I head home."

"Alone…" Her brow lifted.

"You should get back to your date," I said.

"Your loss." She smiled but it had lost some of its sweetness. "Good to see you again, Matteo."

Gina walked away from me, drawing the eye of almost every man in the room. Maybe I was a fool. Maybe I should have taken her up on her offer and tangled with her between the sheets. Sex didn't have to mean anything more than a good time. I knew that.

I knew… and yet, I couldn't do it.

I had no desire to do it.

Fuck. I needed another drink.

Or three.

THE NEXT MORNING, I found myself hungover and alone. After lying in bed for almost an hour, willing myself to get up, I finally dragged my sorry ass into the bathroom and freshened up. I needed extra strong coffee, and something to soak up the liquor.

I'd shared this apartment with Enzo before he'd decided to move out and get a love nest with Nora. It wasn't the same without him, so I didn't stay here a lot, preferring to stay at home with my family. But I couldn't begrudge him. If anyone deserved to be happy, it was E. He had a shitty life at the hands of his old man. Nora was his redemption. His salvation. She was everything he never knew he needed, and I didn't expect him to last long before he made it official and put a ring on her finger.

He was that damn serious about her.

I scrubbed a hand down my face as I padded into the kitchen and turned on the coffee machine. A bang on the door drew my attention. It was barely nine, and I didn't get a lot of visitors.

"Just a minute," I yelled, crossing the room, and opening the door. "Nicco."

"Hey." He grimaced, and I frowned. "What is it? What's wrong?"

"Can I come in?"

"As if you have to ask." I stepped aside and he slipped past me, making a beeline for the breakfast counter.

"I was just making coffee."

"Black, one sugar," he mumbled.

"I know how you take your coffee, Nic. What's up?"

Because this wasn't my best friend. His eyes were ringed with dark circles, and he looked like he'd hardly slept in days.

"Is it Ari? Is she—"

"She's fine. She's back at the apartment, sleeping. We had a late night."

"I bet you did." I smirked, but it melted away when his eyes shuttered with pain.

"Fuck, I don't know what to do."

"Nic, talk to me," I said, feeling like I was missing something huge.

"It's my dad."

"Uncle T?"

He nodded. "He's sick."

"I know. We all do." He had a heart attack earlier on in the year. But he was making a good recovery.

"No, you don't…" He let out a heavy sigh, anguish bleeding from him. "He lied, Matt. He lied to everyone. He isn't okay. He isn't fucking okay at all."

"He's not?"

"It's cancer."

The words echoed in my skull like gunfire.

"C-cancer?"

"Yeah. I found some medical letters."

"He didn't tell you?"

"What do you think?" His expression darkened. Nicco was the levelheaded one out of the three of us. I was the joker, the light-hearted one looking to make people smile. Enzo was the storm. Cold and unforgiving. He didn't trust easily, and his heart was buried under a thick layer of ice.

Then there was Niccolò. He was somewhere in the middle. As the boss's eldest and only son, he knew the responsibility weighing on his shoulders, and he carried it with nothing but strength and honor. He was already a true leader. Men respected him, strangers revered him, and our enemies feared him.

"Shit, Nicco, I'm sorry."

"He said he was fine. He said—" Nicco buried his face in his hands. I gave him a second, waiting. When he eventually lifted his face, what I saw there made my heart squeeze.

"I always knew that one day, I would take his place. But it's too soon. I'm not… ready."

"You've got this, man. Arianne will be right by your side; me and E too. You're not alone in this, cous."

"I thought I had more time."

I got it. If Uncle Toni had to step down, or worse, Nicco would become the boss. That kind of pressure, it left little room to play happy family with your wife. And they were so young.

An idea struck me. "My old man—"

Nicco gave me a weak smile. "We both know Michele isn't cut out to be the boss. Besides, I'm not even sure my father would allow it. No, this falls to me, and me alone."

Silence echoed between us, and then I said, "Whatever you need, cous. I'm here."

"Thank you, Matt. It helps knowing I have you and E in my corner."

"Of course." I nodded. I'd known Nicco since we were babies. He and Enzo were the closest thing to a brother I'd ever have.

"Have you heard from Enzo?" he asked me.

"A couple of texts. He's too busy wooing his girl." I smirked, and Nicco chuckled.

"Who'd have thought it? Lorenzo Marchetti tamed by a female."

"Stranger things have happened."

"You know, it's your turn next. Arianne has some nice friends at—"

"Jesus, does everyone around here think I need help finding a decent girl?"

"Who—"

"Arabella," I scoffed. "She was giving me shit last night."

"She means well." He pinned me with a hard look. "We all do."

"I can handle my own affairs, Nic."

He held up his hands. "I'm shutting up now."

"Good," I grumbled. "I have my whole life ahead of me to think about settling down."

Yet, when I looked at what Nicco and Arianne had, what Enzo had found with Nora… I wanted that. Fuck, I wanted it. But I didn't want it with just any girl. I wanted it with *the* girl.

The one.

All I had to do was find her.

"Listen. When Enzo gets back, I want the two of you to head to Providence. DiMarco is still making noise and we need to remind him that you don't back out on a deal with the Family."

"You want me to go?" I asked.

Zander DiMarco was one of the Family's business associates in Providence. He owned a string of successful strip clubs that brought in a lot of money. The guy was a grade A asshole, but money talked, and DiMarco knew how to make it in spades.

"Yeah, I'd go myself, but I'm not sure that's wise right now."

Because his old man was sick and that kind of burden… it wreaked havoc with a man's soul. Especially a guy like Nicco.

"Yeah, okay," I said.

"You sure you're okay?"

"Yeah."

It was just a trip to Providence. What was the worst that could happen?

You could try and look up Caitlin again…

I immediately shut down that train of thought. It had

been months, and she'd made it perfectly clear she wanted nothing more to do with me. I had to let that shit go—I had to let the idea, the fantasy of her go.

"Who knows, maybe you'll meet the girl of your dreams there." Nicco chuckled, and I flipped him off, adding, "At DiMarco's club? I highly doubt it."

His girls were all beautiful, but I wasn't sure I could handle my woman dancing for other men's enjoyment. And I never wanted to be the kind of man who asked a woman to change for him. I could enjoy the view like every other patron at a strip joint, but I wouldn't find anything more in a place like that.

"How far do we go?" I asked, dreading his answer.

Enzo was our enforcer. He had no problem persuading people—associates, enemies, sometimes even allies—to do our bidding using whatever means necessary. I preferred a softer touch. Negotiation. Coercion. Blackmail if it came down to it. But Zander DiMarco had been pushing against our agreement for a while now. He had warning after warning. If he refused to play ball, then it was likely he'd feel the full wrath of the Family before long.

"Relax, Matt. I'm not asking you to go put a bullet in his head. But DiMarco is becoming a thorn in our side. A thorn my father wants blunting as soon as possible. I'm trusting you can find a way to remind him how things will go if he doesn't play nice. If that fails, I'm sure Enzo can help demonstrate how difficult life will be should he decide to keep disrespecting our arrangement."

"Got it, Boss." My lips curved.

Nicco shook his head, letting out a weary sigh. "I don't think I'll ever get used to that."

"You should probably try."

Because if Uncle Toni was really sick... Nicco could find himself taking charge sooner rather than later.

And I didn't envy my best friend at all.

CHAPTER 3

CAITLIN

"Oh my God, Cait. What happened?" Gisele reached for my face, but I swatted her hand away.

"It's nothing, really."

"Girl, that isn't nothing." She scoffed. "You look like you got mauled by a—"

"Gisele, please…" I silently pleaded with her; aware we were drawing an audience.

I'd done my best to conceal the fingermarks around my throat, but the skin along your neck wasn't the easiest place to cover up. I'd even added a scarf, but the bruising was still obvious. And then there was the slight split in my lip.

Maybe I should have stayed at my apartment and feigned a stomach flu. But sometimes it was easier to placate Zander by putting on a brave face and pretending nothing was wrong.

Besides, it could have been worse. He could have actually let Dominic touch me. He hadn't—and for that, I was grateful. Even if he had punished me for exacting his wishes.

Men.

I would never understand their double standards or the games they liked to play.

But I was okay... a few bruises here and there was nothing.

I'd survived much worse.

"I should get ready for my shift," I said, slipping past her to go to my locker.

"Hey, Cait," she called after me.

"Yeah?"

"I'm here, if you ever need someone to talk to."

"Thanks." I smiled, but we both knew I wouldn't take her up on her offer.

I was Zander's favorite toy. If I spoke out against him, I'd find myself living on the streets without a job again. And although he was the devil in an expensive Italian suit, there were still worse things out there than Zander DiMarco.

Ignoring the curious stares of the other girls, I hurried to my locker and dumped my purse and jacket. I was tying my purple-trimmed black apron when Zander called my name.

"Caitlin, my office," he commanded.

My stomach sank. I was hoping he would leave me alone after last night; he usually did. But I guess fate was feeling decidedly cruel.

Gisele shot me a sympathetic look as I passed her and made my way out of the dancers dressing room along the hall to Zander's office.

"Come in," he said, not bothering to look at me, too busy poring over the paperwork on his desk.

"Did you need something?"

"Sit." He motioned to the couch, and I sat down, folding my hands in my lap.

Zander continued checking his papers, murmuring to himself as he punched in numbers on the calculator.

"All done." He threw the stack down and smiled at me. "How are you today?"

"I'm fine, thank you."

"Good, that's good. Last night was… a misjudgment on my part, and for that, I'm sorry."

"It was nothing."

He let out a heavy sigh, rising from his chair to walk over to me. "You're so beautiful, Cait." Sliding his hand along my neck, he gently gripped my jaw and forced me to look up at him. "I was too rough."

I suppressed a shudder. He was always rough. Most men like Zander were. They liked the power, the fear… they liked to possess women to the point of pain.

"I'm sorry."

His apology echoed around my skull. In all the time I'd known Zander, he'd never once apologized.

I didn't know what to make of it.

He ran his thumb over my bottom lip, letting the pillow of flesh pop as he pulled it away.

"I just get so angry when I see other men watch you."

"I thought you wanted me to dance for him?"

"I did, dolcezza. I did. And you did such a good job.

But the way I feel about you, Caitlin… it's enough to drive a man to the brink of insanity."

I was his.

Despite the fact we hadn't ever officially gone public or labelled our relationship, I was under no illusion that this was anything but the fact Zander DiMarco had decided I belonged to him.

When he'd first found me and took me off the streets, Zander had given me a safe place to stay, and I'd lapped up his attention. But then he'd started to hint at his true intentions. For so long, I managed to keep him at arm's length. Until one night, Zander had grown tired of waiting for me and had taken what he'd wanted all along.

Me.

"You know I'm not interested in any of those men," I said. There had never been a man to catch my attention. Except one, on a stormy night when I'd found myself in a dark alley with another Zander DiMarco of the world. A man who thought he could just take what he wanted.

I would never forget Matteo. He'd saved my life that night, and then gave me one of the best nights of my almost twenty-one years on Earth.

But that's all it could ever be.

I'd refused to give him my number, locking him away in a little box where Zander couldn't touch him.

If he ever found out about that night… It didn't bear thinking about.

A violent shudder rolled through me, and I took a calming breath, trying to keep my expression neutral.

"So why do you keep stalling, dolcezza? It would be so much easier if you moved in with me. We could play happy family. I could go to sleep every night holding you, wake every morning with you in my arms."

Lies.

It was all lies.

Zander didn't know how to do any of those things. He didn't know how to be soft and tender. Even now, his fingers were gripping me a little too tightly, his jaw clenched with frustration.

"I've told you before, I'm not ready."

He knew why.

I'd given him that much.

But I could see from the flash of anger in his eyes, my excuses weren't enough anymore.

"I've waited," he said. "I've been patient and given you space. But a man will only wait so long, Cait. I can't give you up, dolcezza. I won't."

"I should probably get to work."

Wrong answer.

My neck wrenched as he yanked my face upward, my muscles screaming in protest. Tears pricked the corners of my eyes. "Z-Zander please, I have to go to work."

"You work for me, or have you forgotten that? You. Are. Mine. Caitlin. The sooner you get on board with that, the better. Now be a good girl and kiss me." He practically dragged me to my feet, giving me no time to back out as his lips slammed down on mine. His fingers slid into my hair, clutching me like a rag doll. A puppet. My whole life had been nothing more than a show I had no control over. I came to Providence to start over, but the cycle just continued.

And I hated it.

I hated that I attracted a certain kind of man. I hated that I wasn't strong enough to walk away.

But walking away wasn't that simple.

I had nothing. Nowhere to go, no one to turn to. I was all alone in the world except for the few friends I had at DiMarco's.

I went lax in his arms, knowing that fighting would only stoke the anger rising inside him.

"God, dolcezza, it's like I can't get enough of you." His hands ran over my body, clawing at my modest black skirt.

"Zander," I breathed. "It's the middle of the day, everyone is expecting me."

That snapped him out of his trance, and he backed away slightly. "You're right." He smoothed down his shirt. "Later then."

I nodded, not trusting myself to speak. Slipping around him, I straightened my skirt and headed for the door.

"One day, Cait, you're going to give me what I want."

Pretending not to hear him, I hurried from the room and headed straight to the women's bathroom. I needed a minute to collect my thoughts and stop shaking.

"THERE YOU ARE. I was beginning to wonder—"

"Not now, Shaun," I said, busying myself with polishing glasses. DiMarco's was always quieter in the afternoon, so it gave the floor staff a chance to prepare for the night ahead. Glasses were buffed, tables were cleaned, and the refrigerators and liquor shelves were restocked. It was laborious work, but I didn't mind it. It kept my mind busy.

Zander came and went, sometimes sitting at his usual spot in the corner of the club on the raised platform, giving him a vantage point of the entire room. He liked people to know he was the boss, just like he liked people to know he was always there watching them. It was part of his power play.

But during the day, he had meetings, telephone calls, and paperwork to do, so he wasn't around so much. I took pleasure in those moments, and for a second, I could almost imagine being invisible.

I was busy restocking the tealight votives on each table when I felt him. Zander. He'd barely left me thirty minutes before coming to check up on me.

His behavior toward me was growing more erratic. More possessive. And I knew the thin rope of control I still had would soon snap.

He wanted an answer—an answer I couldn't give him, not willingly.

I glanced over my shoulder, and sure enough, he was across the room watching me. His eyes darkened as he swirled the glass of scotch around in his hand before bringing the rim to his lips. I should have looked away, refused to play his game of cat and mouse. But I wasn't about to cower, not now. Not ever.

"Cait?" Gisele tapped me on the shoulder, and I almost jumped out of my skin. "Sorry, I didn't mean to startle you."

"It's okay." I flashed her a warm smile, still able to feel

Zander's eyes drilling holes into the side of my face.

"He's getting more and more obvious," she said between gritted teeth.

"He just enjoys the chase."

"I can try to talk to him? Make him see that—"

"No, no. It's fine. I can handle Zander. But thank you."

"Of course." Her expression was etched with sympathy. "I'd help you get out if I could. But it's—"

"Gisele, I don't expect you or anyone else to fight my battles."

And I would never jeopardize her job like that. Zander wouldn't hesitate to get rid of anyone who tried to get in his way, his best dancers included. Because there were always more girls like Gisele and Marielle… and me. Girls looking to make a quick buck and escape whatever nightmare drove them to a place like DiMarco's in the first place.

A lot of them would argue it wasn't so bad. The club was one of the more high-end joints in Providence, and Zander and his guys afforded them a certain amount of protection—provided they did their job and brought in enough money.

"Ugh, duty calls." Gisele rolled her eyes, and I glanced back again to find Zander glaring at her.

"I'll see you later, okay?" She squeezed my hand before disappearing.

I headed for the bar, trying to keep busy. It was hard with Zander's eyes following me everywhere. Especially so early into my shift.

"Cait, do me a favor and go get some extra napkins, we're short," Shaun said, not looking up from the counter.

"Sure thing." Hurrying into the back, I went straight into the storeroom and grabbed as many packets of napkins as I could find. But when I turned around, Zander was blocking the door.

"Z-Zander, what are you—"

"Relax, dolcezza," he purred. "I just wanted to make sure you're okay. You seemed… tense after our talk this morning."

"I'm fine." I forced a smile. "But I should probably get these back to Shaun before he comes looking for me."

Zander stepped into the room, taking the air with him. "No one's coming back here, Caitlin. It's just you and me." He crowded me into the corner of the storeroom, my back hitting the shelves.

"I… I have to work."

"I'm your boss, and I think you should take a quick break."

"But I…"

"Stop, Cait." His hand shot out, grabbing my jaw. "Just stop."

Tears rushed up my throat as my heart crashed wildly in my chest. I thought I was safe. At least until later.

Fear flooded me, making it hard to breathe.

"I can't stop thinking about fucking Cabrioles with his hands on you. I should never have let him touch you." He brushed his thumb along my cheek. "He wasn't worthy of you, dolcezza."

"It doesn't matter," I said. "It's over. He won't be a problem no more."

Something flashed in Zander's eyes, but he nodded all the same. "Come here." His hand slipped to my neck, curving around my throat. He pulled me closer, forcing me to tilt my face up to look at him.

"The things I want to do to you. The things I want to show you..."

Oh God.

The knot in my stomach twisted. He wasn't going to let me walk away from this untouched. Not this time.

There was a feral look in his eyes. A hunger I'd seen too many times before.

"You're mine, Caitlin. Mine." He lowered his head, pressing his mouth to mine.

Every muscle inside me went rigid as I tried to breathe through the terror. My body trembled at his touch.

"Open up for me," he drawled, licking the seam of my lips, trying to force his way in.

"Zander, not here," I breathed, desperately trying to break out of his hold without seeming too forceful. "I have to—"

He smashed his body into mine, stealing the air from my lungs as he plunged his tongue into my mouth. My head smacked off the edge of the shelves, stars exploding in my vision.

"Zander, no." I tried to fight him, but he was too strong, too heavy, pressing the entire length of his body against mine.

Stars swam in my vision and tears stung my eyes. I heard the familiar clunk of his belt buckle, bile churning in my stomach.

"No," I cried. "Not here, not like—"

He backhanded me so hard my teeth rattled, and pain exploded along my jaw.

"You think you're too good for me? Is that it?" His hands began clawing at my legs, my thighs. My eyes grew heavy, the pounding in my skull making blood roar in my ears.

"I… no… *please…*"

Zander grabbed my face hard, squeezing my cheeks to the point of pain. "I'm going to enjoy this." He grinned, but it was dark and twisted.

That grin was the last thing I saw before oblivion claimed me.

~

"Stay with me, girl." The voice drifted in and out of my consciousness.

Or maybe that was me.

I couldn't figure it out.

Everything was blurry… like swimming underwater with your eyes open.

"Cait?" The voice sounded panicked. "Cait, hold on… we're almost there."

I wanted to ask where, but when my lips moved nothing but a tiny squeak came out. My mouth felt wrong, swollen and sore, and I could taste the coppery, metallic twang of blood on my tongue.

"Oh God," I murmured, agony shredding my insides. "What…? What…?"

"Shh." Someone reached over and squeezed my hand. "It's going to be okay, Cait."

"Where are you taking me?" Shaun's form shimmered in and out of focus.

"He thinks I'm taking you to Providence General. But fuck that," Shaun spat. "He went too far this time, Cait. Too fucking far. I'm going to drive you to Pawtucket and tell him we stopped for gas and you ran."

"W-what? That's crazy." He was crazy.

I couldn't run.

Where the hell would I go? I could barely keep awake.

"You need to disappear, okay? If he finds you... he'll kill you, Cait. I won't have that on my conscience."

"It hurts," I groaned, touching a shaky finger to my hair. When I pulled it away it was coated with sticky, dried blood. "Oh my God."

What the hell had he done to me?

A shudder went through me as hazy memories assaulted me. Hands grabbing, teeth and tongue, his strong body taking what wasn't his to take.

Oh God.

"We're almost there, just try and keep it together, okay?"

But I couldn't do it. I couldn't fight the agony radiating through my body, my face.

"Shaun," I murmured, barely a whisper. "I'm... I'm scared."

"It's going to be okay, Cait," he said. "It's going to be okay."

It was the last thing I heard.

CHAPTER 4

MATTEO

"Morning, Son," Dad said looking up from his newspaper. "I didn't expect to see you this morning. Nicco said you and Enzo were heading to Providence."

"We are but Enzo and Nora stayed an extra night. They should be back anytime, so I told Arabella I can give her a ride to school."

"You're good to her, Son."

"Of course he is." Mom breezed into the kitchen, swatting me with the towel when she noticed me try to pluck off the freshly made cornetti off the cooling rack. "Later," she chided. "You can have one later."

"I won't be here. I'll be out of town for a couple of nights."

Her shoulders bunched together. "Do I even want to know?"

"It's business, Marcella. They'll be fine."

"That's what they always say," she murmured, making herself busy.

Mom had grown up around my uncles and Nonno. She knew what this life entailed. Part of me sometimes wondered if she'd expected to get out when she married my father. But instead, he'd joined the ranks, swearing his allegiance to the Family. But Michele Bellatoni wasn't like most mafioso. He was quiet and contemplative, and he didn't abuse his power. That wasn't to say he hadn't gotten any blood on his hands—you didn't live this life and never experience death—but he wasn't hungry for it the way some were. He was a good guy.

One of the best.

The kind of man I always hoped to become.

"Just keep your wits about you, Son," he said, his eyes flicking to my mom. Once he was satisfied she wasn't paying us any attention, he added, "DiMarco is a wily sonofabitch."

"Ain't that the truth," I mumbled, swiping a cornetti while Mom's back was turned.

My old man chuckled, but then his expression soured. "Stay safe, Matteo, and watch your back."

THE FAMILIAR RUMBLE of Enzo's GTO drew my attention, and I drained my coffee. "Thanks, Mama. I'll see you soon, okay."

She came over to me, taking my face in her dainty hands. "You come back to me in one piece, figlio mio."

"Stop fussing over the boy, woman. He knows the drill by now. Besides, Zander DiMarco is all talk."

Glad he thought so. Because I wasn't so sure. Zander was a showboater. He loved the attention and reputation. In my experience, people like that were dangerous and unpredictable.

But this was my job. My father—the Family—expected me to fall in line and carry out Nicco's and Uncle Toni's orders. You didn't get to argue or shirk your responsibility. Once you swore Omertà, you were all in. *Famiglia prima di tutto*. The Family came first, always.

A heavy knock at the door indicated Enzo was too damn impatient to stay in his car.

"Lorenzo, how was the big city?" Mom greeted him.

"It's the Big Apple, woman," Dad called.

"Big city, big apple, it's all the same." She waved him off, directing Enzo toward the breakfast counter.

"Eat," she said.

"I'm good thanks, Aunt Marcella. I already ate."

"I bet you did." I smirked and he discreetly flipped me off, but I didn't miss the smug look of satisfaction on his face.

Dirty fucker.

But I was happy for him. Him and Nora. After all they'd been through, they deserved to be happy.

"You ready to roll?" He looked at me, and I nodded, snagging another cornetti.

"Let's go."

"Matteo!" Mom called after me, but we were already out of the door.

"So how was the Big Apple? Did you manage to do any sightseeing?" I asked Enzo the second we were in his car.

"Fuck off." Enzo grumbled.

"What? It's a legit question." I chuckled. "Let me guess, you did nothing but sightseeing… Nora was so pumped about the trip."

"She was pumped… a lot." The smug fucker smirked, and I shook my head.

"Did you just make a joke? Fuck, man, I'm going to need to check for your balls because that girl has you all—"

"We saw the sights. I made her come twice on the trip to Ellis Island."

I almost choked on my own breath. "I bet the other passengers loved that."

"Hired a private boat."

"Of course you did."

"If it's good enough for Nic." He shrugged.

"I'm happy for you, man, the two of you deserved to come out on top." Silence settled between us.

I knew Enzo probably wanted to take this trip as much as I did. Things were tense after DiMarco's club got hit in a string of attacks on our businesses a few months back, and since Enzo had been there when it happened… I doubted Zander would be in a hurry to see him either.

But Nicco wanted us to handle it—so here we were. About to handle it.

"She's good for you," I said, glancing over at my cousin.

He was softer around the edges, we all saw it. He was still Enzo—the love of a good woman didn't change that— but he was different.

My chest tightened, but I stuffed those memories down. It had been months since I'd spent one amazing night with a red-haired, green-eyed angel. Caitlin. If that was even her real name.

The three of us—Nicco, Enzo, and myself—had been in Providence and there'd been a bad storm. I'd stumbled across a girl being threatened in a dark alley... and well, one thing led to another, and I'd spent the night at her place. It was the best sex I'd ever had. But she refused to give me her number, and when I'd finally plucked up the courage to drive back down there a few weeks later, to track her down, she was gone.

And I went back to my life without the Irish beauty who had marked my soul.

Enzo's cell phone started ringing, but he took one look at the number and ignored it.

"Who is that?"

"Beats me." He shrugged.

It immediately started ringing again.

"Maybe you should answer it? It could be important."

He plucked the thing out of the center console and barked, "Yeah?"

I smirked. He was such a grumpy asshole still. I guess there were some things not even Nora could change.

"What? Yeah, okay. We're on our way." He hung up and grumbled, "Fuck."

"What is it?"

"When I was down here with Gino, I helped one of Zander's girls out. I think that fucker was hurting her."

"What?"

"Yeah, I don't know for sure what went down. But I

gave her my number in case she ever needed help."

"That was her?"

"No, that was the hospital."

"Fuck," I breathed. "Is she okay?"

"They didn't say much, but she specifically asked for me."

"She's at Providence General?"

"No, she's at County in Pawtucket. So, we're going to have to make a detour."

"Sure, man. Whatever you need." If there was one thing I hated, it was men who beat women.

THIRTY MINUTES LATER, we arrived at the hospital. A nurse directed us to the correct bay and Enzo went off to chat with another nurse. The place was a hive of activity as staff came and went, treating patients. I'd never much liked these places because they usually ended in bad news.

"She's down here." Enzo beckoned me over and we went down another hall. "Bay five." He grabbed the curtain and slipped inside.

"You came," a soft voice said.

"Yeah, I brought a friend with me. Is it okay if he—"

"Sure, I guess."

I went inside the small bay and my heart damn near exploded in my chest.

"You."

"I-I don't understand," I croaked, feeling myself grow hot all over.

"Wait a minute," Enzo frowned. "You two know each

other? But how?"

He was drilling holes into my face, but I couldn't take my eyes off the woman lying in bed. Her face was littered with bruises, and she had fingermarks around her neck.

Fucking fingermarks!

"Matteo?" Enzo gripped my shoulder as my knees went weak.

"Caitlin?" The word barely got out over the lump in my throat.

It was her.

The girl from that night.

She was one of Zander's girls?

A stripper?

It couldn't be.

Yet, Enzo knew her. He'd helped her. And she'd called him.

What the fuck was going on?

"Caitlin?" I said again, my heart crashing violently in my chest as I took in her injuries. She was beat up pretty bad. Someone had done this to her… someone had—

The penny dropped as Enzo's words from earlier came back to me.

"DiMarco did this?" My voice didn't sound like my own as red-hot fury exploded inside of me.

"Why is he here?" Caitlin stared at Enzo, her big green eyes pleading with him. I wanted to roar—to tell her not to look at him like he was her savior—but to look at me.

Fuck.

Fuck!

This was totally fucking with my head.

All I could think about was Zander putting his hands

on her, hurting her. *Abusing* her.

"Enzo, I said why is he—"

"I'll kill him," the words spilled from my lips. "I'll fucking kill him." My fists clenched by my sides as I plotted all the ways I'd make Zander fucking DiMarco pay for ever laying hands on Caitlin. Something slow and painful, something that would make sure he never laid another hand on Caitlin or any other woman for as long as—

"Matt." Enzo's hand clamped down on my shoulder and I glanced up at him, blinking.

"Yeah?"

"Can you wait outside?"

"The fuck?" I balked, glancing between them.

"You're scaring her, cous."

Scaring her?

I was scaring her?

"Caitlin?" I choked out, but she didn't look at me. She wouldn't.

"Come on, Matt. Let's take a walk." Enzo slung his arm over my shoulder and guided me out of her bay.

"No," I protested, glancing back over my shoulder. "I should stay with her. I should—"

"You need to cool it," he said, the second we were out of earshot.

"Cool it? You want me to cool it? Did you see what he did to her? DiMarco is a dead man walking," I seethed, anger coursing through me like wildfire, burning me inside out.

"You don't get to make that call, and you know it." Enzo scrubbed his jaw, his eyes hardening to slits. He didn't like this anymore than I did, but it wasn't his… whatever the fuck Caitlin was to me, lying in a hospital bed.

"Who is she to you?" he asked.

"Caitlin? She's… Fuck," I murmured, trying to rein in my thoughts. "Remember when we were up in Providence last summer, visiting DiMarco? We… I… I spent the night with her."

"You did?" He frowned.

"Don't look so surprised. Despite what you might think, I do know how to use it."

"I didn't… it doesn't matter." Enzo shook his head. "All that matters is that she's safe."

"She called you. Why the fuck did she call you?"

"I told you, I met her a few weeks ago, and got the impression she was in need of a friend. I don't know why but I gave her my number in case she ever needed help."

Which I was so fucking relieved about. But I couldn't help the stab of jealousy I felt that Caitlin had called Enzo… and yet, she'd refused to give me her number all those months ago.

Was this why?

Was it because she was somehow tangled up with DiMarco?

I couldn't make sense of it all. Because all I could think about was her lying there in that hospital bed, beaten and bruised. He was a… Fucking. Dead. Man.

"You know you need to stay cool about this, right?" Enzo pinned me with a knowing look.

"Like you'd be cool about it if it was Nora lying in that bed?"

His expression darkened. "It's not the same, Matt, and you know it."

"It's—" Shit. He was right. It was a low blow—especially after everything he and Nora had been through.

Besides, it wasn't the same because Caitlin wasn't my... she wasn't my anything.

He exhaled a steady breath. "Look, I get it, the two of you have history. But from the surprise on both of your faces, I'm guessing it's in the past."

Yeah, because she'd ghosted me.

But I'd never stopped thinking about her, not for a second.

Maybe that made me a pussy, but we'd shared something that night. Something that had burrowed deep into my soul.

"Let me go talk to her," he said. "She called me for a reason, let me find out why."

Seemed pretty obvious to me, but I didn't argue. No matter how much I wanted to be the one to go to her.

To protect her.

"Yeah, okay. Tell her... shit, tell her, I only want to help. No pressure."

Enzo's brows knitted together as he scrubbed his jaw. "You really like her, don't you?"

I gave him a weak smile and shook my head, "I don't even know her."

WHILE ENZO WENT to see Caitlin, I got coffee and tried not to wear a hole in the floor. But I couldn't sit still.

She was here.

Or rather, *we* were here.

Both of us, at the same time, in the same place. If that wasn't some kind of freaky kismet, I don't know what was.

Except, she hadn't looked pleased to see me.

Not even a little bit.

This isn't about you, asshole. It's about the woman lying in a hospital bed hurting because of that fucker.

I could still vividly remember her from that night. Her soft, pale skin. The taste of her lips. How perfectly her body had fit with mine.

I'd been in fucking heaven, ready to make all kinds of promises, and she hadn't even wanted to give me her number.

I wracked my brain for the exact details of our conversations. She'd told me she worked at some diner… but Enzo had said she was one of Zander's girls.

Did that mean she was one of his dancers?

Shit.

How had I not noticed? Although it wasn't like strippers wore a neon sign over their head.

Slumping down in the chair, I drained my coffee and threw the cup in the nearby trash can. I didn't give two shits what Caitlin did for a living. She was still one of the most real, most beautiful women I'd ever met.

And she's here.

I just needed to talk to her. To find out exactly what happened, and who I needed to hurt. My fist clenched against my thigh as I waited. Whatever she and Enzo were talking about was taking a long fucking time.

When he finally appeared, I shot up off the chair. "How is she?"

"She's… a mess. She won't tell me what happened, but it's bad, Matt."

My heart sank as I clenched my fists against my thigh. "Can I see her?"

"I'm not sure that's a good idea."

"What do you mean? I just want to talk to her and reassure—"

"Shit, Matt." Enzo stepped in front of me, cutting off my route to her. "She doesn't want to see you."

"She said that?"

He nodded.

"I see."

Dejection flooded me. It was one thing to be rejected by her all those months ago. But to see her again, find her here of all places, only to have her shut the door in my face again…

"Hey." Enzo gripped my shoulder. "This isn't about you, cous. It's about her."

"Yeah." The word soured on my tongue, my eyes flicking beyond Enzo to the row of curtains offering privacy to each bay.

"The doctor wants to keep her overnight for observations. Then she agreed to come back with us."

"B-back with us?"

"Yeah, to Verona County. She can't go back to Providence, Matt."

"Say it." My teeth ground together, my entire body trembling with rage.

"You need to calm down—"

"Say it, E. Tell me why she can't go back."

He let out a weary sigh, a dark cloud circling him. "Because she's scared of what DiMarco will do if she does."

Motherfucker.

My fist flew out, connecting with the wall before I could stop it. Pain ricocheted through my wrist and into my arm, and I swallowed a grunt of agony.

"Better?" Enzo quirked a brow.

"Fuck off," I muttered.

"Look at you, cous. She's got you all twisted up inside."

"You're telling me you're okay with that piece of shit DiMarco putting his hands on his girls?"

"You know I'm not. But it isn't that simple. He's a trusted associate. And you know we don't get involved with another man's business. Not like this."

I scoffed, cradling my busted hand near my chest. "That's some bullshit and you know it."

"You should get that looked at." His hard gaze dropped to my hand. "You might have broken something."

"I'm fine."

I wasn't, but whatever.

"I'm going to call Nicco. See how he wants us to play this. You going to stay put and refrain from doing anything stupid?"

"Yeah."

"Good," he said, digging his cell out of his pocket. "I'll be five minutes." Enzo took off down the hall.

The minute he was out of sight, I headed for Caitlin's bay.

CHAPTER 5

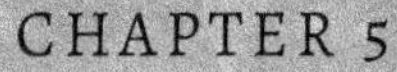

CAITLIN

I woke to the sensation of being watched. Slowly, I cracked a tender eye open, silently hoping it was *him*.

Matteo.

I'd dreamed he was watching me, felt his eyes lingering on my face as I dozed in and out of a drug-induced sleep.

I still wasn't over the shock of seeing him, staring at me with a mix of confusion and lust and longing. And rejection.

God, it had been like a physical blow to the heart.

One I wouldn't recover from anytime soon.

Still, it didn't stop the sigh of relief slipping from my lips when my gaze landed on the petite, brown-eyed girl staring at me.

"How are you feeling?" she asked.

"I'm sorry," I said, clearing my throat. "Do I know you?"

The girl approached my bedside, grabbing a cup and pouring me some water. "I'm Arianne, Enzo's friend."

"Arianne..." Her name sounded familiar. "You're his... friend?"

She nodded. "He thought you might prefer some female company."

"That's... very thoughtful."

"How are you feeling?"

"Like I almost got beaten to death."

The joke missed its intended mark, and Arianne's smile fell.

"That's not funny," she breathed.

"No, I suppose it isn't."

Silence descended over us. Thick, oppressive silence.

"Can you remember what happened?"

Fear raced down my spine as I clutched the crisp, white sheet to my body. "I—"

"It's okay. I'm not here to interrogate you. Enzo said you needed somewhere to stay for a while."

I nodded, wondering if I'd done the right thing telling him that. But he'd come through when I'd needed him, hadn't he?

When he'd given me his number, I hadn't ever planned to use it. Then I'd woken up in the hospital, scared and alone, and the doctor was looking at me with so much pity that when he asked me if there was someone he could call, I'd panicked and given him Enzo's number. After all, it wasn't like I could call anyone at the club.

"I can't go back..." Silent tears flowed down my cheeks as I clutched the stiff, white sheet.

Zander would know I was missing by now. He would know I had run.

"You don't have to; you can come back with us."

"With you… or Enzo?" My voice trembled. What the hell was happening here?

"You can stay with Enzo and Nora, or—"

"Nora?"

"His girlfriend. My best friend. You'd like her." Arianne smiled and it was nothing but warm and reassuring.

Despite the strange circumstances in which we were meeting, I liked her. There was just something about her —something comforting.

"Or," she added. "You can stay with me and Nicco."

"Is that your boyfriend?"

"My husband."

"You seem kind of young to be married," I said, clapping a hand over my mouth at my outburst.

Arianne smiled again. "When you know, you know."

That sounded nice.

"We have a place in Romany Square if you wanted to stay with us, until we can figure out your next steps."

Next steps, right, because I needed those. Because I had nowhere to go. Again.

"You'll get to meet Nicco soon. He's outside talking to Enzo and Matteo."

Nicco… Enzo… Matteo.

Why did those names ring a bell?

No.

No!

Everything slammed into me at once.

"What's your husband's surname?" I asked, hoping to God I was wrong.

Arianne let out a steady breath and then said the one little word that changed everything.

"Marchetti."

~

MY SAVIOR WAS A MARCHETTI.

Both of them.

Well, Matteo wasn't a Marchetti by name, but he was by blood.

If I would've had any idea who Enzo was the day he came to my apartment to check on me, I would never have stored his number in my cell.

Marchetti.

The constant thorn in Zander's side.

I didn't like to listen to backstage gossip or conjecture, but there was no escaping the whispers about the Marchetti crime family.

I should have realized who Enzo was, but I'd been too fragile to pay any attention, assuming he was one of Zander's friends—and he had many—trying to score brownie points.

But a Marchetti.

Jesus.

I might as well have crossed enemy lines because if Zander found out Enzo was helping me—Enzo *and* his family—he wouldn't only be pissed; he'd see it as a declaration of war.

"Caitlin?" Arianne frowned. "You've gone as white as a

ghost."

"I'm fine." I forced a smile, swallowing back a fresh wave of tears. "Just a little tired."

"You'll be safe with us," she said, reaching for my hand. "I promise."

I didn't have it in me to tell her that it wasn't me I was worried about. That if they took me back to Verona County and Zander found out, it would be them who needed to worry.

"Maybe this isn't a good idea," I blurted out.

I had nowhere to go. No money, no belongings, nothing. But it wasn't the first time I'd found myself homeless and penniless.

"What?"

"I don't want to be a burden," I said. "I can—"

"But Enzo said you told him you can't go back. Where will you go if you don't come with us?"

"I can call a friend, maybe. She can get some of my stuff and I can get—"

"Don't you have any family you can call?"

"No." It came out harsher than intended.

"We can protect you, Caitlin."

"Cait. You can call me Cait."

She nodded. "If you don't want to stay with me and Nicco or Enzo, I might have another idea. Nicco's family owns some cabins, secluded, off the beaten track. You'd have your own space out there, no one would bother you. It would give you a chance to figure things out."

It sounded too good to be true, but it also sounded safe. And I needed that right now.

"That actually sounds perfect." I hesitated. "But I don't understand why you'd do this for me… I'm no one."

"Everyone needs a helping hand sometimes." She smiled. "Besides, you're not no one, Cait. Not to Matteo."

Oh God, she went there.

She actually went there.

I'd done a good job up until now, pretending that he wasn't out there, in the hall somewhere. He hadn't tried to see me again. But now Arianne had mentioned him, I couldn't stop thinking about him.

He'd looked so shocked, so confused, but it quickly turned to anger. I think it was the agony in his expression that had made me tell Enzo to make Matteo leave.

I didn't want him to see me like this. Not now. Not ever.

"He told you about me?"

"Actually, Enzo filled us in. Matteo is still… trying to process everything."

"It was one night, a long time ago," I whispered, barely able to look her in the eye.

"For you maybe, but for him, I'm not so sure. You know, he told Nicco about you once."

"He did?" My heart fluttered at her words.

Silly, foolish heart.

But I could still remember how nice he'd been to me that night.

Matteo had made a lasting impression—even if I'd known it could never be anything more than one night.

One perfect storm.

"What other options do you have?" Arianne said softly.

"You said it yourself, you have no family. You can't go back to Providence, and—"

"Okay," I snapped, embarrassed at her accurate assessment of my situation. "Okay."

"So you'll come back with us?"

I nodded. "I'll come. On one condition," I added.

"I'm listening."

"I don't want Matteo anywhere near me."

I RODE with Nicco and Arianne. True to her word, she had kept Matteo away from me—I didn't see so much as a glance of him as we left the hospital.

It was strange. I felt the bitter sting of disappointment at his absence, even though I'd made my position perfectly clear.

What happened between us was history.

Ancient history as far as I was concerned.

It was one night and then we'd gone our separate ways. If I would've known who he was that night, it never would have happened.

So it was a moot point.

He was a Marchetti. And I was… no one.

"How are you holding up?" Arianne asked from upfront of Nicco's sleek, black Range Rover.

"I'm okay, thanks. A little sore but the pain meds help."

The doctor had wanted me to stay in the hospital for another night, but I didn't want that.

I needed to put as much distance between me and

Zander as possible, and Arianne was right—they could help me do that.

Shaun had left me with a small amount of cash, since I didn't have my purse with me. Not that I could use my bank cards anymore. Things like that were traceable.

But it was something.

Pain rippled through me. It wasn't only physical, it was emotional. Heart-wrenching, soul deep agony. The kind that didn't just disappear with a hot bath and a mug of hot chocolate.

What Zander had done to me...

A shudder tore through me and Arianne glanced back at me.

"Okay?"

I nodded, breathing through my mouth.

I didn't know these people, not really. Yet, they'd offered me nothing but understanding and compassion. That had to be worth something.

Didn't it?

"So we'll take you back to our place and let you get cleaned up, and then tomorrow, Nicco and I will drive you out to the cabin."

"Are you sure it's okay for me to stay there? I don't want to intrude."

"It's yours for as long as you want it," Nicco said, his eyes catching mine in the rearview mirror.

Niccolò Marchetti was something else. The way he looked at his wife was the kind of adoration documented in the great love stories throughout history. I couldn't deny the stab of jealousy I'd felt when she'd introduced me to him and he'd pulled her straight into his arms, as if she belonged there.

I'd spent my entire childhood wanting that—wanting one person to love me and me alone. Of course, those dreams were quickly replaced with enough nightmares to warn me off men forever.

Until him.

I immediately shut down those thoughts. What Matteo and I had shared last summer was one night of spontaneous passion. It was impulsive and a little bit reckless and for the first time in a long time, I had thrown caution to the wind and trusted a guy to take care of me.

He hadn't disappointed me, at all. But it wasn't real life, and I was under no illusions that the stranger from Verona County would sweep me off my feet and fight my monsters for me.

"Thanks, I really appreciate it. I just need a few days to make a plan and then I'll be out of your hair."

"Take as much time as you need, Cait. Truly."

Gosh, Arianne was too nice. It had been almost impossible to tell her no earlier.

"You're from Providence?" she asked, making small talk.

"I… no." I touched a hand to my face, prodding the tenderness around my cheekbone. "I was born and raised in Rochester, New York."

"You're a long way from home," Nicco added.

"I travelled around a lot when I was younger." The lies came easily. "Decided to settle in Providence."

"How old are you exactly?" His eyes met mine again.

"I turn twenty-one in a couple of months." I stared out

of the tinted window, watching the world roll by. I knew there was another SUV following us, but nobody said anything about it, so I played along.

Nicco and Arianne were kind of a big deal in Rhode Island. From the bit of backstage gossip I could remember, he was heir to the Marchetti empire, and Arianne was heir to Capizola Holdings.

Their union had been all anyone had talked about for weeks. People thought it was a power play, aligning two of the most influential families in the state. But they hadn't witnessed Nicco and Arianne together. It had only taken a second for me to see it was the real deal and not some business arrangement.

"We're almost here," Nicco said. He'd been quiet since our introduction. Polite, but quiet, nonetheless. I couldn't help but wonder what he really thought about all of this.

If the rumors were true, he was set to become boss of the Marchetti family one day, so he had to know that taking me to Verona County was a risky move.

My stomach churned and I pressed a hand against it, willing my nerves to calm down. At least here, I was safe for the immediate future. I could go to the cabin, heal, and figure out my next move.

I would be okay.

Because while life had given up on me a long time ago, I refused to stop fighting.

The SUV came to a stop outside a quiet apartment block.

Nicco leaned in, kissing Arianne's head. "I'll be inside."

"Okay."

He didn't spare me a second glance as he climbed out,

slamming the door behind him. It reverberated through me, making me flinch.

"Don't mind Nicco," Arianne said. "He's just—"

"Pissed that I'm here." I sunk into the soft leather seat. God, what was I thinking coming here?

"No. No, Cait," Arianne sighed. "That isn't it at all. He has personal experience with…" Her expression softened. "It's not my story to tell. But know that Nicco's issue isn't with you, it's with… the situation."

"If Zander finds out I'm here—"

"He won't. You're safe here, I promise." She smiled. "Why don't we go inside and get you settled? You must be tired."

I wanted to argue—to make her see that Zander wouldn't just give up. He was obsessed with me. Obsessed with the idea of me.

He wouldn't just let me go.

But everything hurt. My face. My muscles and bones. My soul.

I ached in ways I never thought possible, even more than any recital or performance where I'd spent hours twisting and contorting my body into gravity-defying positions.

"Yeah, okay."

Arianne got out of the car and opened the back door, helping me out. I winced, biting back the groan of pain bubbling in my throat.

"The guest room has its own bathroom, so you can take a bath or shower, whatever you want."

"Sleep sounds good."

"Then sleep it is." She smiled, and I couldn't help but smile back.

Their building was fancy. Gold accents and a bellboy outside who opened the door for us.

"Mrs. Marchetti," he greeted Arianne.

"Lowell, this is Ca—"

"Cadence," I blurted out.

"Cadence is going to be staying with us for the night." Arianne didn't miss a beat.

"Very good. Enjoy the rest of your day." His brows knitted slightly, but he didn't comment on the state of my face.

I let out a shaky breath and Arianne grabbed my hand. "It's okay."

"I-I didn't mean to… it's a habit."

"It's okay. Come on, we can take the elevator."

Arianne didn't push. Didn't ask questions or demand answers. She let the silence settle between us. And I was grateful.

So damn grateful.

By the time we reached her apartment, I was ready to crash. She noticed, holding her arm through mine and taking some of my weight.

"Nicco," she called through the open door. He appeared, brows furrowed as he took us in.

"She's crashing."

My head began to swim, thick and sludgy, as I gripped onto Arianne. "I don't feel so good," I murmured, my legs going out from under me.

"Nicco," she yelled.

And I went down, just as strong arms caught me.

CHAPTER 6

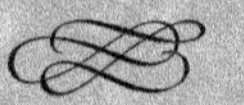

MATTEO

"You can't be here," Nicco said, stepping into the hall and pulling the door to his apartment closed.

"Seriously, Nic?" I balked. "He did that. DiMarco fucking—"

"I know, okay. I know." He blew out an exasperated breath. "You think I don't want to drive down there and make that asshole pay? I do. But we have to be smart, and right now, Caitlin needs us."

"You." I scoffed. "She needs you."

She wouldn't even let me get near enough to talk to her.

It stung.

More than that, it fucking hurt.

"She agreed to stay at the cabin," he said. "Maybe once she has some time to figure things out, she'll come around."

My lips pursed. I wouldn't bet on it.

For some reason, she was shutting me out—the same way she'd shut me out all those months ago when she'd refused to give me her number after our amazing night together.

"Yeah, whatever."

"Matt…"

"I get it. She's hurt and she has every right to be wary of me, especially after—"

I couldn't say the words; it made me sick to my stomach just thinking about it. I don't know how but Enzo had managed to sweet talk one of the nurses into giving him a rundown of Cait's injuries. It wasn't good.

He'd raped her.

DiMarco had beaten and raped her and left her barely conscious.

"But shit, Nic, I never thought I'd see her again… and she's here, and I… forget it." Defeat crashed into me. All the times I'd imagined seeing her again, I'd never wanted it to be like this. But we couldn't turn back time.

"I should go," I said, rubbing the back of my neck.

"That's probably a good idea. Maybe go down to Hard Knocks and work it off."

"Yeah."

"I smoothed things over with Uncle Michele," Nicco said. "He thinks Enzo had to rush back here because Nora's sick. He's going to send a couple guys to go see DiMarco. I don't think it's a good idea for you to be anywhere near him right now. Not until we get to the bottom of what really happened."

"You lied…"

"Until we get to the bottom of things, we need to keep her off the radar."

"I think it's pretty obvious what happened. The guy's a fucking woman beater and he—"

"Matt…" His jaw clenched.

Nicco didn't like this. He didn't like lying to my father or the Family. But if anyone hated this kind of thing more than me, it was Nicco.

"If DiMarco finds out we have her—"

"Don't. I'll handle it. For now, we keep this between us. We'll take her out to the cabin tomorrow. She'll be safe there until we can figure out what to do about DiMarco."

"Thank you," I dipped my head, forcing myself to take a breath. Nicco wasn't the enemy here.

"Matt," Nicco pinned me with a hard look, glancing down the hall. He and Ari had the penthouse suite, so access was only via the elevator, but I understood his wariness. You never knew who was around, listening to things they shouldn't be listening to.

One of his security guys gave us a sharp nod.

"Yeah, okay." I relented. "I'm going."

Nicco grabbed my shoulder before I could walk away. "We'll deal with DiMarco, you have my word. But we have to do it the right way."

The way that didn't have any backlash for the Family.

"Okay. Just do me a favor, yeah?"

"Anything."

"Text me later and let me know how she is." I pulled out of his hold and started down the hall.

"She's really under your skin, isn't she?" he called, and I glanced over my shoulder nodding.

He had no idea.

~

"If this is Nicco's attempt at babysitting me, you're excused," I mumbled to Enzo and Nora as they joined me at my booth in L'Anello's.

"Brooding suits you." Enzo smirked, and I flipped him off.

"E," Nora chided. "Don't be mean. Hey, Matt, how's it going?"

"Oh, you know, the woman I've spent the last eight months trying to forget shows up out of the blue looking like she got into a fist fight with Deontay Wilder and is acting like I'm the bad guy."

She shot Enzo a concerned look before sliding into the booth beside me. "Sounds like you need a strong drink."

"Babe, if the state of him is anything to go by, he already had enough to drink."

"I'm fine," I protested, nursing my empty glass. "But I am out of liquor."

"Get the guy another drink, boyfriend," Nora sassed. "Me and Matt need a little talk."

Oh God.

I loved Nora like a sister, but I didn't want one of her motivational speeches right now.

Enzo's brow quirked and she waved him off with a chuckle.

"The two of you seem happy," I said.

"We are. Blissfully. But I don't want to talk about me and Enzo, I want to talk about you. How are you holding up, really?" She pinned me with her big, brown eyes, and I felt stripped bare. But that was Nora, always seeing right through people's bullshit. It was one of the reasons I'd known from the beginning that she would be good for Enzo. He needed someone with an inner strength and confidence. And Nora Abato had that in spades.

Enzo never stood a chance.

I smiled to myself, and she asked me, "What?"

"Nothing," I replied. "Just thinking how much fun it's going to be watching you domesticate E."

"Don't let him hear you say that." We shared a conspiratorial smile. "Now, back to my question. How are you?"

"I'm… messed up, Nor. Really fucking messed up."

"Oh, Matt. Come here." She slipped her arms around me and hugged me tight. "It must have been a shock seeing her… like that." Nora eased away, offering me a sympathetic smile. "Enzo said it's bad."

"I barely recognized her." But I would've noticed those green eyes and red hair anywhere.

"I can't imagine…" She shuddered.

"She wouldn't even talk to me, Nor."

"Caitlin has been through something traumatic. Her response wasn't about you, Matt, it was about the situation. Trust me, I know."

"I know. Shit, I know." Enzo had said the same thing. But it didn't stop the gnawing pit of despair I felt every time I pictured the horrified look in Cait's eyes when she'd noticed me.

"Tell me about her. About how you two met."

"You mean E didn't give you the CliffsNotes version already?"

"I don't care about his version; I want your version."

I let out a deep sigh, my eyes flicking to where Enzo was chatting with Billy at the bar. He was obviously giving me and Nora a minute.

"It was last summer before the semester started. We were in Providence on… a job."

She rolled her eyes. "I know what you guys do, Matt."

"After we left DiMarco's, I was headed for my truck when I heard a scream. I went to check it out and found some asshole trying to mug Caitlin."

"Holy crap. What did you do?"

"Told him to beat it and offered her a ride home."

"I'm guessing you gave her more than a ride home." Her eyes twinkled.

"Ha-ha, very funny. But yeah, I stayed the night with her. The storm was wild, and she seemed shook up. We played poker and things escalated."

"Then what happened?"

"The next morning, I practically begged for her number, but she wouldn't give it to me."

"You never saw her again?"

"No. I checked out her place once, but she was gone." I'd never told anyone I'd been back to find her. In fact, I'd downright lied when I'd talked to Nicco about her. Told him that she'd blocked my number… when really, she'd up and disappeared as if she had never existed.

"What do you mean gone?"

"She didn't live there anymore."

"That's… weird."

"Right?"

"And she didn't say anything about DiMarco that night?"

"Nope." But I hadn't exactly been upfront about who I was either. "Told me she worked at a diner called Stella's," I added.

"You don't think there's a diner called Stella's?"

"There might be a diner, but I'd put a hundred bucks on her not working there."

"So she lied."

"It would seem so." My jaw clenched.

I still didn't know the truth… because Caitlin wouldn't fucking talk to me.

She didn't owe me anything, I knew that. But damn, I'd thought we'd shared something special that night. Maybe it was one-sided though. Maybe she hadn't felt the connection burning between us.

Maybe I'd spent the last eight months spinning it into something it wasn't. A fantasy.

A dream.

"So what are you going to do?"

"Do?" I blinked at Nora, and she chuckled.

"Don't seriously tell me you're going to stand by and let her slip through your fingers again?"

"You heard the part where she doesn't want to talk to me, right?"

"Yeah, but come on, Matt, this is you."

"What the fuck is that supposed to mean?"

"You're the charmer. The sweet one. The good guy. If anyone can win her over, it's you. After everything she's been through, she'll need reminding that good guys still exist."

"I want to kill him, Nor." My fist clenched against the table. "I want to drive down to Providence and—"

"Matteo, look at me." She covered my hand with her own, prying my fingers open. "That's not you talking."

"Isn't it? You didn't see what he did to her. You didn't—"

"Listen to me and listen good. I know it hurts. I know you want to fix it and try to make it right. But that is not a path you want to walk, Matt, because if you do, you might never come back."

"Everything okay?" Enzo finally returned to our booth.

"Yeah, babe. We're good. Right, Matt?"

"Yeah," I grumbled, accepting my drink from him.

"Jimmy says there's a fight tonight, if you want in." He studied me.

"No, he doesn't want in." Nora balked. "For God's sake, E. Fighting doesn't fix—"

"Tell him I'm in."

"What?" Nora whirled on me. "Have you lost your goddamn mind? You don't fight, Matt. It's not—"

"Relax, babe." Enzo ran a hand down his face. "It'll help him burn off some energy."

"And get his pretty face mangled in the process. This is a bad idea." She glanced between us. "A very bad idea."

Enzo grinned. "But sometimes the bad ideas are the most fun."

～

NORA WAS RIGHT.

This was a really bad idea.

That's all I could think as the brute of a man circled me. Shirtless, his thick, corded muscles rippled as he held his fists up in front of his face.

"I'm coming for you, kid." He gave me a crooked grin.

"Get him good, Matt," Enzo yelled from somewhere behind me. The two whisky chasers he'd insisted I down before climbing into the ring burned inside me. It had given me a false sense of security before my opponent appeared.

I can do this, I'd thought while I wrapped my fists and let Enzo school me on the softest places on a body to punch.

But looking at him now, I realized two things.

I couldn't do this… and whatever was about to come, was really going to fucking hurt.

In a blur the guy flew at me, his fist crashing into my face. Pain exploded along my jaw, my head snapping back.

"Fucking pussy," the guy hissed, dropping back to let me catch my breath.

"Shake it off, Matt, let's go." Enzo clapped his hands, as I hit myself gently a couple of times trying to focus.

I can do this… I can do it.

I pictured Caitlin, her bruised face and sad eyes. Rage flooded me. Red hot uncontainable rage.

Without thinking, I lunged forward, driving my fist into whatever part of the guy I could find. Bone crunched against bone, blood splattering the air.

"Motherfucker," he grunted, his pained cries drowned out by the bloodthirsty roar of the crowd.

I didn't give him time to come up for air, driving my

fists into his face, his ribs, and stomach. Over and over, I punched him, imagining Zander DiMarco's sleazy face.

Fuck, I hated that piece of shit. He'd hurt Caitlin. My Cait.

Deep down, I knew she wasn't mine, but it didn't matter. My heart, my foolish fucking soul had claimed a piece of her that night last summer, or she'd claimed a piece of me. I still couldn't quite process what I felt after seeing her again. But I knew without a doubt, that DiMarco had made a mistake ever laying his hands on her.

Blood coated my knuckles, sweat rolling down my back as I bounced on my feet, sparring with the guy. He gave me a good few hits back, grazing my eye; and catching my jaw a couple of times, once enough to rattle my teeth.

The longer we fought, the more I settled into the bursts of pain. The feel of his soft tissue bowing under my fists. And for a split second, I could understand why my cousin Nicco had once needed this to stave off his own demons.

We both began to tire. I was fit; I liked to workout as much as the next guy, but I'd underestimated how intense going one on one with a guy—almost twice my size —would be.

"Come on, Matt, finish him," Enzo roared, spurring me forward again. We crashed together, jabbing ribs and kidneys.

Pain radiated deep inside my body, but I let it fuel me for one last attack.

"You're mine, pretty boy," the guy spat, slumping away to circle me again.

But I was ready for him.

I was ready to end this.

He came at me, and I ducked his oncoming fist, rolling away enough to counter hit. My knuckles grazed his jaw and I smiled to myself, ready to end this.

But I didn't see his other fist between us.

"Matteo, watch—"

The uppercut sliced into me, rocking my whole body and I began to topple.

"*Matt!*"

I hit the floor, everything inside me cracking, a wave of pain crashing over me.

My eyes shuttered and the last thing I saw was the guy grinning down at me with victory in his eyes.

"Did I win?" I cracked an eye open, wincing in pain.

"You almost had him," Enzo said, fighting a smirk.

"Asshole." Nora slapped him upside the head. "I told you this was a bad idea." She crouched down beside me and pressed a bag of frozen peas to my face. "This will hurt."

I hissed; the pain almost unbearable.

"Ah, don't be such a pussy," Enzo murmured.

I managed to lift my arm and flip him off. He chuckled.

"Tell me it didn't help," he challenged. "Tell me you

don't feel even a fraction better for working off some of that anger."

I couldn't.

Because the truth was, for a minute, I had felt better. I didn't feel so great now though.

"How bad is it?" I asked.

"You'll live," Nora said. "Although you might have one or two new scars on your pretty face." Her lip curved with amusement, but I saw the pity in her eyes.

Shaking it off, I said, "Aww, you think I'm pretty."

"I think you're an idiot. What the hell were you thinking?"

"I was thinking I wanted to drive to Providence and put a bullet through DiMarco's eyes, but since you wouldn't let me do that, I had to settle for fighting the Hulk."

"The Hulk?" Enzo snorted. "The guy wasn't that big."

"Fuck you, stronzo, fuck you."

"Hold these." Nora slapped my hand over the peas and stood. "I need to call Ari and tell her you're awake."

"Shit, you called Nic?"

"Don't look at me," Enzo said, his eyes flicking to Nora.

"What?" She shrugged. "She texted and I wasn't going to lie about where we were."

"Ah shit, Nora."

"Should have thought about that before you decided to get in the ring." She walked off, leaving me and Enzo alone.

"How are you holding up really?" he asked.

"I'm messed up." I stared up at the ceiling. "I can't get

her out of my head, E. I can't stop thinking about what that fucker did to her."

"You really care about her."

"It's crazy, right?" My eyes slid to his. "I haven't seen her in months. But I can't explain it, that night… something inside me clicked into place."

"You sound like Nicco with all that written-in-the-stars bullshit."

"Yeah, maybe." I let out a weary breath.

"What are you going to do?" he asked quietly.

"There isn't much I can do right now. She doesn't want to talk to me, and I don't want to be another guy who demands things from her. Not after…"

"He'll pay, Matt. One way or another, DiMarco will get his. But we have to be smart, we have to take our lead from Uncle Toni."

"I know."

I did.

But it didn't mean I had to like it.

"And until then, I guess you're just gonna have to be patient."

I glanced over at him. "Nora's changed you, cous."

"Fuck off. I've always been full of useful advice."

My brow arched, and he grumbled something under his breath.

"Oh yeah, you've always been a real Dr. Phil type." I smirked.

"I'll keep my final piece of advice to myself then," he said.

"Nah, go on. It might help." I let out a chuckle but

ended up choking on the wave of agony ripping through me.

"You good?"

I nodded, finally catching my breath.

"Well, you know what they say, cous. The best things come to those who wait."

I rolled my eyes at him, shaking my head incredulously. "Who are you and what have you done with Lorenzo Marchetti?" I teased.

"It's regular pussy, Matt. It changes a guy."

"I wouldn't know," I murmured, hating the ache in my chest.

Silently hoping Enzo was right.

That all I needed to do was be patient and wait it out.

After all, I'd waited this long for her to walk back into my life.

CHAPTER 7

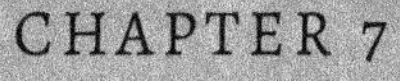

CAITLIN

It took me two days to recover. After passing out in Nicco and Arianne's apartment, I slept… and slept… and slept some more.

They had their family doctor come and check on me, but he said it was to be expected after such a traumatic event.

But this morning, when I woke up in the soft beige sheets, I forced myself out of bed and found Arianne in the kitchen area of their open plan living room.

"Hey, you're up."

"Hi." I smiled weakly, joining her at the breakfast counter.

"How are you feeling?"

"Like I slept for two days."

"The doctor said rest is good."

"You didn't need to do that," I said.

"We were worried. You passed out and—"

"Thank you." I cut her off. I really didn't want to do this... whatever *this* was.

"Coffee?"

I nodded, perching on a stool. My body ached, my muscles tired and weary. Or maybe that was my soul.

"Can I ask you something?" Arianne said as she made our drinks.

"Sure..."

"Before, when we arrived here, with Lowell..."

"The bellhop?"

It was her turn to nod. "You gave him a false name."

"I thought it would be safer." I shrugged.

"No one will hurt you here, Caitlin. I need you to know that."

But I didn't know that.

How could I?

Zander wasn't some two-bit club owner. He was connected. And he was obsessive in a way that terrified me. Not to mention the fact that the Marchetti had direct ties to him. All it would take was for someone to say the wrong thing at the wrong time and word could get back to him...

"Caitlin?"

I blinked over at Arianne. "Sorry, what?"

"I asked if you want sugar and creamer?"

"Oh, yes please."

She pushed the steaming mug of coffee toward me. "I took the liberty of buying you some new things yesterday. I hope that's okay."

"I... you didn't need to do that."

"I know I didn't need to. I wanted to."

"I'll pay you back." I didn't know how, but I would.

"You can take a look at what I got in a bit and if you need anything else before we leave for the cabin, I can get them for you."

"Thank you." The words got stuck on the lump in my throat, tears pricking the corners of my eyes.

"Cait," she said softly, reaching over the counter and resting her hand atop mine. "You're going to be okay."

Another nod. It was all I could manage.

"Are you ready to talk about what happened?"

Pressing my lips together, I shook my head. I wasn't sure I'd ever be ready. Besides, there were too many skeletons in my closet, and if I started down that road… No, I couldn't go there.

Ever.

Sympathy filled her expression, but she didn't push, and heavy silence enveloped us. I loosened a breath when there was a loud knock at the door, but my relief was quickly doused in fear.

"It's okay," Arianne said. "Security only lets up approved guests."

Approved guests? Wow. I didn't know what to say to that, so I sat quietly, watching as she went to open the door.

"Luis." She threw her arms around the immaculately dressed man. "It's good to see you."

"Nicco said you might need me."

"Come in."

She led him over to the kitchen. "Caitlin, this is Luis, our head of security."

I stared at him, unable to speak.

"It's okay," Arianne reassured me. "I trust Luis with my life. He's one of the good guys."

"Hello." It came out weak.

"Miss O'Connell." He gave me a small nod. "How are you feeling?"

I frowned. He knew my name? Interesting.

"I'm okay. Nicco and Arianne have been very kind."

"Coffee?" Arianne asked him.

"That would be great. Where's Nicco?"

"Visiting with his father." Something in her expression tightened.

"How is he?"

"Honestly, I'm not sure."

"Antonio is a fighter." He squeezed her shoulder gently. "If anyone can beat it, he can."

"Thank you."

"I'm to accompany Miss O'Connell to the cabin tomorrow?"

"We'll all go and get her settled. But yes, I'd feel better if you'd stay." She glanced at me. "If that's okay with you?"

"I..."

"I'll keep out of your way. You'll hardly know I'm there."

"O-okay."

The gravity of my situation crashed into me. I was in Niccolò Marchetti's apartment with his young wife, discussing being shipped off to their family's cabin with close protection.

It was too much to process.

And yet, no one had ever gone to such lengths to make me feel safe before.

My entire life had been one big string of disappointments and being let down by the people who were supposed to love and protect you.

"It's going to be okay, Cait."

Arianne kept saying that.

I just didn't know when, or if, I would ever believe it.

"YOU'RE SURE?"

The voices beyond my room made me stop rising from bed.

After a morning of going through the new things Arianne had bought me, I'd retreated to my room to rest. I must have fallen asleep because it was hours later and already dark outside.

"Our contact at the hospital said DiMarco showed up first thing this morning, sniffing around."

A chill ran down my spine, fear stealing the air from my lungs.

Zander knew—he knew, and he was already looking for me.

"But they didn't tell him anything, right?"

"No, patient confidentiality will protect her to a degree, and we paid off the right people to buy discretion, including wiping the CCTV, but if he manages to get anyone to talk—"

"They could place Enzo and Matteo at the hospital."

"Unlikely, but it's a possibility."

I was up and out of the bed before I knew it. Yanking

the door open, I stormed into the living room. Arianne's eyes widened to saucers. "Caitlin, what are—"

"He knows." I looked at Nicco.

He drew in a sharp breath. "It would seem so."

"Shaun?" If anything had happened to him because of me... I wasn't sure I could live with that.

"We don't know yet."

"What do you mean, you don't know yet?"

"We have to tread very carefully. If DiMarco suspects that we're involved—"

"If Zander suspects Shaun lied, do you have any idea what he'll do to him?"

Nicco's eyes darkened. "I have a pretty good idea." He rubbed his jaw. "I know this is hard, but until we figure out how to handle this—"

"Nicco." Arianne inched closer, shooting her husband a scathing look. "I'm sure your friend will be okay and as soon as it's safe to do so, Nicco will send someone to check on him. Won't you?" She pinned him with another hard look.

Hands jammed casually in his pockets, he gave her an imperceptible nod. "We have guys in Providence keeping an eye out, but right now, we have to be discreet."

My gaze bounced between them both as I hugged myself tight.

"Cait," Arianne said softly. "We'll do everything we can to protect you from Zander, I promise."

She kept saying that, but she didn't know what he was capable of, how obsessed he was.

"I need to check in on my father," Nicco said. "I'll be

back later." He went to Arianne and cupped her face in his hands. "Ti amo, Bambolina."

Her eyes fluttered as she kissed him back, and I turned away affording them some privacy. Ignoring the ache—the longing—in my chest.

Their love was a living, breathing thing that bled throughout the entire room. It was impossible to be unaffected by it, no matter how much it made my heart squeeze.

Nicco left and Arianne offered to make us both some hot cocoa.

"Are you hungry? There's some leftover lasagna."

"I'm okay, thank you."

"You haven't eaten much since you got here."

"I don't have much of an appetite yet."

She nodded, handing me a mug of frothy, rich hot cocoa topped with marshmallows.

"Is Nicco's father okay?" I blurted out, my cheeks burning at my sudden outburst.

"Actually, no." Grief washed over her. "He's sick."

"I'm sorry. That must be very difficult for Nicco... and you."

"If you have something you want to ask, ask it."

There was no malice in her words, only gentle understanding.

"Will..." I inhaled a sharp breath. "Does that mean Nicco will..." I trailed off, dipping my gaze.

"Will he take over his father's... responsibilities? Yes."

"And you're okay with that?"

"I knew who Nicco was when I married him, Caitlin."

Her expression softened. "And my answer would always be the same. I love him. And love knows no bounds."

Spoken with a conviction I myself couldn't understand. I'd never known that kind of love and devotion.

"You seem very happy," I said.

"We are. You know, Matt—"

Panic welled inside me as I rushed out, "Please, don't."

"Very well. But you know, Cait, you can't avoid him forever."

Precisely why I couldn't stop thinking that letting them help me was a huge mistake.

"Cait, we're almost here." Arianne gently shook my shoulders, rousing me from a fitful dream.

I hadn't meant to fall asleep on the way to the cabin— it was only a short ride—but the rumble of the SUV had quickly lulled me into oblivion.

Rubbing my eyes, I peered out of the tinted window, watching the dense trees roll by as Luis drove down the dirt road to the cabin.

"There's only one route in and out," she said. "Luis knows this area like the back of his hand. Nicco and his cousins too. There's hot water, electricity, and plenty of home comforts. Cell service should be okay."

The brand-new iPhone felt heavy in my pocket. I hadn't wanted to accept it, but Arianne wanted me to have a way to contact her should I need to. Plus, it gave me a tether to the real world.

Not that I had anything left in the real world.

"My offer still stands. I can stay—"

"No," I said hastily. "You don't need to do that. I need some time… alone."

Arianne smiled. "I understand. Nora was sorry she couldn't make it."

"That's okay." I didn't need a farewell party. It already felt like they had done too much for me.

"Remember, you can take as much time as you need."

I nodded.

The SUV came to a stop and Luis climbed out, coming around to open my door. "Miss O'Connell," he said.

"Thank you."

God, I seemed to be doing a lot of that. Thanking people. Nodding. Agreeing with them. Zander had turned me into a docile, wounded creature.

And I hated him for it.

But what choice did I have but to acquiesce?

Unless I wanted to go it alone with nothing but the clothes on my back and the few dollars in my purse, I needed the help. At least, until I could figure out a plan.

It wasn't like I had much in my apartment in Providence anyway, and a lot of it came from Zander. Things I didn't ever want to touch or see again.

A shudder ran down my spine as I climbed out of the SUV. The frigid air brushed up against me and I burrowed deeper into the thick sweater Arianne had bought me.

I was grateful, I was. But part of me was angry that I was here. Again. Relying on the charity of others. DiMarco's was supposed to be my way out. When Zander had offered me the job, I'd jumped at the chance to fix my desperate need to earn money. But I'd underestimated his motives, and before it was too late, he'd already set his sights on me.

"Caitlin?" Arianne called, and my head snapped up.

"Coming." I followed them to the cabin. It was impressive on the outside, but the inside was something to behold. There was a large, open plan living space with a kitchen in the back, divided by a gorgeous, soft sectional. The open fire was filled with chopped wood just begging to be lit, and the furniture was all rustic to match the open beams.

It was beautiful.

"There's a heating system," Luis said, stoking the fire. "Though nothing beats an open fire."

"Living room and kitchen," Arianne said. "Then the hall leads to the main bathroom, one master suite, and three guest bedrooms.

"You can have your pick of any of the three, but my favorite is the first door on the left." A warm smile graced her face. "Come on."

She led me down the hall and into the first bedroom.

"Wow, this is… stunning." It rivalled the guest room at their apartment. Decadent décor and ornate, hand-carved furniture. It was rustic and welcoming and everything I'd never had before.

"It's yours," she said. "For as long as you need it."

Emotion welled inside my chest, and I glanced away, trying to hide the moisture clinging to my lashes.

But when Arianne said, "I'll give you a minute." I knew I'd failed.

Silence enveloped me. Thick, oppressive silence. I

surveyed the room, my gaze snagging on my reflection in the dresser mirror.

The woman staring back at me looked exhausted, dark circles ringing her dull, lifeless green eyes. Bruises mottled her skin, angry red welts lining her jaw.

She was a mess.

I was a mess.

The tears I'd fought so hard to contain began spilling down my cheeks.

"How did you end up here again? How?" I gripped the edge of the dresser, my eyes shuttering with anguish.

I was a fighter, a survivor, had been since I was just a kid. But over and over, I found myself in these desperate situations. Like a magnet for the broken and bad.

I could hear my mom's raspy voice as clear as day. *"You're nothing but a worthless whore, Cait. That's all you'll ever be."*

But I wasn't that girl. I never had been. She was just too bitter, too angry and high to see it.

"Cait?" Arianne's voice startled me.

"Just a minute." I swiped the tears from my eyes, wincing when I caught the bruising on my cheek. It still hurt, but not nearly as much as my heart.

"Are you okay?"

"I'm coming," I called, forcing myself to take a calming breath.

Checking my reflection one last time, I slipped back into the hall.

"Are you hungry?" she asked. "I thought we could eat before Nicco gets here."

He was picking Arianne up to take her back to

Romany Square. Luis would remain here with me as agreed.

I still didn't know how to feel about being here with a man I hardly knew, but I did know it was preferable to being out in the middle of nowhere alone.

My eyes flicked over to where Luis was tending the fire. As if she heard my thoughts, Arianne said, "Luis is practically family. I wouldn't leave him here with you if I didn't trust him."

"We've got company," he announced, peering out of the window.

"It's just Nicco." Arianne moved toward him, frowning at whatever she saw beyond the window.

"I'll be back," she said, glancing over her shoulder at me. With a silent look at Luis, she slipped out of the cabin and a trickle of fear went through me.

"What's wrong?" I asked.

"Nothing. I'm sure it's—"

But I was already moving toward the window, gasping when I saw the figure step out of the car.

"What is he doing here?" My voice quivered as I clutched my throat.

"I'm sure there's a perfectly good explanation," Luis said.

Yeah, like he couldn't stay the hell away.

Anger unfurled in my stomach, heating my blood and without thinking, I yanked open the door, stepped outside, and hissed, "What the hell are you doing here?"

CHAPTER 8

MATTEO

Arianne let out a soft sigh as Caitlin glared at me, her anger like a storm raging between us.

"Nicco couldn't come, he—"

"How convenient," she spat the words. "So you figured, what? You'd come and try to force me to talk to you?"

"Caitlin, that isn't what's happening here." Arianne stepped forward, but Caitlin jerked back.

"I trusted you." Hurt flashed over her features. "I trusted you and—"

"Antonio was rushed to the hospital," I blurted out. "Nicco couldn't come because his family needed him."

"Oh." Her expression slipped, some of the anger melting away, replaced with guilt. "I… I didn't know."

"It's okay," Arianne said. "Why don't you go inside, and I'll be right there."

"Yeah, sorry." Caitlin's cool gaze swept over me, leaving me chilled to the bone.

She all but ran back into the cabin.

I let out a frustrated breath. "That went well."

"She needs time, Matt." Sympathy shone in Ari's eyes. "She's… confused and hurting."

"I'm not the enemy," I grumbled, feeling totally out of my depth.

"No, but you are a guy she's been intimate with. It's a lot to confront after everything she's been through."

I glanced up at the cabin and dragged a hand down my face. "I guess I'll wait out here."

"Thank you." Ari squeezed my hand. "I'll just say goodbye and then we can go."

Nicco and Alessia, his sister, were already at the hospital with Enzo and Nora. I'd offered to come get Ari and take her straight there.

I'd almost jumped at the chance to come out here with a valid excuse to see her. Probably not my brightest idea ever, but I'd underestimated just how much Caitlin didn't want to see me.

Way to go, Matt.

Luis stepped out onto the porch. "How's Toni?"

"We don't know yet."

Fuck, if anything happened to him, I didn't want to think about the domino effect that would have.

"Tell Nicco I'll be praying."

I nodded, my eyes flicking beyond him to the door. "How is she?"

"Arianne?"

"No, Caitlin."

He frowned. "She's as well as can be expected given the circumstances."

"You'll watch out for her?"

"Of course. Is she… someone to you?" Luis's brow lifted.

"She's…"

The door opened and Arianne appeared. "I'm going to be a few minutes. Come and wait inside."

"I'm not sure—"

"It's fine."

"I'm going to check the perimeter." Luis took off toward the tree line.

"Come on," Ari beckoned me inside.

There was no sign of Caitlin, and I didn't ask. The sting of dejection weighed heavily on my shoulders.

At least she was here, safe. Out of the clutches of that sick motherfucker.

"Is she—"

Caitlin appeared in the hallway, her lips pulled into a tight line.

"I'll wait in the car," Arianne said to me, before turning her attention on Caitlin. "Remember you can call or text me at any time."

Caitlin gave her an imperceptible nod, hugging herself tight as if she was trying to build a physical wall between us.

This wasn't the same woman I'd met all those months ago. She had fire in her eyes and warmth in her heart that night. But now there was no sparkle in her gaze, only pain and sadness. And it fucking gutted me.

Arianne left, the click of the door like a gunshot in the silence.

"Caitlin, I—"

"Let me," she cut me off. "I'm sorry, about before. You didn't deserve that." Her voice trembled.

"Hey." I stepped forward, but she immediately jerked back. "Caitlin, I'm not going to hurt you. I'm not—"

"I know." She inhaled a shuddering breath. "But I can't… I can't."

"Can't what? I'm not asking you for anything. I just want to help. I want to—"

"You should go." The words tumbled from her lips. "I only wanted to apologize for my behavior. I'm not… that isn't me. But everything is messed up and I need some time."

"I get that." But I didn't want to leave, not with so much left unsaid between us.

Caitlin stared at me, through me, silently begging me to go. I couldn't do it though. Not without doing something.

Glancing around the cabin, my eyes landed on the sideboard. I marched over to it, grabbed the pen and scribbled my cell phone number on the notepad. "Here." I tore it off and held it out to her.

But she just kept staring.

Fine. I didn't need her to take it to know she had it.

Pulling one of the magnets off the refrigerator, I pinned it there. "If you need anything, any time, night or day, you can call me. Text me. Leave me a message. It doesn't matter. I'll pick up. I swear."

Her stone expression gave nothing away, but I at least felt a little better about leaving.

"You're not alone in this, Caitlin. Not one bit."

I made for the door, praying she would call after me.

She didn't.

"Any word from Nicco?" I asked Arianne as we made the ride back into the city.

"Nothing."

"Hey." I reached over and squeezed her arm. "He'll be okay."

"Will he?" She sank back against my leather seats. "If Antonio doesn't pull through… he's too young, Matt."

"Do you ever regret it? Marrying into the Family?"

"No, never. That's not what this is." She let out a weary sigh. "I just worry about the toll it will take on him."

"Nic is one of the best people I know, Ari. He'll find his way. Besides, he has you by his side. Something tells me you'll never let him stray from his path."

"I hope you're right."

"Hey, I am. You're like the Bonnie to his Clyde."

"You did not just say that." Her laughter eased some of the tension in the car. "She's going to be okay, right? Caitlin, I mean?"

"Yeah." It came out strangled. "I mean, she'll lay low at the cabin, we'll deal with DiMarco, and she can go on with her life."

"Matt…"

"What?"

"You sound like a wounded puppy."

"I do not." I shot her a scathing look.

She chuckled. "Do you think she'll text you?"

"No."

"So, why d'you do it?"

"Because…" I shrugged.

"Because… you care about her?"

"Because she's the only woman I've thought about in the last eight months, Ari. And maybe that makes me a fool, but I never thought I'd get to see her again. Now she's here, and I can't believe it's just so I can watch her disappear again."

Arianne's eyes drilled holes into the side of my face, but I couldn't meet her stare.

"You're a good guy, Matt," she said, softly. "One of the best guys I know."

"Yeah."

Maybe that was the problem though.

Maybe I was too nice.

Everyone knew, nice guys usually finished last.

"BAMBOLINA." Nicco was up and out of his chair the second he spotted us. He scooped Ari into his arms, burying his face in the crook of her neck.

"How is he?" I asked Enzo.

"It's not looking good." Pain shone in his eyes as Nora rested her head on his shoulder. "He's in surgery still. But he went into cardiac arrest. Medics managed to stabilize him, but they're worried about swelling to his brain."

I glanced over at Nicco and Ari, my stomach sinking into my boots.

"Matt," Alessia appeared around the corner and ran straight into my arms. "You're here."

"Hey, Sia." I hugged her tight. "How you holding up?"

"I…" She burst into tears, sobbing into my sweater.

"Shh, kid. It's going to be okay." I smoothed my hand down her long golden hair. "Where's Genevieve?" I asked no one in particular.

"She went to visit her mom in Pawtucket last night. She's on her way."

Genevieve was my uncle's housekeeper turned girlfriend. Their relationship was still fairly new and at his request no one made a big deal about it.

But she would want to be here.

I led Alessia over to the row of plastic chairs and sat down. She burrowed into my side, still sobbing.

"We can't lose him," she cried. "We can't."

"Uncle T is a fighter. He's not going anywhere, Sia."

But as I said the words, I felt nothing but dread. Uncle Toni was sick, and who knew what would happen when the doctors opened him up.

I dragged a hand down my face, tipping my head back against the wall. My gaze landed on Nicco and Ari. He was holding her like she was his life raft in an angry sea. He already looked older somehow, as if the burden of what was to come had aged him overnight.

I didn't envy him. Not one bit. He had his beautiful wife and a beautiful home, but his life would never truly be his own.

It'll never be yours either. I let out a weary sigh.

"Niccolò, Alessia." Genevieve burst through the doors, running toward them.

"Gen," Alessia jumped up to greet her, burrowing herself in the woman's arms.

"Oh, sweet girl, shh. I'm here, I'm here." They hugged each other tight, silence falling over the seven of us again.

My mind wandered to Caitlin, to our last conversation. I doubted she would ever call or text me, but I wanted to give her the option. It was just something I needed to do.

"Has the doctor been out?"

"Not since they took him to surgery," Nicco said.

"Okay. I want you all to wait here while I go and speak to a nurse."

"I can come—"

"Stay with your sister," she said to Nicco. "I'll be back as soon as I get some answers."

Genevieve pressed a kiss to Alessia's head and gently nudged her back to me. "Watch her," she mouthed, and I nodded.

"She seems pretty calm," Enzo said.

"The calm before the storm," Nicco replied, his eyes vacant as he looked down the hall where Genevieve had disappeared.

"How did it go?" he asked, glancing between me and Arianne.

"Fine. Don't worry about that right now. This is more important."

Enzo caught my eye, and I knew what he was thinking. It was more important. But if DiMarco found out we were hiding Caitlin…

Then the shit would really hit the fan.

GENEVIEVE RETURNED WITH THE DOCTOR. It was good and bad news. The good news was they had stabilized Uncle Toni, but the bad news was they had put him into a coma to reduce swelling to his brain. The next forty-eight hours would be critical to his recovery.

Nicco and Arianne stayed with Genevieve, but I left with Enzo, Nora, and Alessia. She was going to stay with me and my family until we knew more.

"How is she?" Mom asked me as I joined her in the living room.

"Exhausted, scared… but I think it'll do her good being with Bella." My sister would watch out for her. The two of them were thicker than thieves.

"Poor girl. And Niccolò, mio Dio, such a weight on his shoulder."

"I know, Mama." I took a long pull on my beer.

"I can't imagine…" She let out a heavy sigh. "If we lost your papa."

"Don't think about it."

"It's always there, figlio mio. This life… it takes so much from us."

"Did you ever want to get out?" The words rolled off my tongue before I could stop them.

She tsked. "You think that is a choice?"

"No, Mama, I know it's not… I just…"

"Matteo, what is it?"

"Nothing, Mama."

"Is it a girl?" A knowing smile spread over her face. "You know, you're not getting any younger. Your cousins have both settled down now, perhaps it's time for you to think about meeting someone."

"Because it's that easy," I grumbled.

"There must be someone. Nora and Arianne have plenty of friends at the college. Surely a pretty girl must have caught your eye? You know, if you'd stuck it out there, you could—"

"We're not having this conversation." I'd wanted to finish college, I had. But it had proved too hard splitting my time and keeping up pretenses, and given everything that was happening with Uncle Toni, I'd decided to withdraw.

"Why not?"

"Because…" I shrugged. "It's weird."

"You think I don't know about the birds and the bees? About how young men like yourself like to sow your seeds far and wide before you settle."

"That's not the saying, Mama."

"It's my saying." She tsked again, waving me off. "You are a good man, Matteo. Kind and compassionate. You think with your head. You're not like some of these cogliones."

"Mama!"

"What? I speak the truth."

"I love you, Mama."

"I love you too, figlio mio. And I just know there's a good woman out there somewhere for you."

Oh, Jesus. She was like a dog with a bone. For a second, I'd contemplated telling her about Caitlin, but it would only raise her hopes.

My cell phone had burned a hole in my pocket all afternoon. I knew she wouldn't text or call, but it didn't stop my heart from stuttering every time I got a notification. If I had half a brain, I would forget all about her. But I couldn't do it.

I couldn't get her out of my fucking head.

If I were more like Enzo, I would have gone to the cabin and refused to leave until she agreed to talk to me. Or if I were more like Nicco, I would have made some grand gesture she couldn't ignore.

But I wasn't like them. I was Matteo Bellatoni. Loyal friend. Perpetual joker. Heart on his sleeve kinda guy.

And deep down, all I'd ever wanted was to meet the girl of my dreams.

I didn't think I'd meet her only to lose her…

Twice.

CHAPTER 9

CAITLIN

Matteo's number pinned to the refrigerator taunted me.

After he and Arianne had left, I'd contemplated throwing it onto the open fire. But I hadn't, yet.

I felt awful after railing at him the way I did, after finding out that Nicco's father was sick. They were clearly all close—Arianne, Nicco, and his cousins—and I'd acted like a complete bitch.

But everything was so messed up. I wasn't the same woman I was last summer when I'd spent the night with Matteo. So much had happened since then. Things I didn't want to ever have to explain to him.

"You can come inside, you know?" I said to Luis as he swept the leaves off the steps leading up to the cabin.

"I'll be in soon. Better to clear these now before the ground frosts."

"I'll make a fresh pot of coffee."

"Perfect." He smiled.

They hadn't been joking when they said Luis would keep to himself. I'd barely seen him in the few hours that had passed since Matteo and Arianne left.

It was hard to believe that less than six days ago, I was at DiMarco's working a regular shift. And now... now my life was in tatters.

All because of him.

Tears burned my throat, but I swallowed them down. I didn't agree to come here to wallow; I wanted to give myself time and space to heal and come back stronger.

But it was easier said than done. Too much time alone with my thoughts was dangerous. Grabbing my phone off the coffee table, I snuggled into the cushions and opened a new browser, typing in Niccolò Marchetti.

Article after article appeared, some documenting the merger between Capizola Holdings and the Marchetti Empire. The reports surrounding Nicco and Arianne's wedding ranged from it being nothing more than a business deal; to an arranged marriage; to the Marchetti calling in payment of a debt from Roberto Capizola, Arianne's father.

But I'd seen their relationship firsthand. There was no denying how much they loved one another.

I scrolled through some more articles before switching to the image search results. Photo after photo appeared of Nicco attending functions, charity events, gala dinners; there were even some photos of him and Arianne working at a community center in Romany Square. Then my eyes landed on him.

Matteo.

Gosh, he looked handsome in the black dinner suit, his dirty-blond hair swept to one side, his charming smile radiating off the screen. He was different to his cousins. They both had the typical dark Italian genes. But Matteo was much fairer. Like sunshine between two storm clouds. The thought made me smile as I ran my finger over his photo.

Guilt sat heavy in my chest at how I'd treated him earlier, and at the hospital. But I'd been so shocked to see him standing there, I hadn't known what else to do. And after what Zander did to me… how could I look Matteo in the eye?

My eyes flicked over to the kitchen, snagging on the note pinned on the refrigerator. Even if I did text him, what the hell would I say?

I'd lied to him that night. Concealed the truth. And I'd do it again if it meant protecting myself.

With a small sigh, I switched off my cell and padded over to the kitchen. I needed to keep busy, which seemed almost impossible in a cabin in the middle of nowhere. But I'd spied a bookshelf full of books and a stack of puzzles, which was better than nothing.

Placing my cell on the counter, I switched on the coffee machine and went over to the puzzles, choosing one. A two-thousand-piece print of the New York skyline.

Satisfied with my choice, I made me and Luis a mug of coffee each and let him know it was ready.

By the time he came inside, I'd already moved to the coffee table and emptied out all the pieces.

"You like puzzles?" Luis asked, leaning back against the counter and sipping his coffee.

"I haven't done a jigsaw puzzle since I was a child," I admitted.

"Want a helping hand?"

"Sure, why not."

Luis brought his coffee over and placed it on the floor out of harm's way. "Okay, what have we got here." He began sorting the pieces.

"Any idea on where we should start?"

"Outside pieces then build on those, preferably in sections."

"Wow, I didn't realize it was so complicated." I chuckled, adding some outside pieces to his pile.

"I used to sit with my nonna and do puzzles. She loved them. But it's been a long time since I did one for fun."

"I'm not sure two-thousand pieces constitutes the word fun. But I figured it would keep my mind occupied."

"You'll be sucked in before you know it. Here you go, look." He slotted a few pieces together like an old pro. "Now you have a point of reference."

Luis stood and I frowned up at him. "What's wrong?"

"You didn't think I was going to do it for you, did you?" A faint smirk traced his mouth.

"Well, no, but a little help wouldn't go amiss."

"You'll figure it out." He winked and walked off.

Well then.

For the next forty minutes, I worked meticulously to sort the pieces into similar groups. Then I began matching them to the section Luis had completed. It was going to take me forever to finish it… if I ever did. But having a focus would be good for me.

Besides, I could kind of relate to the puzzle.

God, how pathetic, relating to a jigsaw puzzle.

I felt fractured though. Shattered into jagged pieces. It wasn't any one thing that had led me to this point, it was an accumulation of events since my childhood.

But unlike this puzzle, which with time and patience I could fix…

I wasn't sure anyone could ever fix me.

I woke with a start, drenched in sweat and clutching the crumpled bed sheets between my fingers.

"It's just a dream," I urged myself, willing my racing heart to calm down.

But it hadn't been a dream at all.

It had been a nightmare.

Zander's wolfish grin taunting me as he and his business associates circled me like predators hunting their prey. No matter how hard I ran, how fast I pumped my legs, I couldn't outrun them. And then their laughter had morphed into voices I'd spent years trying to forget.

A violent shudder rolled through me as I leaned over and snatched my shiny new cell phone off the nightstand and checked the time.

A little after one.

It was going to be a long night.

Luis was down the hall in one of the other guest rooms. For a moment, I'd thought he was going to sleep out in his SUV which was completely unacceptable.

I'd made us both spaghetti and we had eaten in uncomfortable silence. He didn't pry or push me to talk, and I didn't really know what to say to him. I'd quickly excused myself after dinner and retreated to my room.

Pushing back the covers, I climbed out of bed and wandered quietly into the kitchen. I needed a glass of water to temper the lingering fear of my nightmare.

The cabin was steeped in silence, only the silvery hue of moonlight guiding my way. I helped myself to a bottle of water from the refrigerator, my eyes catching on the note pinned there.

Matteo's number.

His words replayed through my mind.

If you need anything, any time, night or day, you can call me.

It was a bad idea, the worst. But it wasn't like I could text Arianne or wake Luis. I barely knew them.

You barely know him.

But I did know him. Or at least, I had known him for one amazing night. And there was something about the way he'd pushed to talk to me... something a small, broken part of me had latched onto.

It was dangerous territory though.

If I gave him the wrong idea...

Before I could stop myself, I tore the note off the refrigerator and hurried back to my bedroom. It practically burned a hole in my hand and the second I was in the safety of my bedroom, I dropped the note on the bed, staring at it.

"Oh for God's sake, Cait, it's just his number," I murmured to myself.

It represented so much more than just his number though.

If I texted or called him, I would be crossing a line I might not be able to come back from.

But being here, alone with my thoughts wasn't as easy as it sounded.

Burrowing back under the sheets, I clutched my cell phone in my hand. Matteo knew me. He knew the intimate parts of my body, my freckles and blemishes; he'd mapped the curves of my skin with his hands and lips.

But he didn't *know* me.

Not really.

I'd given him a piece of me that night, but she was barely a figment of my imagination—the girl I wanted to be if things were different. The girl I could have become if I'd had a normal childhood with normal, loving, supportive parents.

But I didn't have any of those things.

I had a past full of pain and disappointment and heartache. A past that had shaped me into nothing more than a survivor, clinging onto hope, knowing that she was probably never going to escape the ghosts that haunted her.

Punching in Matteo's number, I hit call… and then realized what a foolish mistake I'd made.

He didn't really want me to call him at any hour. He was probably just being polite, offering me an olive branch seeing as we had some shared history.

It started to ring, but before he could answer, I hung up, throwing my phone across the bed.

What the hell was I thinking?

Hopefully he was asleep and wouldn't see the missed call until—

My phone began to vibrate.

"Shit, shit." I snatched it back up and stared at Matteo's number flashing across the screen.

Dragging my bottom lip between my teeth, I waited for it to stop. It did, and relief sank into me. But a couple of seconds later, it vibrated with an incoming text.

I almost didn't open it, but curiosity got the better of me.

CAITLIN?

MY STOMACH FLUTTERED. I could text him back. A text was safe, non-committal. A text didn't mean anything. Before I could reply though, another message came through.

ARE YOU OKAY?

I HIT REPLY and started typing.

I'M FINE.

LIAR.

· · ·

SO YOU'RE CALLING **me in the middle of night to tell me you're fine? I may have a pretty face, but I'm not stupid, Cait.**

GOSH, the way he called me Cait. As if we were friends. Intimate. As if we'd known each other forever.

That single word wrapped around my heart and didn't let go.

I HAD A NIGHTMARE.

CAN **I** CALL YOU?

N**O, please... I can't...**

O**KAY, no phone call. But we can text? This is okay?**

I CHEWED MY LIP AGAIN.

I GUESS SO...

DID YOU WAKE **L**UIS?

.   .   .

I didn't want to disturb him. I'm a grown woman. I should be able to handle a bad dream.

We all get scared of the dark sometimes, Cait.

Was he trying to wear me down? Because there, in the dark of night, it was working.

He beat me to a reply again.

How do you like the cabin?

It's very peaceful. I found a two-thousand-piece puzzle to keep me occupied.

A puzzle you say? Sounds... riveting.

A faint smile traced my lips as I got comfortable and settled in to text him back. This was safe, reassuring in a strange way.

It wasn't supposed to be, but there was no denying Matteo made it easy.

He had that night all those months ago, and he was doing it again now.

. . .

Caitlin?

He texted back when I didn't reply.

I'm still here…

Good. I thought maybe you'd fallen asleep on me.

Not yet.

Oh, it's like that, huh?

I'm sorry I woke you.

Don't be. I was lying here awake anyway.

You were? It's late.

Yeah, I have a lot of things on my mind.

.   .   .

THE KNOT in my stomach tightened, guilt trickling through me.

WELL, **I feel better about not waking you now.**

I'M GLAD YOU TEXTED.

ME TOO.

IT WAS THE TRUTH, I already felt better.

I MEANT WHAT I SAID. **You can text me anytime and I'll answer.**

I KNOW.

NERVOUS ENERGY VIBRATED INSIDE ME. I'd never had this. Genuine conversation with a guy. There was always something: the expectation of more, veiled threats, or the feeling of something owed. I wasn't used to being... an equal.

In fact, I'd long given up on the idea. In my life, sex and attraction were weapons. Ones that had been used against me too many times.

And then Matteo texted me nine little words that told me exactly how different he was to every man I'd known before him.

DiMarco will pay, Caitlin. I promise you, he'll pay.

I woke up with my phone on the pillow beside me. Matteo and I had texted late into the night. After he'd made his promise to make Zander pay, he'd turned the conversation to safe topics until I'd fallen asleep.

Grabbing my cell, I unlocked the screen and smiled at the message from him.

Good morning. I hope you managed to get some sleep.

I did, thanks to you.

Not exactly how I want to be remembered—for making women fall asleep—but I guess I'll take it.

Laughter bubbled in my chest, but it was quickly dampened by another wave of guilt. He was flirting… and flirting was skirting a line I wasn't sure I wanted to cross.

Not now.

Not ever.

I NEED COFFEE THEN A SHOWER. **Thanks again for keeping me company last night.**

THINGS FELT different in the harsh light of day. I'd been scared last night. Alone and vulnerable. But I didn't need Matteo to chase off the monsters in my sleep now the sun was up.

"Coffee's brewing," Luis called from the hall. He must have heard me shuffling about.

I grabbed a hoodie and pulled it on over my pajamas and padded into the hall.

"Morning," I said, joining him in the kitchen.

"Sleep well?"

"I… yeah, okay."

"I thought I heard something—"

"I got up to get some water."

"Sorry, I should have checked on you."

I snorted. "I'm a big girl. I can take care of myself."

"Noted." He smiled, pushing a mug of coffee toward me. "What do you want to do today?"

"You mean, I have options?"

"You're not a prisoner here, Caitlin."

"No, I know that. I just… sorry," I shook my head softly, "I'm being rude."

"There's some pretty neat trails in the forest, we could check those out."

"You want to take me trekking through the forest?"

That seemed… weird.

"It sounds stranger than it is. Arianne thought you might like—"

"Ah, Arianne put you up to this." I didn't know why but disappointment welled in my chest.

It was silly. Of course she'd suggested it to him. Or ordered him to ask me. I wasn't entirely sure of the nature of their relationship and how it worked.

They seemed friendly, but what did I know about these things.

Nothing, you know nothing.

I ran my thumb around the edge of my mug, not meeting his heavy gaze.

"She just doesn't want you going stir crazy," he said.

"It's only been a day. I'm sure I'm good for a while yet."

"You do have that epic puzzle to complete."

"Exactly."

I'd only picked it off the shelf on a whim, but it was fast becoming a metaphor for my situation.

"Well, I'm going to take a shower. If you want to venture out, just say the word. I'll be around." He tapped the counter, drained his coffee and then disappeared down the hall.

I considered his suggestion again. It was only a walk. What was the worst that could happen?

Besides, I had to leave here eventually.

CHAPTER 10

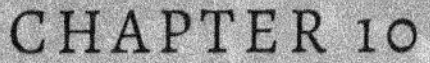

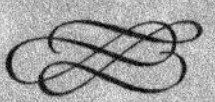

MATTEO

"Expecting a call?" Enzo asked me with a frown.

"No. Just scrolling." I pocketed my cell and tapped my fingers against the counter.

"Seriously, what's up with you?"

"Nothing. I'm fine."

"You seem—"

My cell vibrated and I whipped it out of my pocket, disappointed when I saw Arabella's name.

"Okay, spit it out."

I hesitated, unsure I wanted to put myself out there like that. But it was Enzo, my cousin, one of my best friends.

"She texted me."

"She—" Realization dawned on his face. "Caitlin? For real?"

"Yeah. Last night."

"And what did she say?"

"She had a nightmare and wanted to talk."

"So you… talked?"

"Yeah." I didn't tell him that I hadn't heard from her since our brief message conversation this morning. Even if it was driving me out of my mind that she hadn't texted me back.

"See, I told you all she needed was some time." My expression fell and he added, "Matt?"

"I want more."

"Shit, yeah, you do. But she made it pretty clear last time—"

"I know. I wasn't planning on doing anything stupid."

Like turning up at the cabin unannounced, hoping she would let me in.

And then what…

I jammed my fingers into my hair and tugged the ends, reveling in the slight pinch.

"Did Lucino call yet?"

"Yeah, they arrived yesterday."

"And?"

"It's been a day, Matt. Give them a chance to feel DiMarco out. You know, your old man is going to lose his shit when he finds out—"

"Don't." My jaw clenched.

It was a risk not telling him what really happened, but Nicco was right—we needed to find out what went down first.

It was more than DiMarco deserved, but it wasn't my call to make.

"What are you thinking?" he asked.

"That I want to break his fucking face." I inhaled a shuddering breath.

"For her?"

My eyes snapped to Enzo's, narrowing. "Why are you pushing me on this?"

"Because I've never seen you like this over a woman. I guess I'm trying to understand how you can feel so strongly for someone you spent one night with. It's even worse than Nicco and Arianne, and I thought that was fast."

"Thanks a bunch," I murmured.

"Surely you can see it from my point of view?"

"It's not something I can explain." Frustration coated my words. "We had this… connection."

"The sex was that good?"

"Oh, fuck off."

"Relax." He chuckled. "I'm joking."

"You're being an asshole."

"I guess I'm just trying to understand. None of that shit comes easy for me."

"You have seen yourself with Nora, right?" My brow lifted.

"She's different."

"I would hope so seeing as she's got you locked down heading straight for wedding town."

"Seriously?" He balked. "We've only been together a few months."

"Like you don't want to put a ring on her at the earliest possible moment."

Enzo was a possessive asshole. No way he didn't want

to bind himself to Nora in every way possible, despite his reservations about relationships.

"Fine, you got me there." He smirked. "But it's all her. Only ever her."

"She's good for you, cous," I said. There was silence between us for a moment while we were both lost in our thoughts, before I brought us back to present circumstances. "I still can't believe Uncle Toni is in a coma."

"He'll pull through," Enzo said with arrogant confidence. "He has to."

"Yeah."

But the truth was, I wasn't sure he would.

I didn't think anyone was.

They just didn't want to admit it.

ENZO DIDN'T STICK AROUND. Arianne invited Nora over so naturally he went with her. They asked me but I didn't want to play fifth wheel. Not today.

Not when I couldn't get Caitlin out of my head.

HOW WAS YOUR DAY?

I STARED at the message I'd sent Caitlin ten minutes ago, willing her to reply. It was borderline desperate the way I clutched my phone, waiting. But I couldn't help it.

The thought of her at the cabin, all alone—Luis hardly

counted when he was security—was messing with my head.

When another couple of minutes passed, and she didn't text back, I changed tack.

I'm guessing from your cold shoulder, you're either too wrapped up in your puzzle to reply or Luis decided to take your phone off you.

You got me... this puzzle is addictive.

A smile tugged at my lips.

You know... I heard two hands are better than one.

Good job I have two then, isn't it?

Laughter rumbled in my chest.

You got me there...

Don't you have better things to be doing than texting me?

. . .

AREN'T you bored of your own company yet?

I HAVE Luis to keep me company, remember? He's really good at puzzles.

MY LAUGHTER GREW. This felt good. Safe and easy. She wasn't ignoring me or telling me to leave her alone. I wanted to ask if I could go see her, talk in person. But I didn't want to scare her off, no matter how hard it was to stay away.

I GUESS I should let you get back to your puzzle then.

THE BUZZER RANG and I traipsed over to answer it. "Yeah?"

"It's me," my sister chimed. "I hope you don't mind but I brought Sia with me."

Great. Just what I didn't need—babysitting my sister and cousin.

"Yeah, come up." I pulled the door ajar and padded back to the couch, typing another reply to Caitlin.

SEND HELP. My sister and cousin just turned up to terrorize me.

. . .

SOUNDS like you have your hands full.

YOU HAVE NO IDEA. Any suggestions on how to keep two teenage girls occupied?

SOUNDS TRICKIER THAN MY PUZZLE... trip to the movies? All teenage girls like that, right?

I'M NOT sure Alessia will want to go out.

OH... is everything okay?

IT'S Sia's and Nicco's father, my uncle. He isn't doing so good.

I REMEMBER NOW. I'm sorry to hear he still isn't doing well. Maybe a home movie night instead?

THEIR FOOTSTEPS SOUNDED down the hall, the familiar cadence of Arabella's voice floating into my apartment.

YEAH, maybe. I should probably go see to them. Enjoy your puzzle.

. . .

ENJOY YOUR BABYSITTER DUTIES.

"WHO'S THAT?" Bella asked the second they came inside. I pocketed my cell and went to greet them.

"No one."

"Yeah, I bet." She smirked.

"How are you feeling?" I asked Alessia. She looked exhausted, dark circles ringing her eyes.

"I… I'm okay. They said he should wake up. That's good, right?"

"Yeah, that's real good, Sia."

"Dad gave you a ride here?"

Bella nodded. "He and Mama are heading to the hospital to sit with Uncle Toni."

"Make yourselves comfortable," I said. "I can order some pizza and we can watch a movie? Might take your mind off everything."

"Sure." The helplessness in Alessia's eyes gutted me. She loved her dad, loved him something fierce. If anything happened to him…

I shook the thoughts away. Uncle Toni would pull through. He had to.

The girls got settled while I grabbed a menu from the noticeboard. I might not have had anyone to lean on, not the way Enzo had Nora and Nicco had Ari, but I could do this for my cousin. I could be her person.

"What movie are you thinking?" I asked, diving onto the couch beside Bella.

"Scemo," she muttered, and I chuckled. "How do you feel about Magic Mike?"

"Oh hell no. I'm not watching a bunch of dudes get naked and dance."

"Insecure about your sexuality, brother?"

"Pulce."

"Fine, we'll pass on Magic Mike. How about the latest Marvel film then?"

"I can get on board with that." I kicked up my feet and set about ordering the pizza.

At least entertaining the girls would keep my mind off Caitlin.

"Matt," Bella's voice trickled through my subconscious. "Matt…"

"Yeah?" I bolted upright. "Huh, what—"

"Your cell phone, it's ringing." She thrust it at me, and I blinked rapidly, trying to get my bearings.

I was half-draped on the couch, my neck stiff and my eyes weary. I must have dozed off during the film.

"What time is it?"

"Late; a little past midnight."

"Shit. Where's Sia?" I glanced around.

"She went to bed hours ago. You fell asleep and I was watching Magic Mike, but it just finished. Who's calling?" She motioned to the phone still in my hand.

It had stopped vibrating, but sure enough, there were two missed calls.

Luis.

"I need to take this." Stumbling off the couch, I went over to the kitchen and dialed his number. The second he answered, I breathed, "What happened?"

"Shit, Matteo. I'm sorry I called. She's awake now. She's—"

"What. Happened?" I ground out, instantly going on high alert.

"She was having a nightmare, a real bad one, and I couldn't wake her. I panicked and I didn't want to disturb Nicco, not since Antonio is… and I tried Enzo, but it rang out. So I called you. But everything is fine, she's fine."

Yeah, fuck that.

I let out a weary breath and glanced over at my sister who watched me intently.

"I'll be there soon," I said.

"Matt, I'm not sure that's a good—"

"I'll be there soon." I hung up and pulled up a new message, texting Alessia's bodyguard. The building had its own security, but I wasn't prepared to leave the girls without someone I trusted watching them.

"You're leaving?" Bella asked.

"Yeah, I need to go check on… a friend."

"A friend, right." Her brow quirked. "What's her name?"

Jesus. Bella always had a way of seeing straight through me.

"You don't need to worry about her."

"She's got you all tied up in knots. Seems like I definitely need to worry, Matt."

"Jay will come watch you while—"

"We don't need babysitting, Matt." She huffed.

"I know you don't, but Nicco would have my balls if I left Alessia unsupervised."

"Fine, whatever. Will you be back?"

"I… I don't know. But I'll text you, okay?"

"Okay." She stood up and came over to me, looping her arms around my waist. "You're a good big brother, Matt."

"I'll always keep you safe, pulce."

"I know."

It was my promise to her. I'd seen what this life could do to people—how it could tear families apart. Arabella was innocent, and she deserved a future. She deserved to chase her dreams.

The idea that she could one day be used as a pawn or collateral against the Family terrified the shit out of me.

A knock at the door pulled me from my thoughts and I eased Bella out of my arms, striding across the apartment to let Jay in.

"Mr. Bellatoni."

"Thanks for coming."

"Of course." He nodded stiffly. "It's what Mr. Marchetti pays me for."

"Hey, Jay." My sister gave him a small wave.

"Miss Bellato—"

"How many times do I have to say it, Jay? Call me Bella."

"Very well, Miss Bellatoni."

She grumbled, throwing her hands up in frustration. A smile curved my lips. Arianne was just the same with our security team. She preferred to keep things on a first name basis, but our men weren't used to it.

"I need to go out for a while," I said. "Bella is about to

go to bed, so you won't need to entertain her." I gave her a pointed look.

"Ruin all my fun, why don't you."

"I'll check in with you later." I turned my attention back to Jay.

"I'll handle things here," he said.

"Thanks." I grabbed my jacket and keys.

"I hope she's worth it," Bella called after me, her words hitting me square in the chest.

I didn't look back as I left the apartment with only one thing on my mind.

Getting to Caitlin.

IT TOOK me too fucking long to get to the cabin. By the time I pulled up next to Luis's SUV, it was almost one-thirty.

The cabin was steeped in darkness, only a faint, flickering amber glow coming from inside. I padded up the steps and knocked quietly. Nothing. Pulling out my cell phone, I dialed Luis's number.

"Matteo?" He groaned. "Tell me that's not you—"

"Open the door," I said.

"Cait doesn't want—"

"We both know I'm not leaving until I've seen her, Luis. So do yourself a favor and open the fucking door." I hung up and a second later, the lock unlatched and the door swung open.

"Have you lost your goddamn mind?" He glared at me.

"Where is she?"

"In bed… asleep."

Some of the panic coursing through me abated. "I need to see her." I barged past him, but he grabbed my shoulder.

My eyes met his and he blew out an exasperated breath. "Seriously, Matteo, this is a bad idea. I shouldn't have called."

"What happened?"

Relenting, Luis closed the door and ushered me over to the couch. I wanted to go to her, to see with my own eyes that she was okay. But maybe he was right. Maybe I had been too hasty.

Jesus.

I was a mess.

All over a woman who had made it perfectly clear she wanted nothing to do with me.

"Here, you look like you could do with this." He handed me a beer.

"She's okay?"

"She is now." He ran a hand down his face and sat opposite me in the armchair angled toward the open fire.

"I've never seen anything like it, and I've seen a lot in my time," he said. "She was wild… thrashing and fighting some invisible monster. I couldn't wake her…"

"You did the right thing calling me."

"Did I? The second I told her I had, she lost it."

Fuck.

"Did she tell you what it was about?" Although I had a pretty good idea what haunted her dreams. Or rather, *who*.

"No. Wouldn't say a word."

I took a long pull on my beer, stretching my legs out before me. I felt calmer now I was here, knowing she was sleeping in the next room. The urge to storm in there and check on her simmered beneath the surface still, but I could think clearly enough to know that probably wasn't the best idea—not if I ever wanted her to talk to me again.

"What happened to her?" he asked, his eyes narrowed with grim curiosity.

"We still don't know for certain. But we know enough that Zander DiMarco will get what's coming to him." Anger skittered down my spine. I'd never felt so much wrath as I did for him, and the last few months hadn't exactly been a walk in the park for my cousins and our family.

I glanced back at the hall, imagining Caitlin curled up in bed asleep. If I could just see her for a second, see with my own eyes that she was okay.

"A word of advice from someone much older and wiser than you," Luis said, drawing my attention. "Whatever's running through your head right now... Don't do it."

He was right. Of course he was fucking right.

But I wasn't sure I could listen.

For once in my life, I wasn't sure I could be the better man.

Until a small voice startled me.

"Matteo?"

My heart almost lurched into my throat when I turned and met Caitlin's weary gaze.

"You came," she choked out.

I got up and strode toward her, only stopping when I

was in touching distance. She stared up at me, fear and something I wanted to believe was relief glittering in her eyes.

"Yeah," I said, curving my hand around the back of her neck and drawing her close. "I came."

CHAPTER 11

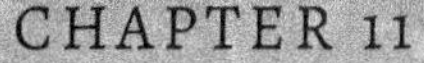

CAITLIN

Matteo held me, his big muscular arms cocooning me, shielding me from the world.

My fingers twisted into his jacket as I breathed him in.

"Shh, Tink, I've got you."

My body trembled as I sobbed into his chest. When I'd woken up with a start, and heard his voice, anger had flooded me… but it quickly melted away when I realized he'd come for me.

I tried to make out I didn't care to protect myself, but really it meant more than I could ever put into words.

Luis gave the two of us some space, mumbling something about retiring for the night. Matteo thanked him before guiding me over to the couch and pulling me down beside him.

"How are you feeling?" he asked.

"I can't believe you're here."

His hand rested against my cheek, his thumb brushing

a soothing line over my jaw. "I told you, I will always come."

Why, I wanted to ask, but I swallowed the question. Part of me knew why; I just didn't want to admit it.

"Do you want to tell me what happened?"

"It was just a nightmare. I get them sometimes."

"About DiMarco?" His eyes narrowed, searching my face for answers I didn't have.

"Zander DiMarco isn't the only monster I've ever faced, Matteo."

God, why did I say that?

He went rigid. "What does that mean?"

"Nothing," I sighed, glancing away. "Forget I said anything."

Matteo slid his fingers under my jaw and gently tilted my face up to meet his. "Talk to me, Caitlin. That's all I'm asking."

My shoulders sagged a little at his admission. Not that I expected him to try anything—I didn't get those vibes from Matteo. Besides, he was clearly very against hurting women. But still, I'd fallen for that act before.

Even though I wanted to trust him—and I did—I needed to keep my wits about me.

"You know, not a single day has gone by when I haven't thought about you," he said quietly, so quietly I almost missed it.

"Matteo." I breathed out slowly. "You can't say things like that to me." Peeking up at him, I studied his face. Strong jaw and glittering blue eyes. His dirty-blond hair fell over his face, and the smattering of stubble on his jaw sharpened his boy-next-door good looks.

"Just did, Tink, and I don't regret a single word." He gazed down at me, and I felt the strange tug between us. I'd felt it that night all those months ago. I'd felt it again when I saw him standing there in the hospital… and I felt it now.

No one had ever made me feel the way Matteo Bellatoni made me feel. And that was a dangerous thing.

"You can't call me that anymore. I don't have the t-shirt."

My Tinkerbell t-shirt was my favorite thing and I'd worn it the night Matteo and I spent together. But it was with the rest of my things at my apartment—the one I could never return to, all thanks to Zander's temper.

"You'll always be Tink to me." Matteo brushed the hair from my face and smiled, and damn if my heart didn't flutter wildly in my chest.

This man. This determined, gorgeous, honest man.

"What?" he asked, and I realized I was gawking at him.

"Nothing, it's late. You probably need to get back—"

"Cait, stop. I came to make sure you're okay. I'm not going anywhere."

"But—"

"No buts." He pressed his finger against my lips and my breath caught. "I can take one of the guest rooms."

"You're staying?"

"Yeah. In the morning, I'm going to feed you breakfast, and then you're going to show me how much progress you've made on that puzzle."

"You're serious?"

"Do I look like I'm joking? Now, let's go." He got up, pulling me with him.

"Uh, go where?"

"To bed. You just said so yourself, it's late." Hands on my shoulders, Matteo gently nudged me down the hall, stopping at my room. "You'll be okay?"

"I… uh, yeah." I glanced back at him.

"Okay." He nodded. "You need anything, just shout… or text. I'll leave my phone on."

"You're going to go stay in one of the guest rooms, just like that?"

Matteo's brow furrowed. "Yeah, why?"

"I… nothing."

I wasn't used to this. I was used to men taking what they wanted, when they wanted it. The desire in his eyes was obvious. The way the air crackled between us whenever we were near. Matteo wanted me—he just wasn't going to do anything about it without my permission.

He chuckled. "I am quite capable of being around you and controlling myself, you know."

Heat flooded my cheeks. "I wasn't… that's not…" Oh God. He was looking at me with so much yearning, I felt stripped bare.

"I should… it's late and I…"

He leaned in, dropping his mouth to my ear and whispered. "Breathe, Tink. Just breathe." His warm breath tickled my skin, sending a shiver through me.

I felt his lips curve as he said, "Although it's nice to know I affect you too."

Trouble.

I was in so much trouble.

"Goodnight, Matteo." I met his gaze, smiling. "And thank you."

I might not have wanted him to come here, but the truth was…

It was exactly what I needed.

THE SMELL of coffee and bacon lured me from a peaceful sleep. My eyes fluttered open as my stomach rumbled and I smiled.

Until the events of the night before hit me and embarrassment washed over me.

I had a nightmare. A bad one. Luis had eventually shaken me awake, but not before he'd witnessed me lashing out at invisible monsters, screaming and sweating as if they were right there in front of me.

And Matteo…

Oh God. Matteo was here.

It was too early to process what that meant, so I opted for coffee first.

After freshening up in the bathroom, I pulled on some leggings and an off-the-shoulder sweater, tamed my unruly curls into a low ponytail and went in search of breakfast.

"Morning," Matteo said from his position at the cooktop. "I wondered if the smell would wake you."

"You cook?" I asked, surprised.

"Don't get too excited, it's bacon and eggs. Hardly à la carte cuisine. Coffee?"

"Sure. Cream, two sugars."

"Two, huh?" He smiled, and my heart fluttered.

"What?"

"Nothing." His smile morphed to a smirk. "I was just thinking you're already sweet enough."

"Matteo." I rolled my eyes, feeling my cheeks heat under his intense regard. "Where's Luis?" I changed the subject, needing to break the simmering connection between us.

"He's around. Don't worry, you're safe with me."

"I know."

His brow lifted but he didn't comment. "Did you manage to get some sleep?"

"Surprisingly, I did."

"Does that happen a lot… with the nightmares?"

"They come and go. There isn't really a pattern."

"What you said before…"

"Please, don't." I sighed, averting my gaze. I shouldn't have said that last night. But Matteo made it too easy. He made me want things—things I could never have.

"Sorry." He continued cooking the bacon, not looking at me again. My stomach twisted, hating the sudden tension lingering between us.

Matteo plated up the bacon and eggs in silence, pushing a plate toward me.

"Thank you," I said, my stomach growling again.

He fought a smile. "You're hungry."

"Starved, actually."

"Glad I could help."

Matteo didn't eat. He just stood there, watching me devour my breakfast. My body hummed with awareness, his gaze caressing my skin.

"So, about that puzzle," he said. "Are you almost done?"

"You're kidding right? It's like two-thousand pieces."

"Eat up and I'll help you for an hour before I have to get back."

"Why?" I blurted out.

"Do I need a reason other than I want to?"

Pressing my lips together, I shook my head.

"I'm going to make a call. I'll be right back."

"Oh God, your sister," I said, remembering he was supposed to be babysitting her last night.

"Relax. Bella is fine. I left her at my place with our cousin and her bodyguard."

My eyes widened to saucers as I spluttered, "Y-you did what?"

He chuckled. "You're cute when you care."

"I… you didn't have to do that. I would never have—"

"I wanted to come, Cait. I can call you Cait, right?"

"Y-yeah." My chest tightened.

A faint smile traced his lips. Warm. Inviting. Like sunshine on a stormy day.

Matteo was gorgeous and having one hundred percent of his attention was completely disarming.

"Finish your breakfast. I'll be back." He tapped the counter and walked off, and suddenly, I didn't feel so hungry anymore.

"Yes!" Matteo whooped, fist punching the air as he slid in another piece of the puzzle.

He was good. Almost as good as Luis. I'd been too mesmerized watching him to really contribute. He caught me watching him more than once but didn't comment, merely flashed me a knowing smile and went back to the puzzle.

"Are you sure you don't need to go?"

"Do you want me to go?"

"No, I just…"

"Caitlin, I meant what I said before. I don't expect anything. This isn't a transaction where I do you a favor and then you owe me. I came because I care. Because ever since that night, I haven't been able to get you out of my mind."

"Matteo—"

"I know," he let out a heavy sigh, "you don't want to talk about it, and that's okay. I can respect that. But I can't ignore the fact that I thought I'd never see you again, and then here you are, under my family's protection. It might not mean anything to you… but it means something to me."

Without thinking, I leaned over and kissed him. Matteo went rigid beneath my touch. My fingers curled into his t-shirt, but then his hands cupped my face, and he took control.

And I let him.

His tongue gently nudged my lips apart, sliding against my own and coaxing a whimper up my throat. He tasted exquisite, his lips firm yet soft, demanding yet patient as he licked my mouth in slow lazy strokes, as if he was familiarizing himself with the shape of my lips and savoring their taste.

My heart galloped in my chest, my toes curling inside the fluffy slippers Arianne had gifted me.

"Fuck, Tink," he rasped, touching his head to mine and inhaling a ragged breath. "That was…"

"Unexpected."

Our laughter mingled together, finding its own harmony.

"You made a fatal mistake," he said.

My brows furrowed. "I did?"

"Yeah, now whenever I see you, all I'll be able to think about is kissing you again."

My stomach dipped, heat coursing through my veins. Matteo brushed his nose along mine, stealing another kiss. This one was more playful, even a little clumsy. But it was still one of the best kisses I've ever had.

I let out a contented sigh as he pulled away.

"You liked that?"

"It wasn't awful." I smiled.

"Good to know." A faint smirk traced his lips.

His phone began vibrating, but he glanced at the screen and ignored it.

"Don't you need to take that?" I asked.

"It can wait."

It stopped vibrating but two seconds later started again.

"I think somebody wants to get a hold of you."

He muttered something in Italian under his breath and clambered to his feet. "I'll be right back."

I watched him answer his cell as he walked toward the window.

"What?" he barked, and I flinched.

It was instinct. An old habit that was hard to break.

Matteo lowered his voice to the point where I couldn't

hear what he was saying, but whatever it was, it didn't look good. His eyes narrowed, his jaw clenched tight as he listened to whoever was on the other end of the line.

"Yeah, okay." He hung up and came back over to me.

"Is everything okay?"

"I need to go," he said, barely meeting my gaze as he loomed over me. A wave of dejection crashed over me.

"Oh, okay."

"You'll be okay? Luis is right down the hall. Maybe he can come finish off the puzzle with you."

"Yeah… I'll be fine." Disappointment welled inside me. "I'll see you out." I went to get up, but Matteo shook his head.

"Don't worry about it, I can see myself out."

By the time I got to my feet he was already at the door. "Matteo," I called, panic rising inside me. "Are you sure everything's okay?"

"Yeah, it's nothing you need to worry about."

My heart sank at the invisible line he was drawing between us.

It wasn't supposed to hurt because I was supposed to keep him at arm's length. But he'd clawed his way inside… and more surprisingly, I'd liked it.

I liked how he made me feel.

Except right now. Now our time together felt tainted, wrong somehow.

It felt like a mistake.

"I'll see you, Caitlin."

Not Cait.

Not Tink.

Caitlin.

As if he hadn't been kissing me only minutes ago.

"Matteo," I blurted out, but he was already gone, the door slamming closed behind him.

I stood there long after the rumble of his car had faded, wondering what had happened to make him leave in such a hurry.

Without even looking at me.

"CAITLIN?" Luis rapped on my door. "I've made some minestrone, if you want to join me?"

"Just a second." I swallowed back the tears burning my eyes and slipped into the bathroom.

It had been hours since Matteo had left, and I'd heard nothing. Not a single text.

It shouldn't have bothered me half as much as it did. After all, I'd been the one who had acted so coolly with him in the beginning.

But something had changed last night when he came for me. At least, I thought it had.

He'd cracked the fortress around my heart and found a way in. And it hadn't panicked me or paralyzed me with fear. Instead, I'd wanted it.

I'd wanted him.

I'd kissed him for God's sake and then he'd gotten that call and left in such a hurry he hadn't even said goodbye, not properly.

I joined Luis at the breakfast counter, smiling weakly when he pushed a bowl of minestrone toward me. "Eat," he said. "And then you can tell me what has you moping around like someone kicked your puppy."

"I am not…" I bit my lip. He was right. I was moping, but with good reason.

"Wouldn't have to do with the way Matteo hauled ass out of here earlier, would it?"

"You saw him leave?"

"Heard him more like." Luis shrugged. "You know, he's a good man, Cait. One of the best people I know. If he left suddenly, he had good reason."

"I wouldn't know, he didn't tell me." My minestrone became mightily interesting as I avoided Luis's questioning gaze.

"This is good," I added.

"It is, but I don't think you'll find any answers at the bottom of the dish."

I peeked up at him. "You're awfully chatty today… and nosey."

"It's my job to know what's going on with my marks." His lips curved with amusement.

"Somehow I find that hard to believe." I smiled back. "Thank you, for the meal."

"You're not alone, Cait. I know it can't be easy, being stuck here with me, but Arianne and Nicco mean well—"

"Oh no, I don't think that at all. What they've done for me…" I swallowed over the lump in my throat. It was more than anyone else had ever done for me. But it didn't change the fact that I couldn't hide out here forever. Eventually, I would have to go back to my life. Wherever that may be.

"They won't let you fight your battles alone. Of that you can be sure."

How could I ask that of them though?

Zander DiMarco was one of their business partners; he wouldn't go quietly. I didn't expect—or want—them to go to war with him.

Only I couldn't see a way out.

Not unless I left…

And never looked back.

MATTEO

"Fuck." I stared down at the dead body, the face barely recognizable. "It's definitely him?"

"Shaun Demetri. Twenty-six years old. Cause of death was blunt force trauma to the head."

"Thanks, Doc," Enzo said, nudging me forward. He waited until we were in the hall to say, "You thinking what I'm thinking?"

"Zander got fed up with chasing her and decided to try and torture it out of him." Acid washed in my stomach.

When Enzo had called me with the news, I'd been so overcome with fear and anger, I had to get out of the cabin before I did something stupid. Looking back, I probably didn't handle it the best way, but I couldn't tell Caitlin, not yet. Not until we confirmed what we already suspected.

DiMarco wasn't going to let her go—he was going to exhaust every possible option available to him to find her.

And eventually, he'd hit the jackpot, and someone would give him the vital piece of information he needed.

That we had her.

"We need to deal with him, and soon," I muttered, jamming my fingers into my hair and tugging the ends.

"I know, but it's not that straightforward."

"What do you mean, it's not that straightforward? He's a woman-beating piece of shit. We don't need to be associated with—"

"Word on the street is he made a deal with Lombardi."

"What?" I balked. "Lombardi? But they're not in Rhode Island."

The Lombardi were a crime family operating out of New Haven, Connecticut. Their boss, Massimo Lombardi, was a real nasty piece of work.

"I don't know all the details, but Lucino said he got wind of Dominic Cabrioles and Jasper Peshie being at DiMarco's a few days ago."

Fuck. Dominic Cabrioles was Massimo Lombardi's right-hand man. If he was in Providence sniffing around DiMarco's club, this was bad news.

Bad fucking news.

"When did you find this out?" My teeth ground together.

"Last night."

"And you didn't think to call me? Fuck, E, I went there and you—"

"Whoa, cous. Don't turn this into something it's not. I didn't tell you because I knew you were heading there and I thought… no, I knew, you needed time with her without this shitshow hanging over your heads. This is bigger than just Caitlin, Matt. If the Lombardi are involved… it changes everything."

"What does Nicco say?"

"Nicco's mind is elsewhere right now."

Of course it was. Uncle Toni was still in the hospital.

"Does my old man know they're sniffing around?"

"Lucino told him, yeah."

I went rigid.

"Relax. He doesn't know about Caitlin yet." He released a steady breath. "Uncle Michele is cautious. He doesn't want to start anything that might cause waves. Besides, he doesn't know who she is to you. If you told—"

"No, I'm not ready. I don't even know if she is anything to me."

Enzo gave me a pointed look. "That's bullshit and you know it."

"I don't mean…" I released a heavy sigh. "I like her, E. More than like her, but she's dealing with a lot of stuff, and she still won't talk about what happened."

"Does it matter?"

We exited the county morgue and headed for Enzo's GTO.

"Of course it fucking matters. I don't want to take advantage of her." Just like I didn't want to be her rebound.

When she'd kissed me earlier… fuck, it was like all my dreams come true. It was all I wanted. But then Enzo called, and it was like being doused with a bucket of ice-cold water. A harsh reminder of everything we still had to deal with—things I wasn't sure Caitlin was ready to face.

How could I even think about being with her until she came to terms with everything.

And now her co-worker—her friend—was dead.

It would kill her, knowing DiMarco had hurt him.

I climbed inside the car and buckled up. Enzo slid in a second later, running a hand through his hair. "It would be so fucking easy to go settle this right now," he said quietly, a deadly edge to his voice. His hands gripped the steering wheel, the blood draining from his knuckles. "I've never liked that piece of shit... but we have to be smart. Especially if he's in bed with the Lombardi."

"This is a total clusterfuck," I seethed.

Enzo glanced over at me. "We'll figure it out. We need to get out of town before DiMarco gets word that we're sniffing around." He stepped on the gas.

The coroner had agreed to be discreet for a fee, but his silence wouldn't withstand torture.

"DiMarco isn't ballsy enough to start picking off people in positions of authority."

"No?" My brow lifted. I had a feeling we didn't know what he was capable of.

"Any word from Nicco?" Enzo asked as I checked my cell.

"Nothing."

"I keep thinking about what will happen if Uncle T doesn't pull through..."

"Same," I confessed. "Nicco is strong." One of the strongest guys I knew. But losing your father and becoming boss was no easy burden to shoulder.

"I used to dream about the day Nicco stepped up and

we became his capos. But I didn't ever want it to happen like this," Enzo said.

I relaxed as we sped out of Providence and hit the highway leading back to Verona County.

"You doing okay?"

"Yeah." I inhaled a deep breath.

"You know why we couldn't go—"

"I know." I snapped, the anger I'd fought so hard to contain spilling over.

We were so close to him... so fucking close, and yet, I had to push my need for vengeance away and focus on the task at hand.

All in the name of the Family.

"I think you should talk to your old man," Enzo said. "If the worst happens and Uncle T... Nicco won't be in any fit state to lead, not straightaway. Which means all decisions will defer to Uncle Michele. He needs to know about her, Matt. About your relationship with her. This is personal and it affects all of us."

I scoffed at that. We didn't have a relationship... did we?

Memories of how good it had felt kissing her invaded my mind, making my body stir to life. She'd been so bold in that moment. I'd caught a glimpse of the girl from last summer. The girl who wasn't afraid to take what she wanted.

When I didn't answer, he added, "You know I'm right."

"Yeah." I dropped my head back against the headrest.

I could already imagine how that conversation would go. My father was a reasonable man. A good man. A family man. But when he found out we had given safe haven to Caitlin, I had no doubt he would have a thing or two to say about the fallout if DiMarco found out. It wasn't that he agreed with hurting women—he didn't, at all—but he would put the Family ahead of emotion. Always.

And when he found out who she was to me—who I wanted her to be—I had no doubt he'd remind me of the Omertà, our code of silence, and what it meant for outsiders.

Caitlin knew who we were. No doubt she had a pretty good idea what we did and how we did it. My father wouldn't look too kindly on a woman who now had valuable information about the Marchetti and at least one of their residences.

Shit.

Maybe I should have told him sooner.

"What?" Enzo broke the thick silence.

"Maybe we shouldn't have brought her back to Verona."

"Do you really believe that? Because I'm not buying it for a second."

"My old man isn't going to like it."

"Then you'd better convince him that you're serious about her."

"What?" My brows pinched.

"If he thinks you're... together, then he can't exactly toss her to the wolves, can he?"

"I can't ask her to play pretend just to pacify my old man." Besides, it would be torture when I wanted the real thing.

"I'll come clean, but I'm not going to ask her to

pretend… DiMarco will kill her if she goes back. We had no choice but to offer her a safe haven."

My father wasn't a monster. He would understand, even if he didn't like it.

"Are you going to text her or just stare at your phone the whole ride back?"

"Honestly, I don't know what to say." Her friend was dead. Tortured at the hands of DiMarco or his men.

"He already knew about the hospital, so there isn't much else Shaun could have told him."

"Somehow I don't think she'll see that as any kind of silver lining."

"She deserves to know," he said.

"And I'll tell her, I will." I just didn't know how. I already had to fix things after the way I hightailed it out of there this morning. Now I had to figure out how to tell her about Shaun.

"She was just starting to warm up to me," I said wearily. "But this… this will ruin her."

"You don't know that. She's stronger than she looks, Matt."

"How can you be so sure?"

"It's in her eyes, cous. She's a fighter."

I didn't like to think about what had made her that way, but I couldn't deny the merit in his words. Caitlin had hinted at something similar herself.

"I still can't believe you left Bella and Alessia with Jay last night. I bet he loved that."

"He had it handled."

"Like you gave him any choice." Enzo chuckled.

A pang of guilt went through me. He had a point—I'd

just up and left them with Jay. Anything could have happened. But all I'd been able to think about was getting to Caitlin.

She blinded me to everything else, and that was a dangerous thing. Because when you were distracted—as I had been since she appeared in my life again—you dropped your guard.

The scenery turned familiar and the ache in my chest abated slightly. Caitlin was safe here. Not even someone as arrogant as DiMarco would be stupid enough to come into the heart of Marchetti territory and try to take her from us.

From me.

I LEFT Enzo to go check in on Nicco and Arianne, and I headed to my parents' house. He was right—I needed to talk to my father. And then, when I'd ironed things out with him, I needed to go to the cabin and break the news to Caitlin about Shaun.

"Ah, Matteo," Dad said as I entered the kitchen. "I was wondering when you'd show up. Your sister said some interesting things this morning."

"She did?" My chest tightened.

"Something about you leaving late last night to go see a woman." His brow lifted as he shook out his newspaper.

"I… we need to talk."

"Sit," he commanded. "Tell me what's on your mind."

"There's something you should know."

He lowered the newspaper. "Go on."

"When we drove out to see DiMarco, we got… interrupted."

"Yes, Nora was sick, was she not?"

"That's not entirely what happened."

His brows bunched together. "I'm listening."

"Enzo got a call from the hospital down in Pawtucket. He'd given his number to one of DiMarco's girls, he was concerned that DiMarco was hurting her."

"I see. And you went to check in on her?"

I nodded, growing hot all over. "I… I recognized her. She and I… we had a thing last summer."

"A thing—" Realization dawned in his eyes. "And how serious was this thing?"

"It was one night." I rubbed a hand over my face. "But I wanted it to be more."

"And she's one of DiMarco's dancers you say?"

"We suspect she's more than that to him. He… he hurt her, badly, and her friend—a guy that works at the club— got her out. But she said she couldn't go back for fear of what DiMarco would do."

My old man went as stiff as a board. "What did you do, figlio mio?"

"We… fuck." I expelled a long breath. "We brought her back to Verona County with us. She's at the family cabin with Luis."

"Sei proprio un coglione! What the hell were you thinking?" he seethed, palm flat against the table.

"You didn't see her lying there, broken and bruised at the hands of that… that fucker."

"But bringing her here? Do you have any idea what you might have started? And Enzo went along with this?"

"We agreed—"

"Matteo," he tsked. "Did either of you stop to consider what happens if DiMarco finds out we're harboring his—"

"Don't." The word rumbled in my chest. "She is not his."

His eyes flashed with understanding. "You feel for the woman?"

"I do." I lifted my chin in defiance. "And sending her back to DiMarco is not an option."

Tension radiated between us and then I added, "He killed the bartender who helped her."

"Che diavolo!"

"It's where we went earlier. We got a heads up from Lucino that the bartender had been reported missing. He turned up dead."

"You saw the body?"

I nodded. "He was pretty messed up. The official report says he slipped down his stairwell and sustained blunt force trauma to his head."

"Merda!" My father's usual composed façade cracked slightly. "This is the last thing we need right now."

"I know. We should have come to you straightaway, but I—"

"You were too busy thinking with your heart and not your head." He cut me with a scathing look.

"I care about her—"

"A girl you barely know. I take it you didn't know she belonged to DiMarco when you tumbled with her between the sheets?"

Jesus. This was so awkward. I didn't want to discuss the details of that night with him. Not when just thinking about her soft skin pressed up against mine, the taste of her lips, made my body stir to life.

I shifted uncomfortably, clearing my throat. "This isn't about my relationship with Caitlin; it's about doing what's right. She needed help and she called Enzo. What were we supposed to do?"

"You should have called me the second you got to the hospital and realized who she was."

"Well, we didn't. And now she's our responsibility."

He scoffed at that. "Just make sure she doesn't become your doom, Son. Who else knows about this?"

"Nicco, Ari, Enzo and Nora, me, Luis… the bellhop would have seen her at Nicco's place. Maybe security."

"We need to contain this before someone talks and word gets out. DiMarco was a loose cannon before, we don't need to light the fuse on him before we figure out how best to proceed."

"I'll call Nicco and—"

"No, I'll handle it. Niccolò has enough on his plate. What's done is done. We all just have to hope DiMarco doesn't find out before we're ready for him to know."

I went rigid at that. "What do you mean… before we're ready for him to know?"

"Son, be reasonable. We can't just take out DiMarco. He has a string of businesses, a network of employees. He has connections. It wouldn't surprise me if he has a contingency plan should we ever feel the need to sever our ties with him."

"One way or another, this will get out," he said. "Unless she disappears, and something tells me you won't stand by and watch that happen. Anything else you want to tell me…"

Shit. "The Lombardi."

"So you did know." My father let out an exasperated breath.

"About the Lombardi sniffing around his clubs, yes."

"Porca puttana! And when were you going to bring this to my attention?"

"I… I've been kind of distracted."

"By a piece of ass." He snorted. "I thought I raised you better than that."

"No, you raised me to respect women and always do right by them. I learned that from you, Papa."

He studied me, shaking his head slightly. "I take it you're going to break the news to her?"

"Yeah, she needs to know the truth." No matter how much it would gut me to tell her.

"Then go be with her." He stood and gripped my shoulder. "If she has captured your heart, then she must be a good woman."

I swallowed over the giant fucking lump in my throat.

Because he was right.

Caitlin had captured my heart. It had taken precisely one intense night with her for me to fall. And not a single day had gone by where my thoughts hadn't drifted to the redheaded angel who had stolen a piece of me.

I couldn't let her vanish, not again.

But it wasn't my choice to make.

CHAPTER 13

CAITLIN

Luis was at the door talking to someone.

Not just anyone.

Matteo.

"Cait," he said, keeping the door half-closed preventing Matteo's access. "There's someone here to see you."

I could have kissed him for giving me the chance to speak up for myself. For giving me the choice. It wasn't something I was used to which only made me appreciate it all the more.

"It's okay," I replied. "You can let him in."

I wanted to hear what he had to say for himself after his stellar performance this morning.

But when Matteo stepped inside, I knew immediately that something was wrong.

"What happened?" I clutched my throat, frozen to the spot.

"Can you give us a minute?" he asked Luis, who glanced at me.

"It's okay." I nodded.

"I'm going for a walk. I won't be far."

"She's safe with me," Matteo said.

Luis gave him a curt nod, but I didn't miss the silent warning in his eyes. It was strange to have someone standing up for me, protecting me. But I liked Luis, I liked him a whole lot. He was easy to be around, if not a little aloof. He didn't probe or push, and he didn't feel the need to fill the silence. It made a difference to be around such a centered male.

He left and the air in the cabin turned thick with tension.

"We should sit," Matteo suggested.

"I'd prefer to stand." I folded my arms around myself, bracing myself for whatever he was about to say.

"The bartender... Shaun..."

"Oh God." Bile rushed up my throat, a wave of nausea battering my insides as I reached out for the counter to steady myself. "He's... dead?"

"I'm so sorry," he started approaching, "I'm so fucking—"

"Don't." I held up my hand. "Just don't."

Shaun.

Kind, funny, big-hearted Shaun. He'd gotten me out of Providence and delivered me to safety... and this was the thanks he got.

"D-did... did he suffer?"

"Cait," Matteo choked out.

"Please. I need to know."

"It would have happened quickly." His expression hardened and I knew he was only pacifying me. But it was probably for the best. I didn't really want to think about what DiMarco and his men had done to Shaun.

Poor Shaun, he didn't deserve this.

It was all my fault.

I should never have let him talk me into running.

"What will happen to him?"

"His family have been notified already."

"And the police?"

Matteo's eyes flared. "As far as the police are concerned, it was an accident. There will be no further investigation."

"But… he was murdered. He was killed by Zander and his…" Tears rolled down my cheeks as reality slammed into me. Zander had done this because of me—to find me.

"Oh no! What if Shaun talked? What if—"

"He didn't know anything past telling you to run. Even if he did talk, he wouldn't have given DiMarco anything more than he already knows."

"He's really gone?" My voice cracked as I stared at Matteo, silently willing him to fix this. To lie and tell me everything was fine.

But everything wasn't fine. And it wouldn't be, so long as Zander was still out there.

An idea popped into my head, and I blurted out, "You can kill him, right? Hire someone to take him out, make it look like an accident or something?"

"It's not that simple—"

"Yes, yes, it is. It solves all our problems."

"Tink." He came closer still, close enough to curve his

hand around my arm and gently brace me. "There is nothing more I want than to put a bullet between his eyes, but I can't. Not yet. Not until—"

"Until what?" I shrieked, a tidal wave of emotion crashing over me. "Until he finds me and points a gun at *my* head? You said you cared about me. You said you wouldn't let anything happen to me. You said—"

"Shh." He pulled me into his chest, holding me tight. My fingers clawed at his sweater as I sobbed violently against him.

"I never asked for any of this… I never wanted it."

"Shh, Tink. I've got you. I'm here." He nuzzled my hair, breathing me in.

My heart stuttered in my chest, overwhelmed by all the emotions flowing through me.

"He won't stop," I breathed. "He won't stop until he finds me, Matteo. And when he does—"

"No." He held me at arm's length, forcing me to look at him. "You do not belong to Zander DiMarco, do you hear me? If he wants you, then he'll have to come through me to get you."

My heart swelled but it didn't last. How could I possibly stand here, swooning, while Shaun lay dead on a steel trolley in the morgue.

Slowly, the tears subsided as I grew numb. This was my fault.

My fault.

"You hungry?" Matteo asked, guiding me over to one of the stools.

"Not really."

"Understandable, but you've got to eat something. How about something light?"

"Fine." I stared off into space.

Food was the last thing on my mind, but it had been an intense few days.

Matteo went to the refrigerator and started collecting up ingredients. "I call this, eggs à la Bellatoni."

"If this is your attempt at making me laugh, you might need to try harder." I sucked in a ragged breath, trying not to succumb to the tears again.

"Shit, Tink, I'm sorry. I don't know what I'm supposed to do here." He blanched, running a hand through his messy, dark-blond hair. Without another word, he rounded the breakfast counter and ran his thumb along the line of my jaw before burying his hand deep into my curls. "I wish I could make this all go away. I wish I could fix it."

"Matt," I breathed, fisting his sweater.

We stayed like that, wrapped up in one another until Luis came back into the cabin and cleared his throat.

"A word," he said to Matteo.

Matteo glanced down at me, and I nodded. "Go. I'm okay."

For a second, I thought he might kiss me, but then he pulled away, following Luis back outside.

I waited, wondering what could possibly be happening now. But I was too distracted to worry. My heart, too broken to care.

Shaun was a good guy. He was my friend. And Zander had hurt him because he'd helped me. I still couldn't believe it. But there was no doubt in my mind now that I could never return to Providence, to my friends there.

I wondered what Zander had told them, how he'd covered my disappearance.

I wondered if anyone cared.

Gisele might. Marielle too. But to a lot of the girls, I was merely the competition. The boss's pet. They didn't understand why he'd taken such a shine to me. I didn't either.

All I knew was, once he'd set his sights on me, Zander DiMarco's obsession with me began.

Matteo came back inside, taking the air with him.

"Is everything okay?" I asked.

"Yeah. Luis needs to head back into the city."

"Oh."

"I'll stay until he returns." His eyes narrowed slightly. "You know, I came back for you last summer."

"W-what?"

He nodded. "It drove me out of my mind that I didn't get your number, so a few weeks after, I drove down to Providence and looked you up. Only to find you were gone."

"You came for me?" Disbelief coated my voice. Just when I thought Matteo couldn't do anything more to convince me he was a good guy, he went and said that.

"I felt something that night, Cait." He prowled toward me, with slow, sure steps. In that moment, he reminded me of a predator stalking its prey. But I didn't feel an ounce of fear, only a shiver of anticipation.

"Something I'd never felt before." He laid his hand on

the side of my neck, gazing down at me. "But you were his… weren't you?"

The utter defeat in Matteo's eyes gutted me. There was so much he didn't understand, things he didn't know, that I couldn't ever tell him.

But there were some truths I could offer him.

"The lease was up on that apartment. I couldn't afford to renew," I said, grounded by his touch. "He said he knew of an empty apartment in his building."

Matteo went rigid, but I kept going. "I didn't have a choice."

Looking back, part of me wondered if Zander was connected with the sudden rental increase on my apartment; if he'd orchestrated the whole thing to get me to move closer to him. It was his MO to act as savior. When really, he was the villain in an expensive suit.

"Did you and he—"

"Don't," I inhaled a ragged breath. "Don't ask me that."

"I'm just trying to understand… that night, you never said—"

"Because I wanted to pretend, Matteo," I snapped. "I wanted to pretend I was just a girl spending a night with a gorgeous, charming guy. A *good* guy. I haven't had much experience with those," I confessed, averting my gaze. Matteo looked at me too intensely, wearing his emotions for all to see.

It was one of the things I found so attractive about him. He didn't play games or try to hold the upper hand. He was honest and real, and he wasn't scared to show or tell you how he felt. It was so refreshing to meet a guy like that.

But part of me also didn't trust it.

Nobody was that perfect, and I couldn't help but wonder what skeletons he had in his closet.

He slid his fingers under my jaw and tilted my face back up. "You think I'm charming?" A smile tipped the corner of his mouth.

"That's what you're choosing to hear out of all that?" My brows furrowed.

"Made you smile though." He traced the seam of my lips with his thumb, and my tummy clenched. "Your past, whatever did or didn't happen with DiMarco, it means nothing to me, Caitlin. All I care about is that you're safe now."

"You don't even know me, Matteo." If he did—if he knew the truth—he wouldn't feel the same.

"I know enough." His eyes darkened, gazing down at me with reverence. "I know what I felt the night I buried myself deep inside you and heard my name fall from your lips, Tink."

He closed the space between us, ghosting his mouth over the corner of mine. A whimper spilled from my lips.

"We shouldn't," I said, not breaking away.

"Tell me one good reason why?" His fingers glided up my neck and threaded into my hair. The way he held me, with such tenderness and possession, made my heart expand.

He wouldn't hurt me. I knew that without a doubt.

But I wasn't worried about myself.

"Let me in, Tink." He kissed me again, harder this time, sliding his tongue past my lips and tasting me. I was powerless to stop him, melting into his touch. The feel of his hands in my hair and his lips on mine.

In one smooth move, he picked me up and started carrying me down the hall.

"Matteo, what are you doing?" I breathed, twining my arms around his neck.

"What I should have done the second I laid eyes on you again." *Kiss.* "Is that good with you?" *Kiss.*

"I…" My heart crashed so hard inside my chest I couldn't think straight.

"It's okay." He nudged my nose with his. "We don't have to do anything you don't want to. I just want to lie with you, Tink. Kiss you. Hold you in my arms."

Gosh, this man. He knew exactly what to say, exactly what to do to make me acquiesce.

"I am kind of tired." Soft laughter spilled from my lips, but my heart ached. For Shaun. For me.

For us.

Matteo was good. I didn't doubt that. He was mafioso, yes, but he had a code of ethics. Morals. But if he knew the truth… if he knew what monsters haunted my dreams, he wouldn't look at me with such reverence.

He paused on the threshold of my room, sweeping his thumb down my cheek and resting it beneath my bottom lip. "You are the most beautiful thing I've ever laid eyes on. I thought it then… I think it now. If you want to stop… if you want space, or want me to go… just say the word and—"

"I want this," I said, pressing my lips to his thumb. He moved it away, but I caught it in my mouth, sucking the tip.

"Fuck," he rasped. "Keep that up, Tink, and all my good intentions will go out the window."

I chuckled again, snuggling closer to him as he walked me inside the bedroom, kicking the door shut behind him. Matteo lowered me onto the bed and gazed down at me, making my stomach clench with delicious anticipation. I couldn't remember the last time someone looked at me with such hunger and desire. As if I was the center of their universe. The most precious thing to walk the Earth.

The feeling coursed through me, making me feel more confident than I had in a long time. "Come here." I crooked my finger at him.

"Patience, Tink," he said, slipping his hands to the hem of his sweater and yanking it off his body. My eyes went straight to the ink decorating his skin. The Eagle swooping over his shoulder and down his chest, the flowers curving around his biceps and trailing down his arm. The wicked skull sitting on his opposite shoulder. Matteo's body was a work of art, and I was the sculptor who wanted to run my hands over every dip and curve to appreciate something so perfectly formed.

"What?" he asked, looming over me.

"You're... beautiful."

"Beautiful, huh?" A smile tugged at his mouth. "I've been called a lot of things in my time, Tink, but I don't think I've ever been called beautiful."

My cheeks burned. "Maybe we should stop talking now." I scooched back to give him space to lie down, and he did, unfurling his big body beside me so we were lying face to face.

"Hi," he said, tucking a stray curl behind my ear.

"Hi."

"I love your hair. Your eyes… Your smile."

I blushed harder at his words. "It took me a long time to accept my wild curls."

"You know, I've heard redheads tend to have a fiery temper." Matteo's brow lifted.

"Maybe, a long time ago." But it had been long beaten out of me.

I hadn't realized I'd dropped my gaze until Matteo gently gripped my chin and lifted my face back to his. "Right here, right in this moment, the past stays where it belongs. This is about you and me."

It wasn't.

It was about so much more than that. But I wanted to pretend. I wanted to join him in the fantasy. Just like I had that night all those months ago.

"Come here." He buried his hand into my hair and curved it around the nape of my neck, drawing me closer. His lips teased mine, kissing the corner of my mouth, my jaw, pecking the end of my nose.

I began to tremble involuntarily, overwhelmed at his touch, at the emotions coursing through me.

"Caitlin?" Matteo pulled away to look at me. "What's wrong?"

"I… I don't deserve this," I whispered, barely able to look at him.

Anger flashed in his eyes, and I jerked back.

"Shit, Cait, I… I'm not angry at you." He pulled me into his arms, holding me. I relaxed against his chest, breathing in his delicious male scent. Matteo smelled of pinewood and spice and all those things a guy should smell of.

"I'm sorry," I murmured.

I'd ruined it—the moment.

But I couldn't get out of my head. I couldn't stop thinking about what would happen when he found out the truth.

When Matteo discovered I wasn't who he thought I was.

CHAPTER 14

MATTEO

Caitlin slept in my arms for hours. I didn't have the heart to wake her. Besides, laying there with her was everything. Knowing she trusted me enough to be so close to her. It was all I wanted.

When Luis had gotten a call from Arianne to return to the city, I'd wondered if Caitlin would feel comfortable being alone with me. Never in my wildest dreams had I expected this.

But now I had it, I wasn't sure I could ever let it—let her—go.

"No," she murmured, twisting in my arms. "No."

"Shh, Tink, you're dreaming." I stroked a hand down her arm.

"No, no. Please… no!" Fear laced her words as she began thrashing, her hands fighting some invisible monster.

"Cait," I said, shaking her gently. "Wake up. You're dreaming. It's just a—"

"No… *NO!*" She bolted upright and my heart leaped into my throat.

"Cait?" I whispered, reaching for her shoulders. Her body tensed as she let out a pained whimper.

"M-Matteo." She stared up at me with wild, confused eyes.

"Hey, I'm here." I sat up, wrapping my arms around her. "I'm right here."

"I… oh God… I'm sorry. I'm so, so—"

"Hey," I touched the side of her face, coaxing her to look at me. "You have nothing to be sorry for."

"I'm a mess. I didn't…" She sucked in a ragged breath. "I fell asleep?"

I nodded, fighting the urge to ask her what she was dreaming about. Or who.

Red-hot anger zipped through me, but I forced it down. This wasn't about me—it was about her. About what she needed.

"Do you want me to get you a drink, some water?"

"N-no, I—" Her eyes darted to my mouth, and she wet her lips. "I…"

My anger was tamped down by the shift in the air between us.

Caitlin curled into my side as I held her, her body trembling, fear radiating from every pore.

"Tell me what happened, please." My voice cracked.

It was driving me out of my mind not knowing the truth. All I wanted to do was help her, to be by her side when things got too tough.

"Tink," I whispered, hating that she still couldn't tell me.

Caitlin shifted in my arms to look up at me. She smiled, but it didn't reach her eyes and she laid her hand against my chest. "I…"

Time stopped, my heart beating violently in my chest.

"Please, just talk to me." I pushed the hair off her face to look at her. To really look at her.

"Matteo, I…" She pressed her lips together, her gaze dropping.

My heart went with it.

She wasn't going to let me in. Even now, after everything, Caitlin wasn't going to let me in.

I went to roll away, needing some space. But she grabbed my arm. "No, please… just…"

"Just what, Cait?" Our eyes locked, the air between us charged with anticipation. She could feel it too, I knew that. But she was too damaged, too scared to act on it.

"Maybe I should go," I sighed with defeat.

"N-no… I don't want you to leave," she rushed out, panic lacing her words. "I just…"

"You just what, Cait?" Dipping my head, I met her eye-to-eye. "What do you want?"

Her bottom lip wobbled, but then she inhaled a deep breath and whispered, "Make me forget, Matteo. All I want is to forget."

She leaned back, until our noses brushed. I inhaled deeply, my heart galloping in my chest. She was offering me everything I wanted, but part of me knew it was a moment of weakness. A moment that, in the harsh light of day, she might regret.

"Please…" She kissed the corner of my mouth, a featherlight touch I felt all the way down to my soul.

"Shit, Tink, you don't know what you're asking of me."

What was I doing? This was what I wanted… all I wanted. And yet, I didn't want to hurt her.

I didn't want to be something she might regret.

Fuck.

"I need this, Matteo." Her eyes shuttered as she drew in a ragged breath. "I need you."

Those three little words snapped the final shred of my resolve and in one smooth move, I rolled her underneath me.

"Hi," I whispered, brushing my nose over hers.

"Hi." She ran her hands up my chest and over my shoulders. Her eyes glittered so much emotion it was like a punch to the chest. "I'm glad you're here," she said.

Fuck. Why did that mean so much to me?

"You really want this?" *You really want me?* I swallowed the words.

Caitlin nodded, showing me with actions, not words that she was all in. Her lips met mine in a teasing kiss, her hand sliding into the hair at the back of my neck. It felt good, too fucking good, and my hips rocked against her. But there were too many layers between us. My jeans. Her leggings.

I climbed off the bed and shuck out of my jeans, feeling like a fucking god as her eyes drank in every inch of my body. Then I moved to the side of the bed, leaning over Caitlin and slowly pulling down her leggings.

"This okay?" I asked. She nodded.

Thank fuck, she nodded. Because now she'd given me

the green light, I couldn't think about anything except feeling her skin pressed up against mine again. Our bodies fused together, moving as one.

When I crawled back over her, she hitched her legs around my hips, pressing her hot center right against my rock-hard dick.

"Fuck, Tink." I gently collared her throat, dragging my tongue up the side of her neck and nipping her ear. "The things I want to do to you."

A violent shudder went through her, and I immediately eased back to look at her.

"Caitlin?"

"It's okay. I'm okay… don't stop." Her pleas were at odds with the fear swimming in her eyes.

Fuck.

Fuck!

I ran a hand down my face, releasing a heavy sigh. "Maybe we should stop."

"No… No!" She locked her hands around the back of my neck and yanked me down. "I want this, I do… it's just…"

DiMarco's attack.

The things DiMarco had done to her had left her mentally scarred.

The thought had my stomach knotting, and I inhaled a sharp breath to try and rein in the anger coursing through my veins.

"I'm not glass, Matteo. I won't shatter if you touch me."

But all I could think about now was his hands on her, taking and hurting. Punishing her. We still hadn't talked about what really happened between them. I wasn't sure I would ever be ready for that conversation, not without doing something reckless. And as my family loved to keep reminding me, I was powerless here.

Caitlin's hand drifted down my abs, her touch burning me inside out as her fingers toyed with the waistband of my boxer briefs.

"Tink," I choked out.

"I trust you, Matteo," she said with renewed confidence. "I trust you."

Lifting her hips slightly, she ground against me, a whimper catching in her throat.

Jesus, she was going to be the death of me.

I was trying to do the right thing…

I was.

But this felt too good—too right. It finally felt like I was exactly where I was supposed to be.

How was that even possible? That a woman I'd met once, could have such an effect on me.

I'd never really considered what spending eight months pining over her meant. I assumed she was just the one who got away. But being here with her, like this, only cemented what I suspected all those months ago.

Caitlin was special.

And she was mine.

"Please." She rubbed on me some more, eliciting a moan from deep inside me.

"No sex," I blurted out, wondering what the fuck was wrong with me. Caitlin frowned, dejection flashing in her green eyes. "We don't have to rush. I want to savor this," I said, trailing my hand up her stomach and gently squeezing her breast, dragging my thumb over her nipple.

"God," she breathed, arching into my touch. "It feels good."

"Just because I'm not going to slide into your warm, wet pussy tonight, doesn't mean I'm not going to make you come so hard you see stars, Tink."

Caitlin shuddered, pressing her lips together and suppressing a moan.

She liked the dirty talk. I'd be storing that little nugget of info for another time. For now, I wanted to give her exactly what she needed.

A distraction.

Dipping my hand between us, I rubbed her over her damp panties. "Already wet for me, Tink?"

"Matteo, God…"

"Not God, baby. Just a guy who really, *really* wants to hear you scream his name." I kissed her, plunging my tongue deep into her mouth as I slid my fingers into her underwear.

"Good?" I checked.

"Yes, don't stop…"

Thank fuck.

I spread her open and found her clit, rolling my thumb in circles until she was panting and writhing beneath me.

"Tell me what you want, Cait."

This had to be on her terms.

She clasped my wrist, pushing my hand south. My fingers grazed her entrance and she moaned.

"Yeah?" I swallowed. "Are you sure? I don't want to hurt you." My brow lifted.

"Please."

Gently, I eased a finger inside her, testing the waters as

I curled it deep. Caitlin froze, breathing heavily as I slowly stretched her, letting her adjust to the feel.

"More," she demanded.

I added a second finger, working her in synchrony with my thumb as it strummed her clit. "Fuck, Cait, you're so tight." Twisting my hand a little, I curled my fingers deeper, rubbing her walls.

Caitlin rode my hand, burying her face in my shoulder, drowning out her breathy moans.

"Look at me," I ordered, nudging her gently. Our eyes clashed and I captured her mouth in a bruising kiss. Our tongues tangled together in slow, lazy licks that had my dick straining against my boxers.

I wanted her, more than I'd ever wanted anything in my life.

The connection between us was like an invisible thread, pulling tauter and tauter. Binding us in ways I didn't understand.

"God, Matteo… it's… *God*." Caitlin began to tremble as she clung to me, breathless.

"Come for me, Tink, come for me now."

She shattered, clenching around my fingers as pleasure washed over her. I kissed her harder, swallowing her moans of *more* and *yes* and *oh God*.

Bringing my fingers to my mouth, I sucked them clean, smirking at the flash of surprise in Caitlin's eyes.

"I need to taste the real thing," I declared, dropping a kiss to her lips before I moved down her body.

Her skin was smooth and pale, pinking under my touch. Teeth and tongue and lips. I swirled my tongue around the peak of her breast, sucking gently. Marking her.

Claiming her.

"Ah, that feels…" Her fingers twisted into the sheets as she arched into my mouth.

My fingers slid back and forth through her wetness.

"It's too much." Caitlin slid her fingers into my hair, yanking slightly.

Our eyes clashed over the line of her body, and I smirked. "You don't want my mouth on you?" I blew a stream of air over her clit, and she moaned.

"I… ah, Matteo…"

"Say the word, Tink, and I'll stop."

She pressed her lips together, shaking her head a little. It was all the permission I needed. I dived at her like a man starved, lapping at her pussy with carnal hunger.

She tasted so fucking good as I dipped my tongue inside her.

"God…" She panted. "Matteo, yes…"

I hooked my hand under her thighs and spread her wider, needing more.

I needed everything she was willing to give me.

Caitlin had stolen a piece of my heart all those months ago, but I was pretty sure that right here, in this moment, she stole the rest.

I PULLED CAITLIN CLOSER, dropping a kiss to her head.

"What?" She peeked up at me.

"Just you… being here with you like this. A guy could get used to it."

"Matteo…"

"It's okay," I said. "I'm not asking you for anything you can't give me."

She relaxed against me. "Thank you, for distracting me."

Hurt crushed my chest.

Is that all this was to her? A distraction?

"It was my pleasure," I laughed off the sting of dejection.

Caitlin pushed up slightly to look me in the eye. "I'm not…"

"It's okay. We don't have to do this."

"Do you regret staying with me?"

"Never," I admitted.

I didn't, but part of me wished things were different. That we'd met under different circumstances.

"You gave me two of the best nights of my life." She whispered the words so quietly I barely heard them.

"I-I did?"

Caitlin nodded. "That night last summer and… right now. I want you to know that, Matteo."

I wanted her to know that I could give her so much more—that I would give her forever if she would let me.

But what kind of person would that make me if I promised her forever when she'd promised me nothing in return.

CHAPTER 15

CAITLIN

I woke up against a warm, hard body.

Matteo.

My lips curved at the memories of the night before. After he'd made me come apart, touch by touch, kiss by kiss, we'd spent hours talking. He'd shared stories from his childhood. I'd talked about the club. Mostly, I'd listened to him talk about his sister and cousins, about the mischief they used to get into.

Matteo had grown up in a big family, and I could tell from the way he talked about them, that family was everything to him.

Especially his younger sister Arabella.

It couldn't have been further from the truth for me.

Maybe under different circumstances, I would have gotten to meet them all one day—to spend time with them, getting to know them.

"Hey," Matteo murmured, his voice thick with sleep.

His hand slid over my hip, dragging me closer into his body. "What time is it?"

"A little after eight," I said, relishing the way it felt to be so close to him, even if it was only temporary.

"I could get used to this," he said, kissing my shoulder. A shiver ran through me at the raw honesty in his words. "How are you feeling?"

"Good," I replied. "I'm good."

I was more relaxed than I had been in weeks. He'd done that.

Matteo had done that with his dirty words, tender touches, and hot kisses. But it was his level of respect for me, and my body, that really got to me. The second I'd recoiled at his touch or flinched when he pressed too far or too hard, he had stopped and checked in with me. It was a revelation to have a guy care like that.

"I was worried you might feel differently this morning." He brushed the hair off my neck and kissed me there.

I rolled over and peeked up at him. "I don't... at all. Last night was... it was perfect. Thank you." I smiled.

"Fuck, Tink, you are so damn beautiful." He leaned in, dusting his mouth over mine.

"I need to brush my teeth," I said, pressing my hands to his chest.

He chuckled. "You think I care about morning breath?"

"You might not, but I do." I kissed his cheek before darting from the bed. "I'll go turn on the coffee machine."

"Stay. We don't have to get up yet." He silently pleaded with me, his eyes hooded with lust and things I didn't want to acknowledge.

But the spell was already broken. I needed some space to think, to clear my head and remember all the reasons why I couldn't allow myself to get swept away in this.

In him.

"I need a girl's minute." I didn't look back as I slipped into the bathroom and closed the door.

At least I hadn't slept with him again. Fooling around was one thing, but sex with Matteo… that would be my undoing. No, I needed to stay strong. I needed to keep some semblance of distance between us. Because if he started asking me for things I couldn't give him, he would start asking me questions I didn't have the answer for.

After taking care of business, I washed my hands and then tamed my curls into a loose ponytail over my shoulder. I felt torn. Part of me was so relieved Matteo was still here, that he had spent the night with me. But the other part knew it would only make things worse when the time came for me to leave.

Shaun was gone.

Zander had killed him… because of me. And I knew it was only the beginning of his rampage to find me. No one was safe around me. Not even Matteo and his family. Because men like Zander didn't play by the rules, they smashed straight through them.

"Tink?" Matteo called, and I smiled to myself. He made everything so simple that it would have been easy to hand over my heart to him right now. But it would only complicate things.

"Cait—"

"Coming," I yelled, unable to keep the frustration out of my voice.

When I slipped back into the bedroom, he was sitting propped up against the headboard, one knee bent.

God, he looked good. Inches upon inches of golden skin stretched over muscle. He could have been something straight out of a sexy magazine shoot.

"Everything okay?"

"Yeah." I smiled a little too enthusiastically. "Why wouldn't it be?" I hesitated, not sure how to do this. It was the morning after. Didn't guys usually make a run for it to avoid this awkward moment?

"Come here." He motioned for me to go to him.

"I should probably—"

"Tink." He dropped his legs over the edge of the bed and sat upright, reaching for me. "Come. Here."

Heat flashed inside me, my stomach clenching. Why did it sound hot when he ordered me around?

I went willingly, like a moth to a flame.

Matteo curved his arm around my waist and pulled me between his legs, staring up at me. "Why do I feel like you're already shutting me out?"

"I… I'm not," I whispered. "It's just… I'm not used to this."

"This?" He frowned, and I nodded.

"The morning after." Heat flooded my cheeks. "In my experience, guys don't usually stick around."

"Maybe you've been picking the wrong guys." He smiled, and it was so playful, so cute, something inside me softened.

Where were you five years ago? I gazed down at him, running my hand through his messy bed hair. He made it look so damn good.

"How are you feeling really?"

"I'll be okay." The lie soured on my tongue. "I just can't believe he's gone." Tears pricked the corners of my eyes, but I blinked them away. If I let myself fall down that dark hole, I wasn't sure I'd ever find a way out.

I didn't kill Shaun—Zander did.

No matter how guilty I felt, I had to remember that.

"What will happen? With Zander?" I asked.

The muscle in Matteo's jaw popped as he released a strained breath. "Honestly, I don't know yet. My family is dealing with a lot right now."

"Because Nicco's father is sick?"

He nodded, pain lingering in his eyes.

"I'm sorry." Without realizing, I scraped my fingers over his skull and a low growl rumbled in his chest. "God, I'm so sorry," I went to pull away, but Matteo grabbed my wrist.

"Don't," he said in a husky voice.

The air crackled around us, thick with anticipation. He wanted to kiss me again. I could see it right there, glittering in his eyes.

"Matteo," I breathed, my heart beating erratically in my chest.

What was happening?

I'd never felt so out of control before.

He pulled me onto his thigh and my arms went around his shoulder to steady myself.

"Hi," he said.

"Hi." A faint smile traced my lips.

"I'm going to kiss you now."

I inhaled a sharp breath, nodding gently. I was under

his spell, unable to break through from the all-consuming thoughts of him. Us. Together.

Matteo slid his hand along my clavicle and down to my chest, right where my heart lay. "I can feel your heart racing... so fast." He marveled, closing the distance between us.

The first touch of his lips was like electricity zapping through me. Kissing last night, in the dark, was one thing. But this... this was something else.

His tongue slipped past my lips, gently lapping at my own. Desire swirled inside me, burning me up.

"Matteo," I moaned into his mouth. "I—"

The shrill sound from his cell phone was like a bucket of ice water dousing the flames circling us. Matteo cursed under his breath, and I slipped off his lap and left the room.

I needed some space to think, and I couldn't do that with Matteo breathing down my neck.

But when I went out into the living room, I startled. "Luis," I gasped. "What are you—"

"Coffee?" he asked me with a smile.

"Sure, thanks." I propped myself up on one of the stools. "When did you get back?"

"About an hour ago."

Which means he knew Matteo spent the night with me.

"It isn't what you think," I rushed out, the strange urge to defend my behavior coursing through me.

"Caitlin." He set his mug down and gave me a knowing smile. "I'm not here to judge. I'm here to keep you safe."

"Morning." Matteo appeared, shirtless and completely unaffected by Luis's presence. "Something smells good."

"Grabbed a few freshly baked pastries from the nearest gas station. Luis motioned to the bag on the counter. "Help yourself. Coffee's in the pot."

"My kind of guy." Matteo squeezed Luis's shoulder.

"You good?" He came over to me and curved his hand around the back of my neck, kissing my temple as I stood there, rooted to the spot. My eyes flicked to Luis, and he gave me a discreet smile.

What the hell was that supposed to mean?

"I… yeah," I murmured, certain he would release me. But he didn't, one-handedly making himself a mug of coffee while keeping his hand on my neck. It shouldn't have thrilled me as much as it did. He was acting like I belonged to him… like we were together.

A fact we both knew could never come true. But it didn't stop him from touching me intimately and it didn't make me push him away.

"You want one?" Matteo asked me, nodding toward the coffee machine.

"Sure."

He finally released me, and I sucked in a shaky breath, stepping back to put some more distance between us.

"How's Nicco and Ari?" He asked Luis as he set about making my coffee.

"They're okay. There's been no change with Antonio though."

Matteo went rigid, releasing a steady breath. "He'll pull through. He has to."

Without thinking, I reached for his hand, squeezing

gently. The pain in his voice, the glittering in his eyes, was too stark to ignore.

His gaze collided with mine, and my heart hammered in my chest at the intensity in his expression. "Thank you," he mouthed, his eyes shuttering.

When they opened again, his whole expression softened as if just seeing me standing there, by his side, instantly made everything better.

It was a heady feeling; one I wasn't used to.

One I wasn't sure I could ever give up.

"Have you ever been?" Matteo asked me as we worked some more on the puzzle. I thought he would leave once we had breakfast, but he didn't.

And it mattered far more than it should.

This—us—it couldn't go anywhere. It couldn't ever be more than… *this*.

He had a life. A family and future. I didn't care about who he was, about what his family did. It wasn't like I'd grown up in a good, law-abiding family either.

No, I didn't care about any of that. And deep down, I wanted nothing more than for him to make good on his word and take care of Zander. At least then I'd be free of his obsession. But I'd never truly be free.

Not in the way Matteo needed me to be.

"Cait?" He brushed my arm, smiling at me. "Is everything okay?"

"Everything's fine." I smiled back, hoping he didn't notice the pain in my eyes.

"So… have you?"

"Have I what?"

"Ever been to New York?"

"Oh, I… I went a few times as a kid. I don't really remember it." The lie soured on my tongue. The truth was, I remembered every trip. Every single one. I remembered the arguments, my mom and her boyfriend fighting, the sound of his hand cracking against her face. The howl of her sobs echoing through the car.

I remembered it all.

Dropping my gaze to the puzzle, I inhaled a sharp breath.

You escaped.

You got out of there and you never have to look back.

"You were born in New York?"

I frowned. "How do you know…? Oh, your friends."

"They meant no harm."

"You're all very close."

"We are." A look of fondness washed over him. "They're my family. You don't have—"

"Matteo," I let out a heavy sigh. "I can't do this."

"Do what? What are we doing, Cait?" His eyes searched mine for answers.

Answers I didn't have.

"I'm so grateful to you and your friends, I am. But this… us…" I took a deep breath, my heart ready to burst, blood roaring in my ears. "Surely you know we can't—"

"Can't what?" His hand curved around my neck, holding me tenderly. Matteo dropped his head to mine, breathing me in. "It's a sign, Cait. Tell me you know it's a sign."

"I…"

Oh God. Emotion balled in my throat, thick and suffocating. He wasn't going to let this go—he wasn't going to let me go. And I didn't want him to. I wanted Matteo to fight for me. I wanted him to prove that there was good in the world. That I deserved more than the shitty hand I'd been dealt.

But that was fantasy.

And my demons were too big to outrun.

His lips brushed mine. Once. Twice. Until his tongue licked the seam of my lips, silently seeking permission. A soft sigh spilled out of me, and he took it as a yes, sliding his tongue deep into my mouth and tangling it with my own.

God, when he kissed me like this… I felt like the most beautiful girl in the world.

I felt safe and cherished… and loved.

"Matteo—"

"Call me Matt," he breathed against my mouth. "That's what my friends call me."

My lips curved involuntarily. "I'm your friend?"

His fingers threaded into my thick curls, pulling me back slightly so he could look me right in the eye. "No, Cait, you're not my friend." His eyes darkened, and I swallowed, my throat suddenly dry.

"You are so much more than that to me."

Oh my.

Matteo took my face in his hands and captured my mouth in a slow kiss, showing me exactly what I was to him.

A kiss I felt all the way down to my soul.

CHAPTER 16

MATTEO

"You're different." Bella narrowed her eyes at me as we ate Mom's bruschette.

"Just happy to see you." I grinned, and she rolled her eyes.

"No, I think it's the girl. The one you left to go and see the other night."

Rolling my lips together, I swallowed the words on the tip of my tongue.

Truth was, it was Caitlin.

I'd spent the morning at the cabin with her, doing that ridiculously impossible puzzle, laughing and talking. We'd avoided the hard topics. Or at least, she had.

Caitlin was a locked box, and no matter how much I tried to break the chains around her heart, she wouldn't let me in.

But I was so gone for her, I'd take whatever scraps I could get.

"Bella," I warned. "Eat your food."

"Don't change the subject, Matt. I know you like her. It's written all over your face. Who is she? Is she pretty? I bet she's real pretty if you—"

"Take a breath, pulce," I teased.

"Can I meet her? I totally have to meet her. Please."

My heart twisted. "No, you can't meet her. Not yet."

Not until it's safe.

I pushed the words out of my head. Caitlin was safe. As long as she stayed at the cabin, no one knew where she was. Even if DiMarco learned that she'd left the hospital with me and Enzo, he still didn't know *where* she was.

He'd have to come through us to find her, and I had no intentions of ever telling him. I'd rather die than give her up.

Fuck. What was I saying?

I had responsibilities. A family to think about. Arabella.

Anger curled in my stomach.

Nothing made sense anymore, not since Caitlin walked back into my life... and yet, being with her felt right. Like I was exactly where I was supposed to be.

It was a complete mind fuck.

"Seriously, Matt, you suck sometimes. This is the first girl you've liked in... well, forever." Arabella pouted, flashing her best puppy dog eyes at me. "I want to meet her. She must be special if she's caught your eye."

Caitlin was special all right.

My heart beat that much faster whenever I laid eyes on her. All those wild red curls, her alabaster skin, and glittering green eyes. She was stunning and so different compared to the kinds of girls I was used to.

Part of me wondered if I'd pushed her too far last night. Especially after what DiMarco had done to her. But Caitlin had wanted it. I'd felt the need pouring off her. And the fact she'd trusted me enough to touch her and make her come apart meant everything to me.

"*Matt!*" Arabella punched my arm and my eyes snapped up at her.

"What?"

"You didn't hear a word I just said, did you?"

"I…"

"Unbelievable." She rolled her eyes. "Sometimes I don't know why I even bother."

"Relax, drama queen." I leaned over and ruffled her hair, the way I used to when we were kids. "It's… complicated."

"Does she have a boyfriend? A psycho ex? Is it Nicco and Ari all over again? Is she the daughter of a rival—"

"Okay, Bella, that's enough with the crazy talk," I said. "Jeez, you need to get out more."

She scoffed. "Like that's an option."

Guilt flooded me.

"I know things are tough sometimes… but is it really so bad to have a family that cares so much?"

"Matteo." She rolled her eyes. "I'm sixteen and I've never even been kissed."

"What the fuck?" I balked. "Why do you want to be kissed? You have plenty of time—"

"And thank you for proving my point." She threw up

her hands. "You think anyone is going to come near me when you act like this?"

"Bella…"

"It's even worse for Alessia. Guys don't look twice at her at school. It's like she has a neon sign above her head saying off-limits. At least guys actually talk to me occasionally."

"What guys?" I snapped.

She shrugged. "Just guys."

"The same guys you want to kiss?"

Jesus, I wasn't ready for this. Arabella was my sister—my baby sister. I still vividly remembered crawling around the yard with her on my back while she pretended to whip me like a horse. She wasn't old enough to date and kiss and… nope, I wasn't going there.

Not until she was at least twenty-one.

"Stop changing the subject. This is about you, not me."

"Caitlin is—"

"Her name's Caitlin?"

Fuck.

Why had I said that?

It just spilled out though because she was always on my fucking mind. Imprinted there with no signs of leaving anytime soon.

Excitement twinkled in my sister's eyes. "Her name is Caitlin? That's pretty. Do you have a photo of her on your phone? Can I see it?"

"No, I don't have a photo of her." But I wished I did.

I laid awake last night for hours, watching her sleep. I couldn't shake the feeling that something bigger was at work here, reuniting us like this. But it was really bad fucking timing.

Uncle Toni was still in a coma. Nicco was barely holding on by a thread. And Lombardi's men were sniffing around DiMarco's.

There wasn't time for me to figure out what Cait and I were to each other. My number one priority had to be keeping her safe. She had already been at the cabin for five days. Eventually, she would want more freedom. Maybe she would even want to leave and go somewhere else, somewhere closer to where she was before.

"So… when can I meet her?" Arabella stared at me with eager eyes, and I chuckled. "What?" she whined.

"Never change, Bella."

My cell phone started ringing and I picked it off the table, checking the caller ID. "I need to take this," I said, trepidation coursing through me. I got up and ruffled her hair again, smiling down at her. "Never change for anything."

"Matteo, Lorenzo." Our Uncle Alonso greeted us the second we stepped into Uncle Toni's study. Genevieve and Alessia were still at the hospital which was the only reason he'd called us to the house instead of meeting somewhere neutral.

"Uncle Al, how's it going?"

"Can't complain."

"Come, sit." He motioned to the table. Nicco; my

father; and Stefan, Uncle T and Al's consigliere, were already seated, their expressions grim. Whatever had happened wasn't good.

"We didn't know you were driving down from Boston," Enzo said.

"Didn't know it myself until Michele called me." The two of them shared a knowing look.

"What's going on?" I said, blood roaring in my ears.

"We need to make some hard decisions, son."

"But Uncle Toni isn't—"

"He's not going to get better enough to return."

"W-what?" I blurted out, feeling like the rug had been pulled from under my feet. "Nic?"

"The doctor said that even if he wakes up, the road to recovery will be extensive." He dragged a hand down his face, his eyes vacant and expression haunted. "Given the new intel on DiMarco and Lombardi, Uncle Michele, Stefan, and Uncle Al decided we need to make the change now."

"Fuck," Enzo breathed.

"Effective immediately, Niccolò is now acting boss," Uncle Al said.

Nicco didn't look happy about it. In fact, he looked downright miserable. But I didn't blame him. It was a huge burden to carry.

"Stefan is going to stick around, try to help you figure out this Lombardi thing. It could be something, it could be nothing."

"And DiMarco?" I asked, immediately regretting it.

My father's heavy gaze found me across the table. He

leaned back slightly, steepling his fingers, and let out a long, steady breath.

"Tell them."

Shit.

I shifted uncomfortably in my chair. I should have kept my mouth shut. But it was too late now—everyone was watching me and if I didn't tell them, he would.

"We have a problem," I said.

Enzo slouched in his seat, burying his face in his hands.

"Out with it," Uncle Al demanded.

"It was my call," Enzo jumped in.

"No, it was my call. I take full responsibility for this. It ends with me." Nicco addressed his uncle and family advisor. "A little over a week ago, Enzo and Matteo went to visit DiMarco. But they never made it to Providence. Enzo got a call from the hospital over in Pawtucket. When they got there, they found one of DiMarco's girls beaten and raped."

I winced at his harsh assessment, my fist curling against my thigh.

"What was she doing in Pawtucket?" Uncle Al asked. "And why the fuck did she call Enzo?"

Nicco looked to our cousin and nodded.

"A few weeks ago, I was in Providence," Enzo said. "I came across one of DiMarco's girls crying in the bathroom. A couple of days later, he asked me to go check on one of his girls at her apartment. It was the same woman. Something felt off about the whole thing, so I gave her my number and said if she ever needed help to call me."

"It was the same girl?" Stefan asked, and Enzo nodded.

"Let me guess, you brought her back to Verona." Uncle Al shook his head with disbelief.

"I called Nicco, and we decided to bring her with us. She had nowhere else to go."

"Where is she now?"

"She's safe," I bit out.

"Interesting." Uncle Al sat back, studying me. "This woman, she is someone to you, Matteo?"

"She's—"

"She's important to me," I said, cutting Nicco off.

"I see."

"And you understand what you risk... for a woman that is neither your wife nor your family?"

"We couldn't leave her there."

"What's done is done." My father's jaw twitched. "The girl is safe in an undisclosed location. We need to focus on finding out everything we can about what Lombardi wants with DiMarco."

"I might be able to help there." Stefan pulled out a manila envelope. "Rumor has it Lombardi is looking to expand. He's made offers on three local businesses in the last three months. A run-down strip joint on the edge of Providence. And a café and gym downtown."

"He's trying to put down roots?"

"Trying to. My contact down at town planning called with his suspicions. Obviously, Lombardi used an alias, but it was traceable."

"Lombardi has to be a fool if he thinks he can just waltz into our territory and get his feet under the rug."

"Fortune favors the bold, old friend." Uncle Al clapped Stefan on the back and flashed him a grim smile.

"Al's right," Nicco said. "He's making a power play. Lombardi must know we'll have real estate covered. Providence is Marchetti territory. It always has been. If he's sniffing around DiMarco, it means he's been watching us. Learning who might not be happy with current arrangements."

"Fuck." My father expelled a breath. "We need to handle this, sooner rather than later."

Nicco nodded. "Enzo, I want you to go there and meet Lucino. Talk to DiMarco and get a feel for where his head's at."

"Sure thing, boss." Enzo smirked.

"I'm going," I said, pressing my palm into the table. If Enzo was going to see that fucker, I wanted—

"No."

"Excuse me?" I glared at Nicco.

"You're going to stay here. I don't want you anywhere near DiMarco until we know exactly what we're dealing with."

"But I—"

"Dammit, Matteo." He slammed his hand down, making his glass of whisky clatter. "That was an order, not a request. You are already too involved to keep a level head."

My teeth ground together behind my lips. He wasn't telling me anything I didn't already know. But I needed this—I needed to look DiMarco in the eye and see it for myself.

And then I needed to make him fucking hurt for having ever laid a finger on Caitlin.

"He's already looking for her," Nicco added. "We think

he killed one of his bartenders; the guy who drove Caitlin to the hospital."

Uncle Al clucked his tongue while my father stared at nothing. This was a clusterfuck, the whole fucking thing.

"How do you want to play this?" Enzo asked, effectively cutting me out from the conversation.

"Sit down with DiMarco and ask him what the fuck he's doing with the Lombardi."

"And if he doesn't tell us what we want to hear?"

"Remind him that his loyalty lies with the Marchetti."

Enzo nodded, tapping the desk. He was different with Nora. Calmer. More settled. But he still had a darkness inside him, a darkness that needed feeding. And Lorenzo Marchetti loved nothing more than getting his hands dirty in the name of business.

"This could cause problems, Niccolò." My father raked a hand through his salt and pepper hair.

"If we give DiMarco even an inch…"

"Sì, you are right. We need to know once and for all what he plans to do. If the Lombardi are in fact trying to make a power grab we need to be prepared."

"And Caitlin?"

I had to ask.

I had to know what they planned on doing with her.

"She can't go back," Nicco said, silently conveying what I so desperately needed to hear.

He had my back.

Regardless.

"Agreed."

Relief slammed into me. I hadn't realized how much I

needed to hear my father say those words until they came out.

"But she can't hide forever. You need to talk to her, Matteo. Find out her plans. Either she stands at your side, or she becomes a liability we can't afford right now."

What the fuck?

I swallowed hard.

It wasn't supposed to be like this.

"Michele is right," Nicco said, pinning me with a hard look. "You need to talk to her and find out her next move."

"And if she won't agree to stand at my side… what then?"

Nicco's expression guttered, and I had my answer. Caitlin was either all in on our side, or she wasn't.

Fuck.

"She's a liability, Matt. Until this thing with DiMarco is over, Caitlin cannot be allowed to leave."

"Right, yeah." My throat was dry, my head spinning.

"And if DiMarco is getting into bed with the Lombardi?" Enzo asked the question we all dreaded.

Nicco inhaled a deep breath, his eyes devoid of emotion as he embodied his father and became the boss.

"Then we prepare to go to war."

"Are you sure this is okay?" Bella asked from beside me. She'd barely sat still for the entire ride. It was the morning after the meeting with my cousins and uncles, and I couldn't stay away from the cabin for a second longer.

"I thought you wanted to meet her." I glanced at her.

"I do... I mean, any girl who has managed to catch your eye is a girl I want to meet. I need to make sure she passes the test."

"The test?"

"Yeah." She snickered, keeping her eyes focused on the scenery rolling by. "The 'is she good enough for my brother' test."

"Jesus, Bella," I murmured under my breath.

Maybe this wasn't such a good idea. But when Nicco and my uncles had suggested I talk to Caitlin, to try to find out what her plans were, my mind immediately went to all the reasons she had to leave. To walk away from me and never look back.

They wouldn't allow that though. Caitlin knew too much, making her a risk they couldn't afford. They wanted her to stay to protect our secrets, but I didn't want that. I wanted her to stay because she chose me.

So I'd brought ammunition in the form of my gorgeous, compassionate, slightly over-protective sister.

Arabella charmed everyone she met, and I had no doubt Caitlin wouldn't be able to resist her wiles. But it wasn't only about me. I knew Cait had to be feeling lonely stuck out in the cabin. Having another girl around might help her relax for the conversation we could no longer avoid.

"Ready?" I said, pulling up outside the cabin.

"Hell yes. I want to meet my future sister-in-law."

"What the—"

She exploded with laughter. "Oh God, you should see your face. I'm joking, Matt. But it's good to know just how serious you are about her."

You have no idea.

I ran a hand down my face, letting out a strained breath.

This was totally a bad idea.

But it was too late now.

CHAPTER 17

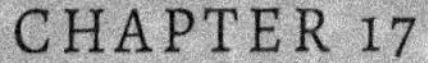

CAITLIN

LUIS ANSWERED THE DOOR AND SMILED. "WELL, THIS IS A surprise."

My brows knitted as I watched him step aside and welcome Matteo, and a young girl who shared his eyes and smile. Her hair was darker though, falling over her shoulders like a waterfall, and she had a vulnerability about her.

Arabella.

This was his sister, Arabella.

"Hey." Matteo dipped his head. "I thought you might appreciate some female company."

"Hello, I'm Arabella, but you can call me Bella. Matteo's told me all about you."

"He has, has he?" I fought a smile.

"No." She chuckled. "It's like getting blood from a stone. But it's really nice to finally meet you."

I glanced between them, surprised at the slight flush to Matteo's cheeks.

He'd told her about me?

"Don't worry," he said as if sensing my sudden discomfort. "I only told her the basics."

Right, and what are those? I wanted to ask. But I rolled my lips together, unsure of what to say. I'd imagined what it would be like to meet his family and get to know those closest to him. But now his sister—his younger sister—was standing there, staring at me, and nothing about this felt right.

I couldn't get to know his sister. What if I liked her? What if we hit it off? It would only be another tether tying me to him. To Verona. I didn't need any more reasons to want to stay here.

Family, love… hope, those things made you weak. And I had no room for weakness, not if I was going to survive the coming weeks.

I'd spent my life running from my past. Trying to escape a family who only ever wanted to hurt me. To use and exploit me. I couldn't risk being found out. No matter how much it meant to me that Matteo was there for me. That he and his family had taken me in and protected me.

"You're very pretty," Arabella said, breaking the tension between me and her brother. "I love your hair."

"Thank you." My fingers went to my curls, pushing them away from my face. "I—"

"What's that?" Her eyes flicked to the puzzle laid out on the coffee table. With Matteo's help, it was well over halfway completed now.

"Just something to pass the time," I said.

"I like puzzles. Can I help?"

"Sure." I motioned for her to go ahead and she sat down and began studying the pieces.

"I'll get us all something to drink."

"I'll help," I blurted out, following Matteo into the kitchen.

"Is this okay?" he asked quietly.

"I… you should have texted first."

"Would you have said yes?" His brow lifted.

He had a point.

I wouldn't have.

"Look. She's harmless. She just wanted to meet the woman I—" Matteo stopped himself and my breath caught.

I didn't think I'd ever wanted to hear words as much as I wanted to hear the ones trapped between his perfect lips.

Heat splashed inside me as I remembered how good it felt to kiss him, to have him kiss me.

"Caitlin?"

Blinking over at him, I shook the unwelcome thoughts out. "Sorry, it's fine. She seems… sweet."

"She is. But don't be fooled by her charm. She has a way of getting under your skin and tricking you into revealing all your deepest, darkest secrets."

I flinched at his words, and Matteo's brow knitted. "What is it? What's wrong?"

"Nothing, I… beer?"

"Sure, one won't hurt. Is there soda or juice for Bella?"

"Yes, I'll be right over." I dismissed him. I needed space. Room to quiet my beating heart.

Being around Matteo was like being close to the sun. You craved the warmth, the seductive feel of its rays, the addictive rush of endorphins. But if you stayed too long, got too close, you risked getting burned.

And I'd been burned one too many times before.

I grabbed their drinks and made my way over to them.

"God, I can't wait until I'm old enough to go to New York."

"You've never been?" I asked Arabella.

"No." Her eyes flicked to Matteo. "But it's not for lack of trying. The men in my family are, how do you say, overprotective."

"How old are you?"

"Sixteen. Yes!" She fitted another piece to the puzzle.

God, I'd been her age when I'd run. Had I seemed so young and naïve back then? Although, Arabella possessed a quiet confidence. And the way Matteo watched her... well, it made my heart ache.

He was a doting brother, determined to protect his family.

It only made him more attractive.

I felt his eyes on me as Arabella and I continued fitting pieces to the puzzle. She quizzed me about my life, about where I was from and what I did for fun, and I dodged her questions with someone with a lifetime of experience of avoiding the truth.

After about an hour, Luis reappeared after leaving the three of us to carry out his daily perimeter walks. He took his job very seriously, but I was relieved to have a friendly face around.

"So, Caitlin, do you have a boyfriend?"

"E-excuse me?" I spluttered, glancing at Matteo for help.

"Bella, that isn't any of your business."

"She can consider it her part of her job interview."

"Job interview… for what exactly?" My eyes narrowed.

An amused smirk tipped the corner of her mouth. "If it makes you feel any better," she added, "I'm rooting for you." Arabella winked at me and went back to the puzzle.

I glanced over at Matteo. He mouthed, "I'm sorry."

Ugh. Did he have to be so gorgeous?

He was making it impossible to forget him.

And even more impossible to leave.

SOME HOURS LATER, and with the puzzle two-thirds complete, my cheeks ached from all the laughter. Arabella Bellatoni was a breath of fresh air. Unapologetic and with zero filter, she told story after story of Matteo and his cousins, leaving no stone unturned. I'd learned more about him today than in any of our previous encounters.

"This has been fun," she said with a proud smile. "We should do it again sometime."

And just like that, the temporary bubble burst.

I couldn't grow close to these people; it would only make leaving them harder.

"Bella, why don't you go give Luis a hand with the dishes."

Luis had made the four of us spaghetti and had insisted on cleaning up too. Bella got up reluctantly and slid her eyes to me. "This is code for, I want to be alone with Caitlin." Her lips pursed playfully.

"Bella," Matteo warned, and his sister skipped off to find our chef for the evening.

"Sorry about her, she gets—"

"It's no problem. It's been nice..." *Normal.* I swallowed the word.

"We need to talk, Cait."

There it was. The moment I'd known was coming.

All day, I'd felt Matteo's eyes on me. Watching. Waiting. Trying to figure out how to broach the subject with me. I'd been preparing myself from the moment he'd stepped into the cabin.

"It's okay," I said with a weak smile.

"Is it?" His eyes shuttered as he inhaled a deep breath. "Because nothing about this feels okay.

"I'll go. If Luis or someone gives me a ride to the nearest bus station, I can catch—"

"Go?" He balked, staring at me with disbelief. "You think I want you to leave?"

"I... I thought... We both know I can't stay here forever."

"You can, Cait. You just have to..." His voice trailed off right as his gaze dropped.

"Matteo?" I whispered. "What is it?" My heart pounded inside my chest. Whatever he was about to say would change everything. I felt it like the first sign of a storm on the horizon, when the air turns thick and heavy.

"Be mine."

"What?" The air *whooshed* from my lungs. "You can't—"

A knock at the cabin startled me and I pressed my lips together to stop anymore words from spilling out.

Be his?

He didn't know what he was asking.

This wasn't a fairy tale where Prince Charming would swoop in and save the day and get the girl.

Because he doesn't know you.

I shook off the icy fingers of regret, the bitter taste of guilt. I didn't owe Matteo anything except a whole heap of gratitude.

Arabella ran for the door. "I'll get it," she called, yanking it open before either Luis or Matteo could get there and make sure it was safe.

"Sia." She pulled the blonde girl inside. "Wait until you meet Caitlin, she's…"

Her words were drowned out from the roar of blood in my ears as I watched Niccolò Marchetti step into the cabin, his wife Arianne at his side.

"You look well," she said, making a beeline for me.

"I'm much better, thank you."

"Caitlin." Nicco dipped his head in greeting.

"This is Alessia, my cousin. Nicco's sister," Arabella dragged the other girl over to us.

"You knew they were coming?" I asked Arabella, and she bit down on her lip.

"It was a surprise. Sia texted me from the car."

"I see."

"It's nice to meet you, Caitlin." Her eyes glittered with so much warmth and understanding, I almost forgot my manners.

"It's nice to meet you. I'm sorry about your father."

"Thank you. He's strong, a fighter… I still have hope."

"Why don't we all sit," Arianne suggested. "Nicco needs to talk to Matt, and I don't know about anyone else, but I'm parched."

"I think there's a bottle of wine chilling," Luis called from the kitchen.

"Perfect. Bring four glasses."

"Four?" Alessia's eyes grew to the size of saucers.

"Just don't tell your brother." Arianne winked, and the girls giggled.

"How are you, really?" she asked me quietly, while the girls got caught up.

"I'm fine. Is everything okay?" My eyes flicked over to where Nicco and Matteo were talking in hushed voices.

"We visited Antonio in the hospital, but it wasn't good news. Alessia was upset so I suggested we take a trip here. There's something about being out here that soothes the soul. Besides, I wanted to see you."

"Y-you did?"

"Don't look so surprised, Cait. You're one of us now."

I didn't know how to answer that, so I breathed a sigh of relief when Luis arrived with the glasses.

"I hope that's sparkling water." Matteo joined us, eyeing the glass in his sister's hand.

"One glass, please." She pouted.

"One. I don't want a repeat of last time."

"What happened last time?" I asked.

"I spent half the night holding her hair back while she worshipped the porcelain gods."

"*Matt!*"

A smile tipped the corner of my mouth. Their relationship was so easy, so warm and full of love. I envied them. I envied everything about Matteo and his family.

"If it's okay with you," Arianne said, "we're going to stay here for the night."

"I… sure." What could I say?

No, I didn't want them to stay because I didn't want to get dragged any deeper into their world? I couldn't do that; it was their cabin. I was the guest.

"Yes!" Arabella punched the air. "We can have movie night and make the guys watch Magic Mike."

"Porca miseria!" Matteo grumbled. "Should I be worried about your level of obsession with Channing Tatum?"

"What?" She shrugged. "He's hot."

Alessia blushed, gawking at her cousin. "He's… okay."

"Are you blind? He's every girl's wet dream."

"Jesus." Matteo hissed, throwing me a 'help me' look.

"Not your type, Alessia?" I smiled, smothering the laughter bubbling inside me.

"She's too hung up on Trist—"

"Bella!" She snapped.

"Trist who?"

"Tristan, Arianne's cousin. He's tall, dark, and super brooding."

"Oh my God, stop. Nicco is right over there."

"And he can hear you." Nicco's jaw flexed. Arianne's eyes crinkled with amusement as she went over to him and whispered something. He kissed her softly before they both came and joined us.

"So, Cait." Nicco folded one of his legs, resting his ankle on his knee. "How are you finding the cabin?"

"It's very nice, thank you."

He nodded once, not saying whatever was on his mind. Something had changed, but I couldn't put my finger on it. And I didn't miss the silent looks he and Matteo were exchanging.

Did it have something to do with what Matteo had asked me earlier?

Be mine.

Such a loaded question.

"Excuse me," I said, standing. I needed a second, emotion crashing into me from all directions.

"Are you okay?" Arianne asked.

"Fine, I'm fine. Excuse me." Hurrying away from them, I slipped down the hall and into my room.

Except, it wasn't my room. Because I didn't have a place to call my own anymore. Not that Zander's apartment had ever felt like home.

I burst into the small bathroom and clutched the basin, staring at myself in the mirror. It had been almost ten days and I still didn't have a plan.

Deep down, I knew the answer wasn't staying here. Letting these people—letting Matteo—burrow further into my heart.

Heaving a deep breath, my eyes fluttered. I sensed him before I saw him. "What do you want, Matteo?"

"Are you okay?"

"Honestly?" I locked eyes with him in the mirror. "I don't know what I am anymore."

He inched closer, taking the air in the room with him. "About what I said earlier—"

"Don't, please don't. I can't do this." My voice cracked,

my agony bleeding out in the space between us. "I can't be who you want me to be. I'm broken, Matt. Don't you see that? I'm broken, and no amount of kind words or gentle touches will fix that. I'm—"

He pulled me into his strong arms, holding me close. My fingers twisted into his sweater as I buried my face in his chest, breathing him in. I was weak, unable to stop myself from taking what he was offering.

"We can help you, Cait. I can help you. You just have to trust me. Let me in, Tink." He held me at arm's length, gazing down at me. "Let me be there for you."

"I…" I can't. The words were on the tip of my tongue, but they didn't come. All I'd ever wanted was this. Someone to care. Someone to lean on. Matteo would never understand what he was offering me, but I knew.

"It's okay, we don't have to do this now." He brushed the tears from my cheeks. "Do you want me to send them away?"

"What? No! I don't… that's not what this is. I just… I have no experience with all of… all of this."

Matteo lowered his head, touching it to mine as his arms banded around my waist. "They're good people, Cait."

I didn't doubt that.

I was a good person, but I still had secrets. Dark, dirty secrets that would send Matteo running for the hills.

What a mess.

I'd never expected to find my hero in all this… but more heartachingly, I'd never expected to become the villain.

When I didn't reply, Matteo brushed his lips over the

corner of my mouth. He wasn't playing fair, bewitching me with his touch; his spicy, male scent; and low, raspy voice.

Matteo infiltrated every corner of my mind, hijacking my heart and taking my soul captive.

But it would be our downfall.

I would be his demise.

"Tomorrow," I said, knowing I couldn't put the inevitable off any longer. "We'll talk about it tomorrow."

"We don't have to go back out there. We can stay right here and—"

"No," I said with a small shake of my head. "We should go back out there."

I could pretend for a little while longer.

CHAPTER 18

MATTEO

I watched Caitlin sleep. She was curled up on the
end of the couch, a blanket thrown over her as she snored
softly.

Everyone except Nicco and I had already gone to bed.

"Is she okay?" he asked.

There hadn't been time to talk earlier. When me and
Caitlin had rejoined my family, the girls had picked out
the movie and Luis already had snacks.

I only had eyes for Caitlin though.

She hadn't answered me when I'd asked her to be
mine. Part of me wondered if she knew my motives and
that's why she was hesitant. But the other part suspected
it wasn't about me at all. She wanted me; I had no doubts
about that. Something was holding her back though.

And I was determined to find out what it was.

"I don't know." I shrugged.

"Do you think she'll agree?"

"Would you?" I laughed dryly. "I didn't want it to be like this. I imagined what it would be like to see her again… but not like this. Fuck." I hissed, running a hand down my face.

"And if she wants to leave?" Nicco studied me, his intense stare almost too much to bear.

I'd churned this over in my head non-stop since bringing Caitlin here. If she wanted to leave, it meant losing her all over again.

"Let's hope she doesn't," I forced out the words past my lips. "I should get her to bed."

"Do you want some help?"

"No, I've got it, thanks."

Nicco stood and nodded. "She watches you too, you know. When you're not looking, she can't take her eyes off you."

His words hit their target and my chest puffed. "Yeah?"

"Yeah." He gave me a sad smile before taking off down the hall.

I stood, looming over Caitlin. She looked so peaceful it seemed a shame to move her.

"M-Matteo?" Her eyes flickered open. "What time is it?"

"Late. Everyone already went to bed."

"They did?"

I nodded, offering her my hand. "Let's get you into bed."

Without argument, Caitlin took my hand and I led her down the hall to her room.

"Where will you sleep?" she asked around a yawn.

I pulled back the covers and flicked my head for her to

get in the bed. Pulling off her hoodie, Caitlin slipped into the sheets and nestled down.

"I'll see you tomorrow," I said.

"Stay."

The word echoed through my skull. My eyes found hers in the dark, and she smiled. "Matteo, will you please stay with me?"

Without a word, I yanked off my sweater and shucked out of my jeans, climbing in beside her. Caitlin burrowed into my side and laid her hand on my breastbone. "Thank you," she whispered. "For everything."

I pressed a kiss to her hair, hardly able to wipe the smile off my face. "You're worth it, Tink. I hope you know that."

A beat passed, and another, and Cait still didn't answer.

"Cait?" I gently shook her. Nothing.

She was out for the count, curled into my side like she belonged there.

It was disarming, the deep sense of peace I felt having her close. We didn't know each other, not really, not beyond the surface. Yet, I felt tethered to her in a way I couldn't explain.

I wanted to hold her like this every night and wake every morning to her green eyes and blinding smile.

I wanted her—plain and simple.

But as I closed my eyes, and allowed myself to fall into oblivion, I couldn't help but feel like I was one breath away from losing her.

∿

MY EYES FLICKERED OPEN, locking on her face. "Morning," I whispered, fighting a smile.

"It's still early, the sun isn't even up yet," she said. "What happened last night?"

"You don't remember?"

"You carried me to bed?"

I nodded. "You were barely conscious."

"Sorry, I didn't—"

"Shh." I pressed my thumb against her lips, unable to smother the groan that worked its way up my throat when the tip of her tongue darted out and tasted my skin.

"Cait?"

"I don't want to talk, Matt," she said. "I just want to feel… make me feel, please." The sheer desperation in her voice reached inside my chest and grabbed my heart in an iron grip.

"You're sure?"

She nodded, dragging my face down to meet hers. Our lips touched, tentative at first. But the second her tongue found mine, my control dissipated. I rolled onto my back, taking Cait with me so that she straddled my hips. Her hands went to my bare chest as she leaned down and brushed her lips over mine again. A featherlight touch, teasing me. Making my blood heat like lava in my veins.

"Sei bellissima." I pushed her red curls off her shoulder and stroked her collarbone. Caitlin threw back her head, whimpering softly. When our eyes connected again, she said, "What did you just say?"

"I said, you are very beautiful."

Slowly, she rocked her hips, dragging her center along

my dick. Even with layers of material separating us, her heat felt incredible.

"What do you want, Tink?" I asked her, curling one hand around her hip to guide her over me harder.

"Y-you," she breathed. "I want you."

My hand grabbed the nape of her neck, pulling her down to me. "You want me, Tink. You want to feel me pushing inside your hot, slick pussy?"

"God, yes... Show me how good it can be..." Her fingers twisted into my chest, clutching and desperate.

Without warning, I held her to me and rolled us, pinning her beneath me. Grinding in slow torturous circles, I brought Caitlin to the edge.

"More?" I quirked a brow.

Mouth hanging open, breathing labored, she nodded.

I chuckled, working my hand inside her panties. "Fuck, you're soaked." Two fingers slid into her with ease.

"No," she wiggled against me, pulling me closer to her body. "I want you inside me. I want to feel you. All of you."

Jesus. She was going to be the death of me. Rocking back on my haunches, I climbed off the bed and pushed my briefs over my hips, kicking out of them. Grabbing my wallet, I retrieved a condom and threw it down on the bed before gently easing off her panties.

A shiver worked through her as I rolled on the condom and crawled up her bed.

"If we do this—"

"Don't," she rushed out, shaking her head. "I don't want to talk about what happens after. I just want to live in the now, Matteo. Can you do that? Can you give me that?"

Jesus, with her staring up at me like that, I would have given her the whole goddamn world.

She had to know that I wouldn't give her up so easily, that I couldn't. Our lives were entwined now, shackled by forces outside of our control.

Caitlin raked her fingers through the hair at the back of my neck, and pulled me down, her lips ghosting mine. "I really need to feel you inside me, Matt."

I filled her with one smooth stroke. Her breath caught as I stilled, just reveling in how tight she felt, how fucking perfect.

Mine.

The word echoed through my skull.

She felt like she was mine.

"I need you to move," she breathed. "Fuck me, Matt. Please…"

I. Lost. Control.

Hitching Caitlin's leg around my waist, I drove her into the mattress with hard, unrelenting thrusts. And she took it. She took everything I gave her, rolling her hips to meet mine, clenching my dick like a fist. It was enough to make me grit my teeth, she felt that damn good.

"Fuck… *fuck*," I panted, straightening my arms to go harder, faster. It wasn't how I wanted to do this; I'd wanted to take my time and go slow. But suddenly, it was like we were on borrowed time. And an urgency to claim her, to take her and make her mine slammed into me. If I marked her, imprinted myself on her, she had to say yes… didn't she?

"Oh God, Matt, yes… *yes*," she choked out, moaning

my name into the dark as our bodies rocked in perfect synchrony.

"Shh," I murmured against her lips, kissing her. "You need to be quiet."

"It just feels so… *good…*"

"I know, baby, I know." Pressing my head to hers, I hooked my forearm under one of her thighs and lifted her leg, allowing me to go deeper. Caitlin buried her face in the crook of my shoulder, clinging to my body as I took us higher and higher.

Nothing, nothing would ever feel as good as this. Her skin was soft and warm, and her pussy fit me like a glove. Her curves were a map I wanted to take my time exploring, until I'd learned every hidden treasure.

Whether she knew it or not, Caitlin was made for me. At least, that's all I could think as I raced toward the edge.

"I need you to come for me, Tink," I whispered against her ear, nipping her lobe. She shuddered, clenching around me hard enough that I groaned.

I slowed the pace, circling my hips a couple of times, grinding my pelvis against her clit. Caitlin held her breath, her body coiling tightly until she snapped apart.

"Yes… Yes…"

I kissed her through it, swallowing her moans, the tiny whimpers spilling from her lips.

"Fuck, Cait… you feel so fucking good." One more thrust and I jerked inside her, coming hard.

We stayed like that, wrapped up in one another, breathing each other's air.

"You good?" I asked her.

A faint smile traced her mouth, but it didn't reach her eyes.

I rolled away, quickly disposing of the condom and then climbed back into bed, pulling her into my arms. "That was incredible."

"Matt…" She blushed.

"I know you feel it, Cait."

"It doesn't change anything." Her brows furrowed. "I'm… and you're…"

"What does that even mean? I can protect you. We can protect you. You don't need to worry about DiMarco."

"You promised we wouldn't do this… not now… not after—" She rolled her lips together, refusing to say the words.

Dejection pulsed through me. How the hell could she deny the connection we shared? It was a living, breathing thing, lingering in the space between us. She felt it. I knew she did.

So why the fuck was she still fighting it?

I wanted her—I'd made it more than clear.

Besides DiMarco, what was she running from?

As I pulled her closer and tucked my chin on the top of her head, it was the only question on my mind.

THE NEXT TIME I WOKE, it was to an empty bed. I let out a frustrated breath and ran a hand over my face. Sunlight poured in through the curtains, a sure sign it was finally morning.

Voices caught my attention beyond the door, and I

climbed out of bed and pulled on my jeans and sweater, making a quick stop in the bathroom before I went looking for Caitlin.

I didn't expect to find her laughing and joking with Arabella as they made pancakes. Leaning against the wall, I watched them, my chest constricting.

"I know you're watching," Bella smirked over her shoulder.

"Busted." I held up my hands, going over to the breakfast counter and sitting on one of the stools. "Something smells good."

"Caitlin was making breakfast and I offered to help." She beamed.

That was Bella, she liked to feel helpful.

"So where did you sleep last night, Matt?"

"Bella." I shook my head.

Caitlin didn't look at me, just kept flipping the batter and adding the pancakes to the growing stack.

"What?" My sister grinned. "It's a simple question."

"Stop," I mouthed, right as Cait met my eyes.

"Hey," she said.

"Hey."

"Okay then, I'll just be… over there, making myself scarce." Bella slipped out of the kitchen and down the hall.

"You were gone."

"I didn't want to wake you." My brow lifted and she added, "Fine, I didn't want things to be awkward."

"Why did you think things would be awkward? I don't have a single regret about last night. Do you?"

"Matt, I—"

"Morning." Luis came in through the front door,

shaking off his jacket. "It's kicking up a storm out there. Hmm, something smells good."

"I made pancakes," Caitlin smiled at him, and a bolt of jealousy went through me. It was irrational, but I wanted her to look at me the way she looked at him. So comfortable and at ease.

Maybe you should have stayed out here with her.

"Help yourself." She shoved the stack of pancakes into the middle of the counter and started on the bacon. Soon, the smell lured Nicco, Arianne, and Alessia from their bedrooms and we all crammed around the counter.

"So good," Arianne complimented her. "Thank you, you didn't need to cook for us."

"It's no big deal." Caitlin shrugged, remaining over by the cooktop.

"Join us," Arabella added. "You can't cook for us and then not eat."

"I'm not hungry."

I stared at her, willing her to look at me. But she dug in her heels, looking everywhere except in my direction.

Last night had been close to perfect, the way our bodies had moved as one, her soft whimpers and the heat burning between us. The sex was incredible, but it had been so much more than that.

Now, she was acting like it was nothing. Refusing to ackowledge this thing between us. And it pissed me off. I didn't want to force her hand. I wanted her to come to me willingly.

Deep down, I wanted her to want this.

To want me.

"Did Matteo upset you?" Arabella chuckled. "Because I know he isn't the easiest person to—"

"*Bella*!" I snapped, growing tired of her bullshit.

"Jeez, what crawled up your ass and died?" she murmured. "I was only joking."

I swallowed the mouthful of pancake and helped myself to a glass of juice to wash it down. This wasn't quite how I imagined the morning after the night before going. Caitlin deserved more. She deserved hearts and flowers and all that stuff women dreamed of.

The silence stretched out before us as everyone glanced between me and Caitlin. It was awkward as fuck, and I breathed a sigh of relief when Arianne suggested they take their second mugs of coffee into the living area.

"Remind me never to bring Arabella out here again," I muttered to Nicco.

"Did you talk to her?"

"Bella?" I frowned.

His brow quirked and my stomach sank. "No. I tried but she's shutting me out."

"So, you still don't know what she plans to do?"

"She's scared," I whispered.

"Maybe so, but she has to make a choice."

"Is it really a choice?" I stared at him, my best friend. Surely, he had to know what he was asking of me. Of her.

"If she wants to leave, Nic…" I couldn't lose her, not when I'd only just found her again.

"That's her choice, Matt. But if she wants to leave, you need to make it clear what that means."

"I know. Fuck, I know, okay? I just… I need more time."

"We're running out of time. E is heading to Providence soon and then he and Lucino will head straight to see DiMarco."

"One more day. I need one more day."

"Fine. But you need to talk to her, or I will."

"Can you take Bella back with you?"

"Of course." A strained expression washed over him.

"Shit, Nic, I'm sorry," I said. "I know how hard this must be for you."

"He's still alive, there's still hope."

But the emptiness in his eyes told me he'd already given up. He believed Uncle Toni was gone, and it was just a case of his body catching up to what his soul already knew.

"They deserve more." He stared over at the girls, his sharp gaze lingering on Alessia and Arabella.

"Yeah." I swallowed. Nicco knew how I felt about Arabella growing up in this life. I wanted nothing more than to wrap her in cotton wool and protect her at all costs. But it was easier said than done. In this life, people were used as pawns. Collateral. Leverage. If someone—our enemies—wanted to come at us, they would do it through hurting one of our loved ones. Nicco and Enzo had not experienced that firsthand.

It was why my old man was so pissed about Caitlin. We'd brought her here, to one of our safe houses. We'd pulled her into this world, which not only made her a target...

It made her a liability.

CHAPTER 19

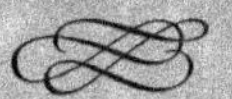

CAITLIN

I watched everyone file out of the cabin. It had been strange, having them all here. I couldn't deny that a part of me had liked it. I liked Arabella's easy way and Alessia's quiet demeanor. I liked Arianne and how kind and compassionate she was. Even Nicco had warmed to our small gathering. And Matteo... I didn't know where to start with him.

Last night had been more than I could've ever dreamed. He wasn't gentle. He didn't handle me like fragile glass. He'd taken what he'd wanted and given me everything I never knew I needed. It had been amazing, being worshipped like that. Every kiss and touch, every roll of his hips, the feel of him moving inside me, was imprinted on my mind—and my soul—and I couldn't imagine forgetting it anytime soon. But the harsh light of day always brought with it a reality neither of us could escape. He was Matteo Bellatoni, a Marchetti by blood. And I was… well, he could never know the truth.

"I'll see you soon, okay?" Bella hurried to my side, hugging me tightly. "You're good for him," she whispered. "And anyone can see that he cares about you a lot."

Emotion balled in my throat.

"See you," I said, the words almost getting stuck.

Arabella regarded me for a second, giving me a warm smile before Matteo called for her. His eyes connected with mine, a bolt of something going through me.

Wasn't he even going to say goodbye?

Disappointment sat heavy in my chest. We hadn't had time to talk—not that I knew what to say. I knew what he wanted; he'd made that more than clear. But I couldn't do it. I couldn't give him more than right here, right now.

The door banged shut, a gunshot to my heart. I hadn't realized how much I'd missed company until they'd all showed up last night. Luis was nice, and he made me feel comfortable, but it wasn't the same. Back in Providence, I had friends. I had Gisele and Mari and Shaun.

God, Shaun.

I clutched my throat. I'd shut those memories out, but now all I felt was the bitter sting of regret. He'd died because of me, and no one had even mentioned it. As if death was just business as usual. I guess for them, in their line of work, maybe it was.

Everything was such a mess.

Letting out a weary sigh, I hugged myself tight and made my way back to my room. I couldn't stay here for much longer. Every day that I did, Matteo, his family, burrowed their way a little deeper. The door clicked open, and I heard footsteps on the wooden floor. It was probably Luis.

But then his voice washed over me.

"Caitlin?"

I turned slowly, my eyes colliding with Matteo. "What are you—"

"You thought I was leaving?" His brows knitted as he stopped short of me.

"I… I assumed you were going back with your family, yes."

"We need to talk." He ran a hand down his face.

"I know."

I did, and I hated it. I didn't want to talk. I didn't want him to ask me questions I didn't have the answers to.

"Where's Luis?" I glanced over his shoulder.

"He's accompanying them back to Verona. We're alone, for now." His conflicted gaze dropped to my lips, and my tongue darted out, wetting them.

When he looked at me like that, I wanted things. Things I could never have. Not now. Not tomorrow. Not ever.

"Please," I whispered. "Don't look at me like that."

"Like what?" Matteo took a step closer. "How am I looking at you?"

"Like you want things." I craned my neck to look him in the eye, the air thick and heavy around us. "Things I can't give you."

"You are so beautiful, Tink." He tucked my curls behind my ear, cupping my neck as his thumb stroked my jaw, lingering on my bottom lip. "I wish it didn't have to be this way. I wish we'd met under different circumstances. But we didn't…"

"No." My voice cracked, my heart beating wildly in my chest.

"Come, sit." He took my hand, leading me over to the couch. I sat down, barely able to think over my racing pulse. "In a different life, I'd court you, Tink. I'd spend my time getting to know you, getting you to trust me. We'd date and take our time learning about each other. But we don't have that luxury. Not with DiMarco out there looking for you."

A shiver ran down my spine as I sucked in a harsh breath.

Matteo squeezed my hand gently. "I will never let him hurt you, Cait. But by bringing you here, we dragged you into this thing. My elders, they will only protect you if you're—"

"If I'm what?" My lip quivered as I took in his gutted expression.

"If you're my woman."

"W-what are you saying?" I blanched.

"You're either with me, Cait, or you're not."

"I'll go." I shot up. "I'll leave and you won't have to—"

"You think I can just let you walk out of here, out of my life?" Pain etched into his expression. "It doesn't work like that, Tink. I'm not—"

"You're not what, Matteo?" I snapped, feeling indignation burn through me. "Am I a prisoner here? Is that what this is?"

His gaze dropped and I had my answer. He wasn't going to let me go. Either I accepted his proposition of being his woman or I would be kept here until God only knew when.

"It's just until this thing with DiMarco is over." His eyes implored me to understand. But I couldn't... I couldn't make sense of... of this. "If we let you leave and he... finds you... you know things about us, Caitlin. You know where Nicco and Arianne live, you know about my sister and this place.

"For as much as I hate it," Matteo inhaled a ragged breath, "my family are right. It makes you a liability."

"You think I'd tell him anything? I hate him, Matt. I'd rather die than ever tell him a single thing." I shrieked, hot tears rolling down my cheeks.

"And that's exactly what will happen if he finds you." Matteo roared, glowering at me, and I jerked back as if he'd slapped me. "Shit, Cait, that's not... I didn't." He jammed his fingers into his hair, tugging the ends. "I don't want to argue with you. I want us to figure this out. *Together*. You know how I feel about you, Caitlin. I guess I'd hoped—"

"That I'd what? Jump into bed with you straightaway and play happy family? You just said it yourself, I'm a liability. You should never have brought me here." I sneered.

"WE DIDN'T HAVE A FUCKING CHOICE," he bellowed. "You think we could just leave you alone in that hospital, knowing what you'd been through? What he'd done?"

"This is my life, Matteo. My. Fucking. Life. I know how to protect myself. I've been doing it long enough." My chest heaved with the weight of my words.

"Cait, what are you hiding?" He reached for me, but I shook him off. "Just talk to me, please. You think I don't see the shadows in your eyes? You're hiding something. Tell me. Let me help."

"I think you've done enough." I averted my gaze, unable to look at him as I wrapped my arms around my waist, holding myself together.

"This isn't how I wanted it to be. But things are going down that are out of my control. If you leave and DiMarco finds you... the Family won't risk that. They can't."

"I got it," I hissed. "You don't trust me." My eyes locked on his. "Well, you really should have thought about that before bringing me here. I didn't ask to meet your family, Matt. I didn't ask you to bring Arabella here. I didn't ask for anything other than time to figure out what I was going to do next."

"I'm sorry." His eyes bored into mine, stripping me bare. "I just wanted to... fuck," he breathed, "I don't even know what I'm doing."

I wasn't being entirely fair, I knew that. But I'd wanted so much to believe Matteo and his family were different. That I could trust them.

Yet here we were. With an ultimatum hanging between us.

If I didn't fall into line, if I didn't agree to be with Matteo, then I would be a prisoner here until DiMarco was no longer a threat.

However long that would be.

A week.

A month.

Two.

I couldn't stay here for that long. I'd go out of my mind. Especially now that I knew the truth.

Matteo didn't want me, not really.

He just wanted to make this easier on me. He wanted to ease me into the idea of us. Even if it was all for show.

"I need some space." I started backing away.

"Cait, please. We need to talk about this."

"No, we really don't." I sniffled, willing myself not to break in front of him more than I already had. "I think I understand everything perfectly."

"Cait…" he called after me, but I turned on my heel, and didn't look back.

I should have run when I had the chance. Stupidly, I hadn't considered when they first brought me here that Luis was here not for my protection—he was here to make sure I didn't try to escape.

Now, all I could see was him as the guy standing between me and freedom.

I wasn't even sure I wanted to leave. I had nowhere to go. I had no contacts, no friends across the country where I could pitch up and sleep on their couch for a few nights. All I had was the instinct to survive and do whatever it took to stay under the radar.

DiMarco's had been the perfect place to blend in. Until

it wasn't. If only I hadn't caught Zander's eyes, I wouldn't be here now. I'd still be working the floor, laughing and joking with Shaun while we watched Gisele and Mari work the crowds of hungry men into a frenzy. It wasn't the dream, but it was something.

It was better than the life I'd spent years running from.

Matteo had left earlier. I'd heard him and Luis talking in hushed voices, only catching the odd word.

Don't let her out of your sight.

Back to Verona.

Call me if she wants to talk.

Watch her.

I hated it. Hated that I'd become such a burden to them. I didn't ask for this—I didn't ask for any of it.

I blamed Enzo. If he had never showed up at my apartment all those weeks ago and given me his number, I never would have ended up here.

No, you probably would have been dead by now.

I inhaled a sharp breath. Like it or not, Enzo and Matteo had saved me that day. They had offered me a lifeline that I couldn't refuse.

So why had I gotten so angry earlier when Matteo had laid out the truth for me?

He wasn't a normal guy. His family were one of the most talked about crime families in New England. Of course they weren't just going to take me in for a couple of weeks, let me find my feet, and then send me on my way with a smile.

They were the mafia for Pete's sake. You didn't graciously accept their help free of charge. You earned it. You became indebted for it.

You *paid* for it.

But I wasn't for sale, and I most certainly wasn't about to pretend to be involved with Matteo to get in their good graces.

"Caitlin?" Luis's gruff voice drifted down the hall. "I made risotto."

"Not hungry," I yelled back.

"You can't stay in there forever." I could almost hear the humor in his voice.

This wasn't funny.

Nothing about this situation warranted laughter. Not a single thing.

"Watch me," I mumbled, throwing myself down on the bed. My cell phone vibrated, and I picked it up.

I'M SORRY. M xo

UGH. It would have hurt less if he was a typical asshole jerk who had broken my heart. But Matteo wasn't a bad guy.

He was just the wrong guy.

Another text came through and I narrowed my eyes.

Is the idea of being with me really that unappealing to you?

FUELED BY RAGE, I texted back.

. . .

THAT'S NOT **the point and you know it...**

No, I don't. Because you refused to talk to me. You think I like this? I don't... but my hands are tied.

ANOTHER ONE CAME STRAIGHT THROUGH.

REGARDLESS OF WHAT **my family wants, this is about you and me. I know you felt it last night, Cait. You can't deny that we're good together... I was sure of it eight months ago, I'm even more sure of it now. What are you so scared of?**

I SQUEEZED MY EYES SHUT.
  Everything.
  I was scared of everything.

I THOUGHT **what we had was real. I thought I could trust you.**

I HIT SEND, immediately regretting it. But I was hurt and on the defense. Matteo wasn't a bad guy, I knew that. Everything was such a mess though. Just when I was about to truly let him in, to give myself to him, he landed me with the ultimatum, reminding me this wasn't a fairy tale… and he wasn't my white knight.

Sadly, there were no heroes in this story.

And no happy endings.

CHAPTER 20

MATTEO

"That bad, huh?" Enzo asked me as I lay sprawled on the couch.

"She's pissed."

"Are you surprised?" He chuckled.

"Yes… No… Fuck, I don't know what to think." Dragging a hand down my face, I let out a heavy sigh. "There's something between us, E. Something real. I thought… I thought she might be willing to explore that."

"You blindsided her."

"Did you know it would go this way when we brought her back to Verona?"

"I knew once Uncle Michele and Al got wind of it, they'd want assurances. You know that's how it works."

"Yeah…" I guess I'd just hoped it wouldn't be like this. "What the fuck am I supposed to do now?"

"Give her some space. Caitlin has every right to feel betrayed. Let her cool off."

"I just don't like the idea of her out there all alone."

"So, we'll send the girls. I'm sure Arianne won't mind going out there and Nora is dying to meet her. They can even take Alessia and Bella."

"I guess…"

"What is it?" He paused. "What aren't you telling me?"

Dropping my eyes to the bottle in my hand, I weighed on whether to tell him or not. But I needed to talk to someone.

"I slept with her."

"Of course you did." I could almost hear his eyes roll.

"What the fuck is that supposed to mean?"

"You look at her the way Nicco looks at Arianne. The way I look at Nora. She's yours, Matt. She just hasn't figured it out yet."

"And if I lose her because of this?"

"You won't."

"How can you be so sure?"

"You might be a soft pussy, but you still have Marchetti blood in your veins. We don't give up what's ours without a fight."

His words sank into me. Was he right? Was it only a matter of time before Caitlin realized what I already knew?

We were supposed to find each other again. Even in the dire circumstances, we were both supposed to end up right here. Together. I refused to believe it was anything less than Fate working her will.

"I'll be lucky if she'll ever talk to me again," I huffed, draining my beer.

Enzo chuckled again. "So make her."

It was my turn to roll my eyes. "And how does that go down with Nora?"

"She'd tell you she hates it when I get all bossy, but secretly, she loves it. Gets her all hot for me."

"Okay, that was too much information."

"She especially likes it when I tie her up and—"

"Jesus, what is wrong with you? I don't want to hear your sex stories."

"Did Caitlin already put your balls in her purse? Because you sound like a fucking pussy."

"Fuck off," I grumbled. Just because I didn't want to share all the details about my sex life. I respected women too much to do that.

"What's happening there anyway? Shouldn't you be stalking DiMarco's?"

"Not a lot, not yet. Anyway, I wanted to speak to you first. Make sure you've got your head screwed on right."

"I feel like I'm losing my damn mind."

"Women, cous, they'll do that to a guy."

"You'll call me if you find out anything?"

"You know it."

"And DiMarco?"

"Let's hope he refuses to give us the intel on Lombardi, so I get the pleasure of reminding him of our agreement."

"Make it hurt." I snorted.

"I will. DiMarco will get his, Matt. Whether it's tomorrow or next week or sometime in the future."

I dipped my head in an appreciative nod.

A knock at the door startled me, and I padded over to the door to open it.

"Enzo sent reinforcements."

"Seriously?" I groaned down the line.

"What? I thought she could give you another pep talk."

"Here," I said, handing her the phone. "He wants to talk to you."

"Hi, babe. I'm missing you." Nora moved deeper into the apartment, dropping her purse on the counter. "Yeah, I miss you too."

Her voice lowered and I heard her giggle as they exchanged sweet nothings.

Lucky bastard.

Nora let out a soft whimper as he no doubt let her know exactly how much he was missing her.

"Babe, we have company," she scolded, covering the receiver to mouth, "Sorry, Matt," at me.

"No apology needed." I forced a smile. "I actually need to get off soon. I promised Bella I'd pick her and Alessia up and take them for ice-cream."

"How're things with Caitlin?"

"Don't ask."

"That bad?"

"She'll come around," Enzo shouted down the line, so Nora put him on speaker.

"She's been through a lot. Cut her some slack."

"I know."

I did. But that only made it worse. I wanted to help her, to be there for her and support her. I didn't want to be on the sidelines.

"Gattina, how do you feel about going out to the cabin to spend some time with her and the girls?" Enzo asked. "Matt thinks she could use the company."

"Hell yes." She grinned. "Count me in. Some female

perspective might help her see things a little differently too."

"No meddling," I warned. "She already doesn't trust me. I don't need you giving her any more ammunition."

Nora gasped. "I'm offended you think I'd mess it up. I can be quite persuasive when I put my mind to it. Ask Enzo." She smirked, and my cousin snorted down the line.

"I think we both know who's in charge around here," he said. "I'm telling you, cous," he added. "If you really think she's the one, fight for her. Fight until she doesn't have any choice but to give in to you."

"Who are you and what have you done with my cousin?" Amusement filled my voice.

"Here," Nora handed me back the cell phone. "I need to pee. Bye babe, video call me later and we can do that thing." She took off down the hall and I turned off the loudspeaker.

"That thing?" I muttered. "Please tell me you're not going to have phone sex while you're supposed to be scoping out DiMarco?"

"I'm telling you cous, one day, I'm going to marry that woman and put my kid in her stomach." He let out a contented sigh.

Jealousy snaked through me.

I wanted that.

I wanted it all...

With a woman who probably hated me now.

"YOU'RE NOT COMING INSIDE?" Bella asked as she climbed out of the truck. It was the day after Enzo had suggested the girls visit Caitlin, and I had to admit it wasn't his worst idea ever.

"No, I... No."

"What happened with you two anyway? I heard Nicco and Ari talking and—"

"Just adult stuff."

"Adult stuff. Really, Matt? You're barely four years older than me."

"Listen, Bella, I could use your help a little here. Caitlin is... well, she's pissed at me."

"And you want me to try to smooth the cracks?"

"Something like that." Was this what my life had really come to? Asking my little sister to score me brownie points with the woman I couldn't stop thinking about?

"I only want her safe, Bella. That's all that matters to me."

"She'll come around." Arabella smiled. "No one can resist your charm for long."

"Thanks." I chuckled, but it sounded strained. "Go on, get inside."

"Are you sure you don't want to come inside and see her?"

My eyes went to the cabin. "I don't think that's a good idea."

Sadness crept into my sister's expression. "Okay. But don't worry, I'll work my magic on her." Bella winked before taking off toward the cabin.

This was a good idea, bringing the girls here. I didn't want Caitlin to think she was our captive. And she'd seemed at ease around Ari, Alessia, and Bella. Of course, I had no doubt Nora would insert herself into our fledgling relationship, or whatever was left of it. But I'd take whatever I could get.

Nicco kissed Arianne before watching her disappear inside, then he got into the truck.

"You're not taking the Range Rover?" I asked.

He shrugged. "I figured we could ride together. Then you can bring me back later."

Sneaky.

But I couldn't deny that having an excuse to come back out here was welcomed.

As I pulled onto the dirt road leading back to the highway, I glanced in my rearview mirror and saw Caitlin watching us.

I had to fight the urge to pull a U-turn and go back for her, to demand she heard me out. But she wanted time, and I would give it to her.

"She'll come around," Nicco said as if he heard my thoughts.

"I'm not so sure." I glanced in the mirror again, but she was gone.

Maybe she'd never been there at all.

"I know you… feel something for her. But what do you really know about her, Matt?"

My brows furrowed. "What the hell is that supposed to mean?"

If anyone got it, I thought it would be Nicco. He'd fallen for Arianne in a heartbeat, not realizing who she really was until it was too late.

Theirs had been a case of star-crossed lovers. The

tragic kind. The kind that ended in death and heartache. But they had survived. He'd gotten the girl and the life he wanted with her.

So yeah, I thought he might understand how it felt to fall so deeply into someone without ever truly knowing them.

"Don't look at me like that," he rolled his eyes. "I don't have the luxury of being sentimental, not now." Not since his father had been taken sick. "I have to make decisions in the best interests of our business. Decisions that protect everything the Family has built. You know that."

"I know. Fuck, Nic, I know that. But if anyone understood, I thought… it doesn't matter." I released a strained breath, keeping my eyes on the road.

"I get it, I do. I'm just worried. She has you all twisted up in knots and I know that feeling well. It leaves you unable to see straight." It was his turn to sigh. "All I'm saying is, tread carefully. You said it yourself, she's hiding something. I don't want you to be blindsided."

"Yeah." I didn't expand.

His words left a bitter taste in my mouth. So it was okay for him and Enzo to pursue women who they knew deserved more than this life, but the first time I actually showed any interest in a girl, it was deemed irresponsible?

Fuck that.

Caitlin was entitled to her secrets after what she'd survived at the hands of DiMarco.

Nothing she could tell me would change how I felt; of that, I was sure. Because you didn't pick the people you cared about, the people you loved. It wasn't something you could control or switch off. It was something you couldn't fight. Something you couldn't ignore.

"I just keep thinking what happens after, you know? Once this shit with DiMarco is handled. What then? If she doesn't want me, what will you do?"

"I'm not a monster, Matteo. This you know."

"I know. But you are the boss now. I understand that comes with responsibility."

"Once we decide what to do with DiMarco, Caitlin will be safe. I'll see to it personally. You have my word."

"You'll make her disappear," I said, the pit in my stomach stretching.

"It's the only way, Matt, and you know it. Unless—"

"Unless she decides to stay and be with me."

That was it then.

If Caitlin didn't choose me once this was all over, she'd be gone, and I'd never see her again.

Nicco, with the help of our trusted associates, would make her disappear. Give her a new life in exchange for her silence.

I guess I should have felt lucky she wouldn't find herself buried in a ditch somewhere, never to be found again. But I couldn't find it in myself to feel anything but a stab of regret.

Surely the universe wouldn't be so cruel to bring her back into my life and then take her away again?

"I'm sorry," he said. "I'm sorry it has to be this way."

"Me too," I murmured as realization sank deep into my bones.

Everything was changing.

It had always been the three of us—Nicco, Enzo, and

me—against the world. Then he met Arianne, and Enzo found Nora. But I was okay with that because seeing them happy was worth being the fifth wheel. I didn't feel like an outsider then. But now, sitting there with Nicco, the guy I'd loved like a brother for my entire life, I couldn't help but feel the power imbalance between us.

He was no longer just my cousin, my best friend, my family. He was the boss. He couldn't let his familiarity or attachment to me get the better of him, and I knew him well enough to know he wouldn't.

Just like I knew if Caitlin refused to give us a chance—refused to give me a chance—after this shit with DiMarco went away, I'd probably never see her again.

~

WHAT DID **you do to her?**

I STARED at Bella's text message, reading the words over and over again.

WHAT'S WRONG?

SHE SEEMS... **sad.**

FUCK.

. . .

There's **some stuff you don't know…**

Arabella's reply came straight through.

Isn't there always.

Even over a cell phone, I felt the bite to her words.

Is she okay?

I don't know. **She seems off, but she won't talk about it. I tried to talk about you, and she completely shut down.**

I tipped my head back against the couch and let out a weary sigh. When we'd gotten back to Verona, I'd asked Nicco to drop me off at the apartment. I hadn't officially moved out of my parents' house, but sometimes, I needed the space.

But space from Caitlin was the last thing I wanted. It felt like there was an ocean between us.

Just be there for her. **She's had a rough time of it. She needs a friend.**

. . .

ALESSIA AND ARABELLA might have been younger, but they were wise beyond their years. I guess that's what happened when you grew up in a family like ours. We tried to protect them as much as we could, but they both had a knack of uncovering the truth.

God help the men who stole their hearts. A shudder went through me. I didn't want to think of my sister falling in love. Not now. Not ever. But I wasn't stupid enough to know it wouldn't happen one day.

My cell vibrated again, and I opened the message, my breath catching at my sister's reply.

MAYBE SHE NEEDS MORE than a friend.

I SCREWED MY EYES SHUT, forcing myself to take a deep breath. That's all I wanted—to be Caitlin's guy. To be there for her, to protect her.

To love her.

This was bigger than the both of us though. Bigger than what I wanted, or Caitlin needed.

It was about the Family. The Family I'd sworn my loyalty—*my life*—to.

But it had never felt more of a burden than it did in that moment.

CHAPTER 21

CAITLIN

"She did not," Arabella and Alessia giggled as I told them about the time Marielle had kicked a guy in the balls for getting too handsy with her.

Nicco and Matteo probably didn't want me corrupting their little sisters with stories from the strip club. But it wasn't like I had anything else to tell them. My childhood wasn't normal. There were no cute stories about my high school boyfriend and prom. I didn't have a romantic first-time story or any anecdotes from being on the cheer squad or being student body president.

"What happened to the guy?"

"He had to ice his balls."

Nora stifled a chuckle while Arianne looked a little horrified.

"Sorry," I said. "I didn't mean to—"

"Relax, babe," Nora said. "This is the best thing I've

heard all day. Besides, serves the asshole right for touching instead of looking."

I liked Nora. She was feisty in a way I'd always wished I was. She and Arianne had turned up armed with wine and the five of us had spent the last couple of hours sitting around, drinking and talking. It was nice. Normal even.

But I couldn't shake the feeling that it was Matteo's attempt at softening me up to the ultimatum he'd dropped on me.

"Who's that?" Alessia asked Bella who was clutching her cell phone.

"No one." Her eyes flicked to mine but quickly dropped when I frowned.

Matteo.

Even now, he was keeping an eye on me, using his sister to do his bidding.

I didn't know how to feel about that.

But I couldn't deny that part of me liked that he cared so much. Not that it changed anything.

"This is nice," Nora said. "Taking a break from city life."

"You mean from Enzo." Bella snickered.

"I mean, I love the guy, but let a girl breathe." She grinned. "But the sex… holy mother of God, the sex is—"

"Okay, Nor." Arianne leaned over and covered her friend's mouth. "I think that's enough wine for you, and definitely enough share time."

"They're not kids, Ari. They know all about the birds and bees. Hell, I bet they've already—"

"Okay." Arianne grabbed Nora's arm and yanked her

up. "We'll just be in the kitchen. Getting Nora a nice, big glass of cold water."

"Yes, *Mom*." Nora rolled her eyes, as she let Arianne pull her away.

"God, I want to be Nora when I'm older," Bella let out a deep sigh. "She's just so… confident, you know? She knows what she wants, and she goes after it. I admire that."

"It's a good quality to have," I murmured, draining my glass. Something told me I was going to need a lot more where that came from if I was going to survive tonight.

"What would you go after, Sia?" Bella mused. "If you could have anything, what would it be?"

"I don't know." Nicco's sister gave a half-shrug. "I've never really thought about it."

"Oh, don't give me that. There must be something… or maybe, someone." Arabella waggled her eyebrows.

"Is there a boy at school you like?" I asked.

"Try man," Bella coughed, smirking.

"Bella!"

"What? I think Tristan is hot too."

"Tristan, who is he… remind me again?" I said.

"Arianne's cousin. The man is fine with a capital F. But he's older. Too old. And he's technically family now. I guess it's weird."

"I don't like Tristan, Bella. You're being ridiculous."

"It's not like Matteo or Nicco will ever let us date anyway." Arabella flopped back into the heap of cushions and looked up at the ceiling. "No one will ever be good enough in their eyes."

"You won't be sixteen forever," I said. "In a couple of

years, you'll be your own woman. Old enough to make your own decisions."

Her eyes slid to mine. "You have met the three of them, right?"

"They just care. You should feel very lucky to have them." My chest constricted with every word.

If only I had a big brother or an older cousin to look out for me, things might have gone differently.

But I didn't.

And I couldn't spend my life living in the past, when I was constantly trying to figure out how to live in the present.

"Did you ever dance at the club?" Arabella asked me out of nowhere.

"I… uh, at first, for a little bit. But I didn't like it."

"You didn't?" She leaned up on her elbows.

"No. You see, I used to dance. Before I moved to Providence."

"In a strip club?"

"No, in a dance company."

"What kind of dance?"

"Anything. Ballet. Jazz. Lyrical. Contemporary."

"That's so cool. I always wanted to be a ballerina when I was a kid, but I have the coordination of Bambi."

"I'm sure you don't."

"Oh, she does," Alessia piped up, chuckling.

"You said you *used* to dance?"

"Yeah." My heart cracked. "I had to stop."

"Why?"

"I… I moved here and life got in the way."

The truth was, I hadn't had the extra money for

lessons. And then, once Zander found out I loved to dance, he'd put me to *good use*. And I hated him for it. I respected the dancers at DiMarco's, admired them even. They owned their bodies and used them to their full advantage. But dancing was something I never wanted to be used against me, ever again.

Something I would never forgive him for.

"There's an amazing theater in the city. They have an in-house ballet company. One of the best in New England. We should go one time. I'm sure Nicco could get—"

"Bella," Alessia chided, shaking her head.

"That would be nice," I said, wanting to break the sudden tension.

Thankfully, Nora and Arianne chose that moment to rejoin us. "What did we miss?" Nora asked.

"Caitlin is a dancer." Bella beamed. "A ballet dancer."

"No way."

I nodded, tucking my hair behind my ears. "An old hobby I don't get much time for these days."

Sympathy flickered in Nora's gaze. She hadn't pressed me about anything; neither had Arianne. But it was always there, in the space between us. The elephant in the room.

"Hey, we should speak to the guys about a girls' night out sometime. Maybe if—" Nora stopped herself, guilt shining in her eyes. "Shit, my bad."

"What?" Bella asked. "What is it?"

"Nothing." I forced a smile. I didn't want them to worry, and I didn't want her or Alessia to look at me any differently. Because I wasn't sure I could face becoming a victim in the eyes of these innocent pure girls, still full of dreams and hopes and so much goodness it radiated from them like sunshine.

Arianne switched the conversation to a safer topic, telling us about her work at the Verona County Transitions Initiative. But I wasn't paying much attention.

Neither was Arabella, as she discreetly texted someone on her phone.

When she was done, she glanced up at me, her expression wavering for a second. But then an easy smile slid over her face as if she hadn't just been caught red-handed texting her brother.

THE NEXT DAY AT LUNCH, I didn't expect to find Luis waiting for me with a garment bag.

"W-what is that?"

"A surprise." His eyes twinkled. "We leave at six-thirty."

Leave?

"Where are we going?" My stomach fluttered, but I didn't know if it was with excitement or apprehension. Maybe even both.

"Like I said, it's a surprise." He left the bag draped over the back of the couch and slipped out of the cabin, leaving me alone.

I moved closer, plucking the small envelope from the clear pocket in the bag.

LET me make it up to you. M xo

. . .

Shivers raced up and down my spine as I slowly pulled the zipper, revealing a gorgeous, deep-green gown. It was fit for a princess, the bodice fitted and woven with delicate lace. The skirt was thick and luscious.

It was beautiful.

Confused, and a little out of my depth, I snatched my cell phone off the counter and texted Matteo.

What happened to house arrest?

His reply came instantly.

Give me a chance to get this right, please...

Why? Why is this so important to you?"

I glanced back at the gown, hardly able to believe my eyes. No one had ever bought me such a beautiful gift.

I didn't know what to think. Was this Matteo's attempt at buying me or was he merely trying to apologize and do something nice for me? Arabella hadn't mentioned him again last night, and I certainly hadn't brought it up. I was grateful for their company, even if watching them leave was a cold reminder of my situation.

Another reply pulled me from my thoughts.

I CARE, Caitlin. Let me prove it.

I CLUTCHED MY CELL PHONE, biting down on my bottom lip. He wasn't going to give up without a fight, and the truth was, I didn't want him to.

I wanted him to fight for me. I wanted Matteo to do what no person had ever done for me.

Before I could talk myself out of it, I texted back.

OKAY.

GREAT, see you later... and Cait, I can't wait to see you in the dress.

I WAS IN TROUBLE.

So much trouble.

Matteo made it so hard to hate him. But could I do it? Could I become his... woman? It would put me in the public eye more. There would be photos and press reports. If I was around Nicco and Arianne, there was every chance I would become noticed.

The smart decision was to reject him and the dress and wait it out.

I wasn't for sale.

Not now, not ever.

But Matteo was different—I knew he was.

It was one night.

One night of freedom. One night to pretend that I was just a girl, and he was just a guy.

I couldn't remember the last time I'd gone on a date, a real honest-to-God date.

It had been too long, that much was certain.

I was pretty sure guys didn't usually forward their dates brand-new dresses. I spied the shoebox on the sideboard… and *shoes*. Oh God, he'd sent shoes.

"You're full of surprises, Matteo Bellatoni," I murmured to myself, lifting the lid and admiring the black kitten heels with a red sole. A red freaking sole.

What was happening?

This morning, I'd been on the verge of making a run for it to escape Matteo and his overbearing ruthless family. This afternoon, I was swooning over a new pair of Louboutins and a dress fit for a princess.

I wanted to tell him he couldn't buy my affection, but the truth was, I wanted it. I wanted one night to play dress up and forget the shitshow that was my life.

Which is why I found myself texting him back.

I'LL BE WAITING.

THE KNOCK at the door sent my heart into overdrive. I'd taken my time getting ready. A long soak in a bubble bath, followed by a glass of wine thanks to Luis, while I finished getting myself together. I'd left my hair down, sweeping one side off my face and pinning it into place. My curls were thick and luscious, and my makeup was simple and understated.

I felt beautiful.

I also couldn't shake the feeling that this was a huge mistake.

But when I opened the door to reveal Matteo dressed in dark jeans and a black shirt and dinner jacket, there was no going back.

"For you," he said, holding out a single red rose.

"Thank you." I blushed, inhaling the floral scent before taking it over to the breakfast counter and adding it to a glass of water. "Are you sure this is okay?"

He nodded, his eyes dancing over my body. "Caitlin, you look... wow."

A faint smile tugged at my mouth.

"Tonight, we're just Matteo and Caitlin, okay?" He stepped forward, reaching for my face and brushing the stray hairs away. His eyes glittered with desire and in that moment I felt beautiful. "Nothing else matters," he leaned in and whispered against my cheek, kissing me softly.

"Okay." I gazed up at him, lost in his deep-blue eyes. He looked so good and smelled amazing. It was like a dream. A really good one I didn't want to wake up from.

I didn't have those often.

"Ready?"

It was my turn to nod. Matteo took my hand and led me out of the cabin.

"Miss O'Donnell," Luis smirked as he opened the back door to the sleek black SUV.

"Seriously?" My brow lifted at Matteo, and he chuckled.

"It's just a precaution."

Right. Because I was in hiding so that Zander didn't find me.

My heart ratcheted.

"Maybe this isn't such—"

"Shh." Matteo smoothed his thumb over my hand. "You're safe, I promise. No one will even know we're there."

"And where is there exactly?"

"You'll see. Come on."

He nudged me into the SUV, sliding in beside me. I half-expected for him to keep some distance between us, but Matteo was full of surprises, taking my hand again and keeping it in his lap. As if he needed a physical tether to me.

The thought made me smile. That I could bring this strong, gorgeous mafioso to his knees.

Don't get carried away with yourself, Cait. I ignored the little voice on my shoulder and sank back into the leather seats, determined to follow Matteo's lead tonight.

Thirty minutes later though, when we pulled up outside The Montague Grand Theater, I struggled to keep my composure.

"Matt," I gasped, cupping a hand over my mouth as I stared at the lit-up billboard hanging over the beautiful, imposing building.

"Romeo and Juliet," I murmured, "I-I don't understand." I gawked at him.

"Arabella said you used to dance. In fact, I think her exact words were, 'Matt, she's a ballerina. A real-life ballerina.'"

Soft laughter spilled from my lips.

"I managed to pull some strings." He gave me a shy smile. "I hope it's okay?"

"Okay?" My throat was dry. "It's… it's the nicest thing anyone has ever done for me. I don't know what to say." I glanced back up at the signage, hardly able to believe my eyes. Tickets to these performances didn't come cheap and I knew he'd probably called in some big favors to make this happen.

I couldn't stop smiling.

"Luis, take us around back please. Pascale is meeting us at the stage door."

I frowned and Matteo squeezed my hand. "Precautions. We have a private box that comes with VIP treatment. Besides," his voice dipped, sending a shiver through me. "This way I get you all to myself."

CHAPTER 22

MATTEO

I couldn't take my eyes off Caitlin. The dress clung to her curves as I guided her into our private box. The tickets had cost me a small fortune, but the second Arabella had texted me telling me that Caitlin liked ballet, the idea had taken root.

Nicco had forbidden it at first. I wasn't supposed to be parading Caitlin around the city. So I'd done what any desperate man would do—I begged.

Luis could drive us right to the stage door, and we could slip in and out before anyone was the wiser. Pascale Moretti, the theater director, was a family friend. My mama loved the ballet, but my father only ever brought her for a special occasion: anniversaries or birthdays. I'd only been once, as a child. I remembered being in awe of the opulent building. There was a giant chandelier in the foyer and a split staircase that ran around each side of the entrance. It was all very art nouveau with its gold-plated décor and stylized balconies and railings.

"Right this way, Mr. Bellatoni," Pascale led us up the staircase and down a long hall, pushing open a small door. "You'll find the bottle of Bollinger chilling along with the other items you requested."

"Thank you, Pascale." I took his hand, gripping it firmly. "I appreciate it."

"Of course, Mr. Bellatoni. Enjoy the production."

"Thank you." Caitlin smiled, her eyes glittering with wonder.

I liked that look on her, and wanted to put it there more often.

"Come on, the show is about to start." I ushered her onto the balcony.

"Oh my God, Matteo. This is—" She grasped the rail and looked out over the stage. It was the best seat in the house, a perfect view of the stage and orchestra seated down in the pit below.

I stepped up behind her, sliding my arm around her waist and I dropped my mouth to her ear. "It's beautiful, isn't it?"

"I've never seen anything like it."

I've never seen anything like you. I swallowed the words, leaning closer to breathe her in.

We'd only just arrived, and already, I never wanted this moment to end.

"We should sit," I said, guiding her over to the chairs. I needed a second. Being so close, with her looking like that, it was hard to rein in the storm of emotions raging inside me.

I wanted to kiss her, to take her in my arms and plunge my tongue deep into her mouth and taste her. I wanted to drown in her and never come up for air.

Did she have any idea the effect she had on me?

It was like I wasn't in control of myself. The urge to touch her, move closer, burning through me like wildfire.

"Champagne?" I asked her, trying to get a grip on myself.

"Yes, please." Caitlin handed me a glass and I popped the cork from the bottle, filling her glass. After I filled my own, I lifted it into the air.

"A toast."

"What are we celebrating?" She batted her eyelashes at me, and I almost drowned in her green eyes.

"One night of possibilities."

"Possibilities?" Her brow quirked, a smile touching her lips.

"Yes," I leaned in, ghosting my mouth over hers. "A night of endless possibilities." My eyes held Caitlin's, the air crackling between us the way it did whenever we were close. I wanted to kiss her. Fuck, did I want to kiss her.

The lights dimmed, the opening notes of the violin rising above the eerie silence. Caitlin grabbed my hand, squeezing tightly as the prima ballerina entered center-stage. I turned my palm, threading our fingers together, taking whatever I could get from her.

Her expression was animated as the story unfolded. I felt every emotion that played on her face. Every high and surprise. Every gasp and sigh. Caitlin leaned forward more than once, as if trying to get closer. The first act stole her breath and her heart… and she stole mine.

I wanted this woman. I wanted her in a way I couldn't explain. There was still every chance she would reject me, but I had to try.

The curtain fell and applause filled the theater. Caitlin shot to her feet, clapping and smiling. Silent tears rolled down her cheeks.

"Here," I said, turning into her to wipe them away with the pad of my thumb.

"That was so beautiful. I... I don't know what to say."

"There's still another act to go yet." I chuckled, letting my thumb linger on her skin. "Are you hungry?"

Her eyes went past me to the small table tucked in the shadows.

"Come." I led Caitlin back to her chair and retrieved the plate of chocolate covered strawberries.

"Anyone would think you were trying to seduce me, Matteo Bellatoni."

"Is it working?" I smirked, bringing one of the straw-berries to her lips. I didn't consider myself a jealous guy, but in that moment, as Caitlin opened her mouth and took a bite, I was burning with jealousy all over a piece of fruit.

"These are good." She let out a soft moan, and I almost came on the spot. "Here, you try one." Caitlin plucked another strawberry off the plate and fed it to me.

"You're right." I grinned, licking the juice off my lips. "This does taste good. But not as good as you." Sliding my hand along her neck, I pulled her face to mine, kissing her softly.

A whimper bubbled in her throat as she parted her lips for me. Our tongues tangled; deep, lazy strokes that had me wishing we were somewhere a little more private. Not that anyone could see us up here.

"I could kiss you all night and never grow tired of it."

"Matt," she breathed, slipping her hands up my chest.

"Tell me you feel it, Tink. I know you do." I pulled back to stare her in the eye. Caitlin's cheeks were flushed, her eyes bright with desire. She wanted me, there was no denying that.

But did she want me enough?

"Thank you, Matteo. This is beyond my wildest dreams."

"I'm just glad you agreed to come. Despite what you might think about me, about my family, I really do care about you, Cait."

She gave me a small nod before popping another strawberry in her mouth. The conversation was over, the second act about to start.

But there were still so many things left unsaid.

"I THINK that was the most beautiful thing I've ever seen," Caitlin said as the lights came on. We hadn't kissed again, but I'd held her hand throughout the whole second act. Savoring every second with her that I could.

I didn't want the night to be over.

Because deep down, I knew my grand gesture wasn't enough to convince her to give me—to give us—a shot.

We made our way back down to the SUV in thick silence. Caitlin was lost in her own thoughts, and I was too preoccupied with what came next.

Luis greeted us right at the door, effortlessly guiding Caitlin into the back of the SUV while I followed. "How was it?" he asked, the second he climbed into the driver's seat.

"It was wonderful." Caitlin let out a contented sigh, and I took her hand again, testing the waters.

To my surprise, she didn't pull away. But she refused to look at me, and that alone spoke volumes.

"Tell me about it," I prompted as the SUV's engine purred beneath us.

"About what?" Caitlin finally met my gaze.

"Dancing."

"It was a long time ago." Sadness bled into her expression.

"You were a ballerina?"

"I trained in ballet, along with other disciplines of dancing."

"Why did you stop?"

"Why do we stop doing any of the things we love?" She let out a small sigh.

"Caitlin, you can talk to me." I gently squeezed her hand. "You can trust me."

It was the wrong thing to say.

Caitlin snatched her hand from me and laid it in her lap, staring out of the window. Luis caught my eye in the rearview mirror, frowning.

He'd come to care for Caitlin, anyone could see that. It was him and Arianne all over again.

We rode in silence for the next ten minutes. I didn't want to push her to talk about her past, but I had hoped tonight would be an olive branch. My cell vibrated and I dug it out of my pocket.

So... did she love it?

I SMILED. I couldn't help it. My sister was one hundred percent team Matteo and Caitlin. She'd even gone as far as to ship our names. Although I wasn't sure Maitlin or Caitteo had a nice ring to it. But it was nice to know someone was rooting for us.

SHE DID.

I TEXTED BACK.

THAT'S IT? Seriously, Matt. You need to give me something else. Did you kiss her?

BELLA!

WHAT? I need to know these things. I like her and she's good for you.

. . .

"Let me guess," Caitlin whispered. "Bella?"

"She's grilling me about my art of seduction." I smiled, hoping to thaw some of the ice between us. "Joke," I quickly added when she didn't reply. "I'm joking."

"What are we doing, Matteo?" Caitlin's eyes shuttered as she inhaled a shaky breath.

"Well, I thought we were watching the ballet, but—"

"Matt, I'm serious. This can't work. You have to know that."

"You're wrong, Cait." I grabbed her hand again, refusing to let her go this time. I didn't care that Luis could hear me, I needed to say this. I needed to make her see.

"What I know is that I can't stop thinking about you. I wake up and the first thing that pops into my head is you. I fall asleep with your face in my mind. Whenever we're near, I want to touch you. It's like my hands get a mind all of their own, needing to be close to you."

"Matt—"

"No, Cait." I pulled her hand to my chest, right over my heart. "Look me in the eye and tell me you don't feel it?" I stared at her, willing her to admit it. "Tell me you don't feel it and I'll walk away. You can stay in the cabin until DiMarco is taken care of and then you can go on your way. You'll never have to see me again. If that's what you want, then—"

"I feel it."

Those three little words should have meant everything to me. But the pain in her eyes made my heart sink.

"Why do I feel like there's a big 'but' in there?"

"You're such a good man, Matteo." Caitlin took my hand in hers. "But I'm…"

"What, Caitlin? Just say it." *Put me out of my misery.*

She sucked in a ragged breath and forced a smile. "It doesn't matter. Tonight was amazing. I'll never forget it." She leaned over and kissed my cheek.

And I let her.

I didn't argue or try to convince her.

Because surely wanting someone to take a chance on you wasn't supposed to be this hard?

BY THE TIME we pulled up outside the cabin, Caitlin had fallen asleep on my arm.

"Caitlin," I whispered, gently nudging her. "We're here."

"Huh?" She blinked up at me, confusion glittering in her eyes. "What time is it?"

"A little after midnight. Wait here, okay?" I dropped a kiss on her head and climbed out of the SUV, going around the other side. Pulling the door open, I helped her out.

"I'm sorry I fell asleep."

"Don't be," I said, tucking her into the crook of my arm and guiding her inside. Luis made himself useful by lighting the fire while I walked Caitlin to her room.

"Thank you for tonight," I said.

I'd hoped this night would end differently. That maybe she'd invite me to stay, and I'd get to taste her again. To do all the things I wanted to do to her.

But I wouldn't be that guy. I couldn't.

If she didn't want all of me, then I had to accept that.

"Are you okay getting inside?" I asked, jamming my hands in my pockets to stop myself from reaching for her.

"Matt, I—"

"It's okay, Cait. I get it. You don't want me." At least not the way I wanted her to want me.

"It isn't… I'm sorry. I can't—"

"Shh, Tink." Cupping the back of her neck, I drew her into me. "It's okay." I breathed against her temple. "I'm glad I could give you tonight."

"Matt." Her fingers twisted into my shirt as we stood there, silently saying everything we couldn't say aloud.

"I think Bella wants to come and see you again tomorrow. But if you'd prefer, she doesn't—"

"No, I'd like that." She gazed up at me and I wanted to believe the hunger in her eyes was for me.

"Go. I'll speak to Luis before I leave and let him know to expect Bella tomorrow." I forced myself to take a step backward. "Good night, Caitlin."

"Good night." She watched me back up down the hall before slipping into her room and closing the door.

I let out a strained breath, running a hand over my jaw. I'd really thought tonight would change things for her.

Feeling utterly defeated, I made my way into the living room.

"You're leaving?" Luis asked me.

"Yeah, I think it's best I go." I moved for the door, pausing when I reached it. "Has she told you anything about her past?"

"Not much, why?"

"No reason," I said. "Bella is going to drop by tomorrow. Keep your eye on her."

He nodded. "You have my word."

"Thank you."

"You know, Matteo, I've been around a while, and well, maybe I've learned a thing or two about women."

My hand paused on the door handle. "Really, old man?" I smiled but it was only a polite one.

"Some women are so damaged by their pasts that they can't see when a good thing is standing right in front of them. They'll push you away, make you think they don't want you… when deep down, all they really want is someone to fight for them. To chase them down until they have no choice but to face the truth."

"That's… enlightening, *Dr. Phil*," I teased.

"It's not your job to fix her, Matteo. It's your job to care enough to help her fix herself."

I gave him a small nod before slipping into the inky night.

Help her fix herself.

I wanted nothing more. But in order to help her, she had to trust me enough to open up first.

Not repeatedly shut me out.

CHAPTER 23

CAITLIN

"What is all that?" I gawked at the bags in Arabella's hands.

"I thought we could have a pamper day."

"A pamper day." I blinked as she breezed past me as if we'd been doing this forever.

Part of me wondered if it was weird that Matteo's sister wanted to hang out with me, but the truth was, Bella was a ray of sunshine, and I enjoyed her company.

So much so, I'd jumped at the chance to see her again.

Strangely, being around her also made me feel close to Matteo. It was the sweetest kind of torture, being close to the most important person in his life, knowing that I'd always be on the outside looking in.

But who could tell a bubbly, sweet sixteen-year-old no?

Not me apparently.

"Yeah, you know. Like face packs and manicures, and I

got some of those truffles from the Chocolate Boutique in the city. I figured you could sneak me a glass or two of wine." She waggled her brows.

"One. *One* glass. I'm the responsible adult here. I take it Luis won't be joining us?" I peered over her shoulder.

"He's walking the perimeter or polishing his Glock or whatever it is he does."

"Polishing his Glock," I muttered under my breath, stifling the laughter bubbling up my throat.

"You know what I mean." She rolled her eyes, dumping the bags on the chair. "So… how was last night?"

"It was lovely."

"Lovely?" Bella balked. "Matteo bought you the best seats in the theater and you thought it was… lovely?"

It was my turn to roll my eyes. "Okay, it was amazing. I loved every second."

How I'd felt watching the dancers flit across the stage was like no other feeling, and it touched something deep inside that Matteo had done that for me. But it was complicated.

"So what's the problem?"

"What do you—"

"I saw my brother today. He looked… sad."

"Oh." My heart cinched.

"I don't get it. You're perfect for each other." She began unpacking all her pamper supplies while I fetched a bottle of wine from the refrigerator. Luis kept it well stocked thankfully.

"One glass." I slid it across the table to her.

"I can keep a secret, you know."

"I'm sure you can."

"So what's holding you back? I mean, anyone in the same vicinity as the two of you can feel it." I frowned and she added, "The sexual tension."

"I'm not sure you're supposed to be talking about sexual tension at your age."

"*Please*. I know what sex is, Cait."

"Are you… having sex?"

"Oh my God, no! I'm saving myself."

"You are?"

She shrugged. "It's no big deal. I mean, I like guys. I have crushes and I even kissed a few guys at my school. But I've never felt it before."

"It?"

"Yeah, that magical moment where the stars align and everything else fades into nothing and you're the only two people left in the world."

"That's beautiful."

I wish I had that. But my childhood had been filled with nothing but dark, desperate days. There had been no room for magic or stars aligning.

"Some of my school friends think it's silly. But I want what my mom and dad have, and Nicco and Ari, and Enzo and Nora. That once in a lifetime kinda love, you know?"

"Then you should hold out."

Arabella beamed at me. I hadn't really noticed before how much she sought validation. I guess it was a side effect of growing up in a family like theirs.

"Okay, let's do face packs first and then I'll give you a manicure."

"Sounds good." I accepted the packet from her and slid

out the cool, refreshing face pack. "Hmm, it smells good enough to eat."

"Wait until you try a truffle. I make Matteo buy me some whenever he's in the city."

Every time she mentioned his name my heart faltered. I'd been unfair to him last night, brushed off his affection after an amazing night together.

It couldn't have been more perfect. Yet, it still wasn't enough for me to shake my fears. It was better this way, it was.

Once the mess with DiMarco was rectified, they would send me on my way and Matteo would move on and find a girl who could meet him halfway. A girl who didn't have copious amounts of baggage and a tragic backstory like me.

Not one that could upend everything he and his family had worked for.

"Caitlin, what is it? What's wrong?"

I didn't realize she could see my expression with the face pack plastered to my skin, but Bella looked concerned.

"I'm fine." I forced my emotions back into their locked box, right where they needed to stay.

She nodded, taking hold of my hand and slathering it in lotion. "I know I'm younger than you and that I'm Matteo's sister, but you can talk to me, Cait. I would never betray your confidence."

"That's very kind of you, but I'm okay. I promise."

For a second, she looked a little hurt at my unwilling-ness to open up to her. But it quickly melted away as she moved onto color options for my nails.

"My friend Gisele would love you," I mused.

"Your friend from…"

"How very sleuthy of you." Laughter crinkled my eyes. "I worked with Gisele."

"Have you spoken to her? Maybe she can visit and we can—"

My expression fell. "I don't think that'll be possible, Bella."

"I'm sure Matteo would arrange it if you asked. He cares about you, Cait. I know he does."

"It isn't that simple."

Bella hesitated for a second and then she asked me four little words that made my stomach drop. "Are you in danger?"

"I… I'm safe now, that's all that matters."

Bella finished painting the nails on my first hand and placed the bottle of varnish down, sinking back against the chair. "Sometimes I hate this life. I hate that I'll never be normal. I'll never get to be just a normal sixteen-year-old girl. There's always security, or my brother, or my cousins. It's suffocating sometimes.

"But then I feel guilty, because I know that some people have none of that. And I know that although they drive me crazy sometimes, my family would do anything for me."

Emotion balled in my throat as I swallowed down the tears burning the backs of my eyes. "You're very lucky to have so many people who love you, Bella. Don't ever take that for granted."

"I won't." She smiled, grabbed the varnish and started on my other hand.

While I sat there wondering if she knew just how lucky she was.

"SOMETHING SMELLS GOOD," I said, joining Bella in the kitchen sometime later. I'd offered to make us something to eat, but she'd said she wanted to cook for us, so I indulged her.

She made everything so easy.

Too easy.

Just like her brother, I could feel myself falling a little bit more in love with her every minute we spent together.

"It's one of my mama's favorite recipes. Simple but delicious." She put on her best Italian accent, laughing at herself.

"Well, it smells good."

"I enjoy cooking. I find it calming."

"And here I would have thought sixteen-year-old girls were into boys and makeup."

She glanced over at me and quirked a brow. "Weren't you listening to anything I said earlier about my brother and cousins."

"It won't be like that forever. Believe me, one day you'll be a force they can't control."

"Damn right I will."

"Although I'm surprised he hasn't been blowing up your cell phone."

"Actually, I told him to give us some space."

"You did, huh?"

"Yeah." She grinned. "I'd like nothing more than to see

you and my brother get together, Cait. You're good for him. And I think he could be good for you too. But I also happen to think you're really cool. I meant what I said before… I'd like for us to be friends."

I gave her a tight-lipped smile. "Can I help you do anything?"

"Refill our wine glasses?" A smirk touched her lips.

"Nice try, young lady. But I already let you have two glasses and I'm sure your brother will have something to say if I send you home drunk."

"Fine, I'll have soda. And I think I saw some parmigiana in there. Grate some of that please."

"I can do that." I got to work, topping up our glasses and locating a cheese grater.

"You know, for all my family's faults, I'll always treasure memories of big family meals." She smiled wistfully. "Before she died, my nonna loved to cook for everyone. It was always chaos, too many people and not enough seats. But we made it work."

"You're very lucky, Bella."

"Sorry. I didn't mean to upset you."

"You didn't. You can't be sad over something you never had, right?" I gave her a strained smile.

"You must have some nice memories of growing up?"

"Nothing worth mentioning." My chest grew tight, and I hoped she would change the subject.

To my relief, she did.

"Okay, I think we're done here." Bella tossed the pasta one more time before serving it onto two plates.

"Aglio e Olio."

"This looks great, Bella. Thank you."

"Maybe next time, you can join us at my house for dinner. I know my parents would love to meet you."

I shoved a mouthful of pasta into my mouth and murmured, "Mm-hmm, maybe."

I couldn't lie to her, but I could evade the truth.

We ate and talked, sticking to safer subjects like Bella's school life, and then cleaned the dishes and headed back into the living room and got comfortable on the couch.

"Luis has been gone a while," I checked the time. "What do you think he's doing out there?"

"Probably sitting in the SUV listening to the radio." Bella popped another truffle into her mouth. "Thank you for letting me come by today."

"You don't need to thank me," I said. "I've enjoyed your company very much."

"Even if you and my brother can't figure things out, I'd like to be friends, Caitlin. If you want, I mean."

Guilt snaked through me, coiling around my heart as I choked out, "Sure."

I was a liar.

A liar and a coward.

But I didn't know how to be anything else.

A heavy thud outside the window startled me and I placed the glass down. "Did you hear that?" I stood, moving closer to the window.

"It's probably just Luis clearing the leaves again." Bella grinned.

"Very true." I pulled back the curtains and peered into the night.

"Anything?" Bella asked, and I shook my—

Thud.

My heart lurched into my throat as I let the curtain drop.

"It's just Luis, I bet." Bella made for the door.

"Wait," I called, but it was too late. She yanked it open. "Luis, what the hell are you… oh, you're not Luis."

My blood turned to ice as I went to her. "Bella, what's—" Fear slammed into me as my gaze landed on the guy standing on the porch. "W-what are—"

"You're a very hard woman to track down, *Caitlin*."

I stared at him, my heart crashing violently in my chest. This couldn't be happening.

It couldn't—

Bella.

Oh God, Arabella was here.

"Please," my voice cracked as I gripped her shoulder to keep myself upright, fear threatening to bring me to my knees.

"Please don't do this."

CHAPTER 24

MATTEO

"Anything?" Nicco asked as I tried Luis for the third time.

"Nothing, and neither of the girls are picking up either."

When Bella hadn't replied to my last four text messages, I'd eventually caved and called Luis. He wasn't answering either.

"They're probably busy."

"Busy doing what? They're stranded in a fucking cabin, Nicco." My leg bounced as I watched the scenery roll by.

The cabin was secure. No one except for a handful of people knew the way in or out. Nicco was right—there was probably a perfectly reasonable explanation.

So why couldn't I shake the feeling something was wrong?

"You need to rela—"

"Don't tell me to relax," I snapped. "That's my sister and—" Whatever the hell Caitlin was to me.

"We're almost there," he said.

"If anything has happened to them…"

I couldn't go there.

There had to be a logical explanation, there had to be.

The blare of my cell phone cut through the tension.

"Anything?" Enzo asked, the second I hit answer.

"Nothing yet, we're almost there," I said. "Have you got eyes on DiMarco?"

"Yeah, he's been at the club all day."

"He doesn't leave, understand?" Nicco's voice was deadly calm, a complete contrast to the chaos raging inside me.

"You got it, Boss. The second you get there, call me."

"We will." I hung up and sent my sister and Caitlin another text message.

"Where the fuck are they?" Fear trickled up and down my spine.

"We're almost there." Nicco pulled off the highway and followed the road down to the cabin, his security car following behind. At least we had back up. Four pairs of eyes were better than two.

I slipped my hand in my jacket and felt the pistol strapped there. It was a part of the job I never enjoyed, but it was necessary.

"See," Nicco said the second the cabin came into view. "The SUV is still there. They have to be here."

But I felt zero relief as the Range Rover rolled to a stop and I climbed out. Everything looked normal: the SUV was parked in its usual place, and the cabin door was closed. It didn't stop the hairs along my arms all standing to attention.

Something was wrong.

"Miss Bellatoni and Luis's GPS trackers show her as still here," Nicco's security guard, Dario, said as he stepped out of the car.

Guns drawn, they approached the cabin first. Knocking twice, they waited. When there was no answer, he glanced at Nicco. He nodded and Dario grabbed the handle, testing it.

The door swung open. "Luis?"

Nothing.

"Miss Bellatoni, it's security. Please respond so we know you're okay."

Still nothing.

"We're coming inside." They stepped inside and swept the living room while Nicco and I hung back.

"I have a bad feeling about this," I said, pacing back and forth.

"Clear," someone called, and we went inside.

"Shit, Nic." My eyes immediately found Bella's cell phone. I only knew it was hers because it had one of those pink, glittery cases.

I grabbed it and checked the screen. "She didn't pick up any of my messages."

"Fan out," Nicco ordered his men. "Check every—"

"Mr. Marchetti," Dario called. "You'll want to see this."

We rushed over to the hall, and I froze at the sight of blood smeared over the floor.

"It leads down here." We followed the sticky red trail to the back of the cabin, right to the storage closet.

"Fuck," I cried out at the splatters of blood.

"Looks like there was a struggle." Dario grasped the door handle, gently twisting it open. He gave his partner a nod and checked inside.

"Luis, shit."

He was unconscious, slumped up against the bench, bleeding out of a nasty cut on his forehead.

"He needs medical attention," Dario said, trying to rouse Luis.

Nicco already had his phone out, calling the Family's doctor. "He's on his way. Get him comfortable." He looked to me. "A word outside."

I followed him out of the room, every cell in my body zipping with nervous energy.

Caitlin and Bella were gone. Luis had been hurt. It didn't take much to figure out what had happened here.

"DiMarco found her," I snapped.

"Maybe. Maybe not." Nicco ran a hand through his hair, staring out of the window.

"Come on, Nic. It's fucking obvious that he found her, and he... he fucking took them. My sister and my—" I stopped myself, inhaling a ragged breath.

"I need to call Enzo." Nicco studied me. "You good for a minute?"

Good?

I wanted to break something. Preferably that fucker's neck.

"Promise me we'll get them back, Nic." My voice

cracked, fear bleeding into every cell in my body. "Promise me that we'll get them back."

He gave me a small nod, but as he walked out of the cabin, cell phone pressed to his ear, I realized he hadn't answered me.

"Papa," I jumped up and strode toward my father, falling into his open arms.

"Shh, figlio mio. We will find them." He gripped me tightly as the emotion I tried so hard to keep contained, rushed to the surface.

"What do we know?" He held me at arm's length, his hard gaze sliding to Nicco.

"Luis was jumped outside the cabin. He came to and tried to fight off two guys, but one hit him with a tire iron. He's got a nasty contusion to his head, but Doc says he'll be okay."

"Have Enzo and Lucino started interrogating DiMarco?"

"No, they're waiting for us," Nicco said.

"What are we waiting for then? Let's go." I went to barge past my father, but he shouldered me.

"Basta! This isn't helping, Son, you need to calm down."

"Seriously? You're going to tell me to calm down when DiMarco has Arabella? Who knows what he's doing to them. He could be—"

"Shh, Son." My father pulled me into his chest, cupping

the back of my neck as a shuddering breath went through me.

If he'd hurt them… I couldn't bear it.

I'd spent my entire life protecting Bella, trying to keep her innocent and out of harm's way.

And now she had been taken… because I'd dropped the ball and allowed her to come here, to be around Caitlin.

"Don't." My father nudged me away to look at me. "Don't do that to yourself. We all agreed it was safe to let her come here. Security is tight, the location is unknown, and we've been careful. You're not to blame, Son."

Careful… but not careful enough.

Fuck.

My fists clenched, my lips thinning. Nothing, *nothing* anyone said would stop the weight of guilt crushing my chest.

"Make sure Luis is taken care of. We need to head to Providence immediately."

"Thank fuck," I breathed, heading for the door. But my father snagged my wrist, stopping me.

"Cool heads, Matteo. We need to keep cool heads, capisci? With DiMarco in talks with Lombardi, we can't rule out that there is more at play here."

"What are you saying?"

"We talk first. Give DiMarco a chance to tell us what he knows."

"I think that's pretty obvious." I scoffed. "He kidnapped them. He took them and left Luis for dead, and you want to… to talk?"

Un-fucking-believable.

"Despite what you might think, figlio mio. I want to resolve this with the least bloodshed. For all we know, it could be a trap. Would you so willingly storm in all guns blazing if you thought it might end up with all of us dead?" His gaze cut me to the bone.

"I… I need to do something."

"And you will." He gripped my shoulder. "When we figure out their motives."

"Fine," I grumbled. "But if DiMarco is responsible, he's a dead man."

My father's eyes went over my shoulder to Nicco, something passing between them. But I didn't stick around to ask what; I needed some fresh air before I combusted.

They wanted to talk, to appease that asshole, when he deserved nothing more than a bullet through his skull. But I wasn't the boss and there was protocol.

Fuck.

Fuck!

I slammed my fist against the side of Nicco's Range Rover, pain skittering up my arm. I was about to hit it again, when my phone vibrated.

For a second, hope went through me. But it quickly died when I saw Enzo's name, not Caitlin's.

WE'LL GET THEM BACK**, cous. You have my word.**

I WANTED to heed his words; I did. But I'd never felt more helpless than I did in that moment.

~

By the time we arrived in Providence, it was late, but downtown was alive with activity. The lights and music, the steady hum of cars passing, was all white noise to the blood roaring in my ears.

It had been too long.

At least three hours since Luis last checked in.

A lot could happen in three hours.

"What now?" I asked Nicco, who was white knuckling the steering wheel as we stared at the sign above DiMarco's club.

"We go pay him a visit."

"Thank fuck." I went to climb out, but Nicco grabbed my arm.

"Not you, Matt."

"What the fuck?" I gawked at him in disbelief. He couldn't be serious.

I needed to see him. I needed to look DiMarco in the eye when he confessed his sins.

"You're too close to this. Let me and Michele go in. You stay out here until—"

"That's bullshit and you know it."

"Matt—"

"No, Nic, *no*! Are you telling me that if it was Alessia and Arianne missing you'd just sit by while me and Enzo handled it?"

His jaw clenched as he tipped his head up and let out a strained breath.

"Exactly," I snapped. "I'm coming."

"Fine, fine. But you follow my lead, and you leave your

piece here." He motioned to the glove compartment. "I mean it, Matteo. We cannot afford to start something until we know where the girls are."

"Okay," I conceded, unsheathing my pistol and shoving it inside.

He nodded, climbing out of the Range Rover. I followed, meeting him around the front. Nicco motioned to my father and his security guard and the four of us approached the entrance to DiMarco's.

"Mr. Marchetti." The doorman nodded out of respect. "Is the boss expecting you?"

"It's an impromptu visit. We'll make our own way inside, thank you."

"Very well." He stepped aside, letting us enter. My heart pounded in my chest with every step deeper into the club.

We spotted Enzo, Lucino, and Stefan seated in one of the VIP booths. They signaled us over, but Nicco told us to go on ahead.

"Matt." Enzo stood to greet me, pulling me into a hug. "You good?"

I offered him a tight smile. "I will be once we get them back."

"And we will, cous. We will."

It was the only possible solution. Because the alternative… I couldn't even go there.

"Gentlemen." A busty brunette sauntered over to us. "What will it be?"

"A round of Blue Label whisky," Lucino said smoothly, playing the game. Keeping up appearances. When all I wanted to do was start smashing things up until someone told me where the fuck my sister and Caitlin were.

"Of course." She left us and I pinched my temples as I scanned the club. "Have you spoken to him?"

"He's acting the part. Came to make sure we had everything we wanted and left us to it."

"He didn't seem ruffled?" my father asked.

"Cool as a fucking cucumber." Lucino sucked on his cigar, blowing a plume of smoke into the air.

"He's a fucking snake."

I glanced over at where Nicco was talking to a guy in a sleek black suit. My cousin was the epitome of a leader. Calm. Composed. Head held high and shoulders rolled back. Whether he liked it or not, Nicco had slid into the role of acting boss with total ease, and part of me was relieved that he was the one handling this and not Uncle Toni.

Because despite what he said, Nicco knew what it was like to find yourself torn between duty, family, and the woman you loved.

Did I love Caitlin?

I wasn't sure.

What we had was new, uncertain, and unknown. But part of me felt like I've always known her, that she'd always been a part of me. So maybe it wasn't love right now, in this moment, but I didn't doubt for a second that I could grow to love her.

The second Zander DiMarco appeared, every muscle in my body went taut.

"Easy, cous," Enzo hissed, clamping his hand around my arm. "Let Nicco handle this."

"This was a bad idea," I ground out, curling my fingers into the edge of the table.

Fuck, I wanted to hurt him. The way he'd hurt Caitlin.

"Just breathe," Enzo warned, gripping my arm harder. "If we're going to find them, we need him."

Nicco and Zander were locked in a standoff, the two of them pulled to their full height, staring the other down.

"Should we intervene?" Lucino asked.

"Nicco can handle DiMarco."

Sure enough, DiMarco threw up his hands and walked away. Seconds later, Nicco joined us, sliding into the booth.

"So?" my father asked, rapping his fingers against the table.

"He isn't happy we showed up unannounced."

"Maybe he should have thought about that before getting into bed with Lombardi."

"I didn't tell him we know. I want to feel him out first."

"So we wait?" Enzo said.

"I told him to close the club early."

Lucino let out a low whistle. "Brave move, ki—"

"Kid, really?" Enzo sneered. "He's the fucking boss."

"Perdonami. I meant no offense."

Nicco gave him a nod. "DiMarco needs to realize who's in control here, and it isn't him." Nicco snatched up his glass of whisky and sat back, watching as the place started emptying out.

I couldn't picture Caitlin working here. The men ogling her and objectifying her. Did they touch her? Whisper dark, depraved things in her ear as she served them drinks?

My fists clenched, anger rising inside me.

He didn't deserve this. He'd hurt Caitlin, we were pretty certain he had Shaun killed, and he was aligning himself with the Lombardi crime family.

And we were giving him the benefit of the doubt by talking to him. It was a fucking joke.

I didn't consider myself a violent man. I usually preferred trying to find more amicable ways to end disputes. But this was my family, the woman I wanted to be mine. I couldn't see past DiMarco hurting her, putting his fucking hands on her and making her bleed and bruise. And now he'd taken Caitlin and my sister. My sweet, innocent Arabella.

He didn't deserve the benefit of the doubt—he deserved to die a slow, painful death, begging for mercy down the barrel of a gun.

We waited until the club was empty. Anticipation rippled in the air like an angry storm circling in the distance.

The servers cleaned up around us, casting suspicious looks in our direction. I didn't blame them. They all knew of DiMarco's connections, so they knew what it meant when business was closed down before closing hours.

"Give us the room," Zander barked as he stepped out of a door marked 'private.'

Everyone scuttled out of sight, leaving DiMarco alone save for his two security men who hovered near the entrance.

"Gentleman, let's talk." He helped himself to a glass of Blue Label whisky and swaggered over to us as if he didn't have a care in the world. "I have to say, Niccolò, if I would've known you were coming, I would have rolled out the red carpet."

"Stronzo," Enzo grumbled, lurching forward, but Nicco shot him a warning look.

"We have heard some concerning things, Zander. Things that we want to give you a chance to explain."

"I have no idea what you're talking about." He swept a hand through his hair.

"Let's not play this game." Nicco loosened his collar. "We know all about Lombardi."

"Business is business," Zander shrugged, "and his men came looking to spend good money."

"I noticed Shaun wasn't working tonight," Enzo said. "He's a good man."

"He was," Zander didn't miss a beat. "One of the best. Such a shame what happened."

"Something happened?"

"He was in an accident. Tragic really."

"He died?"

Zander nodded. "It's been hard for us all."

"Condolences," my father said. "It always hurts to lose someone."

"It does."

Jesus, this fucking asshole was good.

"But I'm sure you didn't come here to discuss my employees."

"I'm going to lay it out straight for you," Nicco said, sliding his hand into his jacket. He pulled out his gun and laid it on the table pointed at Zander, keeping his finger on the trigger. "What are your plans with Lombardi?"

"Easy, Niccolò. You don't want to do something you'll

later regret." DiMarco smirked, lifting his hands up. "We talked, nothing more. Lombardi is looking to branch out into the strip club business. He asked for my advice."

"That so?" Lucino snorted.

"It's the truth. I know our agreement is irreversible. Just like I told Lombardi, Providence is Marchetti territory."

"Seriously? You buy a single word this sleazeball is telling you?" I sneered.

"Matteo," my father warned.

I ground my teeth together, fighting the urge to leap across the table, grab Zander by the throat, and demand answers about Caitlin and Arabella.

"Where are they, Zander?" my father said.

"They?" His brows pinched. "What are you talking about?"

"Cut the bullshit, figlio di puttana! We know you took them." My father glared at him with enough venom that it rippled around us like a living, breathing thing. "You're playing a very dangerous game, DiMarco. I suggest if you don't want to end up with your brains splattered all over the wall, you pick up your cell phone, call your men, and get them here immediately."

"Listen, Niccolò, Michele, I don't know what you're talking about, but I—"

"Basta!" Nicco slammed his hand down, sending the glasses clattering together. "We wanted to give you the chance to fix this, to—"

His cell phone began blaring, his eyes narrowing on whoever's name was flashing across the screen. "Get him up." He motioned to our security guys, and they approached the booth, manhandling Zander onto his feet.

"Now, now, Niccolò. I don't know what you're—"

"Can it," my father spat as he stood and brushed down his jacket.

"You can't do this," DiMarco kept protesting, thrashing against his man-made restraints. "We have an arrangement. One I've never reneged on."

Nicco picked up his gun and stalked toward him, his eyes cold and deadly.

"N-Niccolò, I swear, man! I don't know what you're talking about."

Quicker than a flash, Nicco had his pistol pressed against Zander's forehead, the safety clicked off. "Let's get one thing straight, *amico*, I don't like liars. And you, Zander DiMarco, are the very worst of them."

"Fuck…" Sweat began beading along his forehead, fear glittering in his eyes. "Fuck, Nicco, I swear, I don't know what—"

The blare of Nicco's cell phone cut through the room again. He dug it out of his pocket and frowned at the name on the screen. "I need to take this," he said. "Watch him."

Enzo stepped into our cousin's place. "Don't move a fucking muscle, stronzo."

"And here I thought we were friends." Zander smirked.

The bastard smirked.

Fucking asshole had a death wish.

"Friends?" Enzo cocked a brow. "I don't associate myself with women beaters."

"What the fuck is that supposed to mean?"

"Oh, I think you know exactly what it means."

"E, back up, son." My father stepped up to his side, whispering something to him.

"It's nothing they don't want." DiMarco laughed darkly. "Nothing they don't beg for."

One second I was standing off to the side, watching Zander sneer at Enzo. The next I was in front of him, my fist flying into his face.

"*Matteo!*" someone yelled, but I was lost to the anger raging inside me. I couldn't see. I couldn't think about anything other than hurting Zander.

"You sick motherfucker," I roared, slamming my fist into his nose. Blood sprayed everywhere, pain radiating through my wrist, splitting open my barely healed knuckles. "Where are they?" I grabbed him by his collar, almost wrenching him out of the guards hold. "You tell me right now where they are or I'll fucking end you, you piece of shit."

Confusion flickered in Zander's eyes, blood pouring from his nose and trickling down his chin. "Who are you... *Caitlin?*" Recognition dawned on his face.

"Don't you say her name. Don't you dare fucking say her—"

"Easy, cous." Strong arms grabbed me from behind, dragging me backwards as DiMarco stared at me.

"You good?" Nicco got in my face. "If Enzo lets you go, are you going to stand down?"

Lips thinned, I nodded. He released me slowly, and I inhaled a ragged breath.

"We need to talk," Nicco said to me. "Alone." He

motioned for me to follow him to the opposite side of the club.

"I lost it, Nic, I know. But he's—"

"What do you know about Caitlin, Matt? Really know about her?"

"W-what? How is this important right now?" I gaped at him.

"Just think for a second. What has she told you about her past? About where she comes from?"

"She was raised in Rochester, New York. But that's about all I know. She doesn't like to talk about it. Why?"

Nicco dragged a hand down his face, fixing me with a sympathetic gaze. "I had Tommy run her name."

"What?"

Tommy was the Family's investigator. There wasn't much about anyone or anything that he couldn't dig up.

"Don't act so surprised. I wanted to know who we were taking in, who we were protecting. She's been around Arianne, my sister… Bella. It was the right call, and you know it."

He had a point, but I hadn't considered he would have Tommy look into her past.

"What did you find out?" I asked.

Nicco's eyes dropped to the floor, and when he glanced back at me, I knew.

I knew whatever he'd found changed everything.

"He found something, Matt. Until almost four years ago, Caitlin O'Donnell didn't exist."

"What do you mean, she didn't exist?"

"The trail ends."

"But that's impossible. Unless…"

No.

It couldn't be true.

Until Nicco said eight little words that confirmed my worst fears.

"Unless she isn't who she says she is."

CHAPTER 25

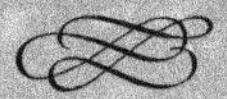

CAITLIN

"Bella?" I whispered into the dark. "Arabella, can you hear me?"

"C-Caitlin?" She sounded woozy. "Where are we? W-what happened?"

I squinted against the darkness, trying to find my bearings. We were in a small room, maybe a large closet or laundry room. I was pressed into the far corner, the wall at my back. A sliver of light trickled under the door, casting dark shadows around the room.

"I'm over here," I called out, my skull rattling with every word.

I winced in agony. The back of my head throbbed from where I'd banged it trying to fight off our captors. Of course, I'd lost. They were big and burly, and I was small and fragile. Still, I'd fought with everything I had, kicking and screaming. I'd even got one of them in the balls, but it made no difference. The other man had thrown me down with such force, I'd slammed my head against the floor and knocked myself out.

At least, I assumed that's what happened, given that when I came to, we were no longer in the cabin and in this cold, dark room instead.

"C-Cait, I'm scared."

My heart cracked.

Bella didn't deserve this—she didn't deserve any of it. It was all my fault she was here. I should never have accepted help from Enzo and Matteo. I should have refused to let them bring me back to Verona. But I'd let myself believe in the fairy tale. I'd let myself believe they could protect me.

A hand grazed mine and I strained to see Bella crawling toward me. "Thank God." I grabbed her, pulling her into my arms. "Are you hurt?"

"My... my face. One of them hit me when I bit his hand."

"You bit him?"

"Well, yeah. I wasn't about to let them take us without a fight. H-he hurt you. You were lying there, and I didn't know if you were dead or—"

"Shh." I pulled her closer, whispering soothing things against her matted hair. "It's okay. It's going to be okay." The lie soured on my tongue.

Because I didn't know that. I had no idea where we were.

"I-I don't understand what's happening." Bella sobbed into my shoulder, clinging to me.

"Shh. Shh." Silent tears rolled down my cheeks.

I needed to figure out where we were, and who had taken us.

If it was Zander, I could negotiate with him. Offer him what he wanted in exchange for Bella's freedom. Surely, he had to know that Matteo and his family would find out Arabella was missing, and when he realized who she was, the smart thing would be to hand her over if they wanted to avoid the Marchetti's wrath.

But if it wasn't Zander…

No.

It wasn't possible.

There was no way he had found me. I'd been careful. I'd covered my tracks and left my old life behind.

It was Zander.

It had to be Zander.

I inhaled a sharp breath, pain radiating through my skull again.

"They'll know, right?" Bella's voice trembled. "Matteo will know we're missing, and they'll be looking for us and… oh God, Cait. What if they don't find us? What if…" She choked over a huge sob, her body wracking under the power of her tears.

"Try and calm down, okay?" I said softly, smoothing my hand down her back. "We need to try and stay strong."

Heavy footsteps outside the door sent all my bravado crumbling though.

"Who is that?" Bella whispered.

"Shh, okay. Just try to be quiet."

There was a rattle of a lock and a heavy clunk and then light poured into the room. I threw my arm up, trying to give my eyes time to adjust to the stark brightness.

"Water and something to eat," a gruff voice said, his dark shadow filling the door. I didn't recognize him, but I wasn't surprised.

Zander had a lot of friends I didn't know. Bad men who worked for him in the shadows, doing despicable things.

"Where are we?" I asked, trying to keep the fear out of my voice. But he started to close the door. "No, wait, please. I'm hurt. My head—"

"Not my problem," he grunted, yanking the door closed.

"Bella, ease up a second." I gently pushed her off me. "We need to drink." I managed to shuffle over to the tray and retrieve the two small bottles of water.

"Here, take one." I held it out for her.

"It's so dark, I can barely see." She fumbled, her fingers brushing mine.

"There, you got it. Now drink. Small sips, okay?"

"Why is this happening? I-I don't understand."

"I… I'm sorry." My heart broke in two at the pain and confusion in her voice.

"I'm here… because of you?" She gasped as if she hadn't realized until now. "No, that's not possible."

"I'm so, so sorry. If I would've known… I didn't mean for this to happen, Bella. You have to know that. I didn't… I wasn't…" My breaths came in ragged pants.

"Who are you, Caitlin?" she whispered, scooting away from me.

Tears streaked down my face as I tipped my head back against the wall and let out a pained whimper.

Someone you're better off not knowing.

"FIREFLY, WAKE UP." A finger stroked down my cheek. "I've got a job for you."

Fear paralyzed me as I clutched the blanket to my changing body. I was only fifteen, but I had the curves of a young woman. I hated them. Hated how my mom's boyfriend and his friends looked at me.

"I don't want to," I cried, refusing to open my eyes.

"I need you to do this for me, firefly. You want to make me happy, don't you? After all I've done for you and your mom." He grabbed my arm, wrenching me up.

"Stop, you're hurting me."

He tsked, the bitter scent of cigars and liquor wafting over my face. I fought down the urge to gag. He didn't like that, didn't like me acting repulsed by him.

"Stop acting like a spoiled brat then. I have a job for you, and you'll be a good fucking girl, and do it unless you want me to cut your momma off. And we both know how she gets without her fix."

A shiver went through me. He was right, of course. If Mom didn't get her fix, she was insufferable.

Pushing my wild curls out of my face, I looked up at the man who had raised me. Raised me... and ruined me.

Pain coiled through my chest as I choked out, "Fine. I'll do it."

What other choice did I have?

If I didn't, it would only be me who suffered. And no matter how cruel my mom could be, no matter how much her barbed words hurt, she was still my mom.

My family.

He cupped my face, dragging his thumb down my cheek, the glint of his gold ring standing out against the darkness surrounding him.

"That's my good girl. Now get dressed. It's showtime."

I BOLTED UPRIGHT, sucking in fresh lungfuls of air. My head felt strange, like it might roll off my shoulders at any given moment.

"Caitlin?" a voice called from somewhere in the darkness.

"B-Bella?" Her name was like ash on my tongue. "I… I don't feel so good."

"You've been sleeping. I thought… I thought—"

"I'm here. I'm right here."

"Caitlin?"

"Yeah?" I sank back against the wall again, my muscles screaming in protest. I felt stiff, groggy, and sore.

"Who's firefly?

The icy fingers of fear wrapped around my throat. "What did you just say?"

"I said who's firefly? You were crying out in your sleep. Murmuring it over and over."

"I was?" A violent shudder rolled through me. It had been a long time since I had that dream.

"It's nothing," I said, refusing to let those thoughts penetrate my mind.

"It didn't sound like nothing."

"How long was I out?"

"I don't know. One, maybe two hours."

Shit.

"Did anyone come back?"

"No one. Although I heard voices beyond the door. It sounded like they were arguing."

"Did you hear any names?"

"None, why?"

"It doesn't matter." Defeat coated my words.

I'd never felt more powerless than I did in this moment, and I'd experienced some dire circumstances in the past. But Arabella was innocent. She didn't deserve to know this terror or fear. And I hated myself for ever dragging her into my life.

"I want you to know something," I said, biting back the tears threatening to fall. "Whatever happens, I'm going to do everything I can to make sure you make it out of this safely, okay?"

"W-what does that mean, Cait? What things? What are you going to do?"

I squeezed my eyes shut, tears dripping down my face. When they opened, a new sense of resolve washed over me.

Zander wanted me.

Bella was just collateral. I would make sure he had no reason to hurt her. I would do whatever it took to see to it that she walked out of here alive and unharmed.

But if I was going to negotiate, I needed to speak to him. I needed to look him in the eye and give him what he wanted.

"Whatever happens," I said to Bella, as I staggered to my feet, "I need you to keep quiet, okay?"

"What are you going to do?"

"What needs to be done. Just keep quiet and promise me you won't antagonize them."

"Cait, I'm not—"

"Promise me, Arabella."

"Okay, okay. I promise."

Before I could second guess myself, I grabbed the tray off the floor and smacked it against the door. "Hey, hey," I yelled, "I need to speak with the boss. I need to talk to him."

"Caitlin, are you mad?" Bella cried. What are you—"

"Shh," I hissed. "I need to attract their attention. I can fix this, Bella. I can make it all okay." I banged the tray against the door again. "Hey, come on, let me out. I need to—"

"What the fuck?" someone grunted from the other side of the door. I stepped back as it flung open.

"Do you have a fucking death wish?" He cocked a thick brow at me.

"I'm ready to talk."

"Oh, you're ready to talk, are you?" A sly smile tugged at his mouth. "That's not how things work around—"

"We both know the boss wants me to cooperate, so tell him. Tell him I'm ready to do whatever he wants. All I ask is that she's released. She isn't any part of this."

He studied me, muttering something about women under his breath. "Come with me." He grabbed my shoulder and yanked me out of the room.

"Caitlin!" Bella screamed as the guy dragged me down the hall.

"Grayson, grab the other one," the guy barked at a guy standing at the end of the hall.

"No, no, she's no part of this. You have to let her go," I shrieked.

"Not my call, darlin'."

We reached another door and he banged it once.

"Enter," a voice boomed, and the guy shouldered it open, dragging me inside. He pushed me hard and I crashed to my knees, pain slicing through me.

Inhaling a couple of breaths, I slowly lifted my head. "You," I gasped, hardly able to believe my eyes. "But it's not possible."

"It's been a long time, firefly."

That single word sent a bolt of fear straight into my heart, and in that moment, I knew... I knew I couldn't protect Arabella. My mom's boyfriend didn't care about right or wrong, or morals, or girls with their whole lives ahead of them. He only cared about business and keeping his associates happy.

I glanced over at Bella as she huddled in the corner of the room and my heart broke as I silently begged for forgiveness I knew would never come.

"I'm sorry," I cried. "I'm so sorry."

CHAPTER 26

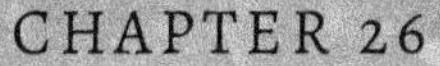

MATTEO

"What's taking so long?" I tapped my foot against the floor, draining another whisky.

"That isn't going to help anything." My father eyed me with concern.

"Well, it's either this or I go beat some answers out of DiMarco. Take your pick."

After Nicco had delivered the blow that Caitlin wasn't really Caitlin O'Donnell at all, our men had dragged Zander away to his office, where they had secured him until we could figure out what the hell to do.

But if he didn't have Caitlin and Bella... who the hell did?

Nicco appeared with Enzo trailing behind him.

"Anything?" I leaped up.

"Nothing that makes sense." Nicco motioned to the booth, and we all sat down. "Tommy was able to pull her cell phone number from DiMarco's staff records."

"He hacked his system?"

Nicco nodded.

"Okay," I frowned, not really following.

"There was nothing unusual at first. But then when he pulled her cell phone records, he noticed she called the same number on the same day of every month, for the last couple of years."

"Did he get a name?" my father asked.

"Yeah. Olivia Walsh. Born and raised in Rochester, New York until she moved to New Haven, Connecticut in the nineties. He's running a more extensive search as we speak."

"I don't understand." I raked a hand through my hair. "What is she running from?"

"That's what we need to find out. I want you to talk to DiMarco," Nicco said.

"Hang on a minute, Boss. You really think that's a good idea?" Enzo glanced between the two of us.

"In his own way, I think DiMarco cares about her. Or, in the very least, he's infatuated with her. Matt can appeal to that side of him."

Enzo snorted. "Or it'll send DiMarco straight off the deep end."

"He's the only tangible connection we have to Caitlin right now, and if he didn't take them, maybe he knows something that might help us find out who did."

"What about the girls that work here? They knew her, someone might know something," I said.

"Already got Lucino and Stefan on it."

Good. That was good.

"Do you think you can talk to him?" Nicco levelled me with a sympathetic look.

What choice did I have?

If Zander had information that could help us, I had to put my anger aside and reach out to him. Man to man.

"Yeah," I breathed, hoping to God I was right. "I can do it."

"Good, come on." Nicco got up and waited for me. "Michele." He glanced back at my father. "Keep in touch with Tommy. I want to know what he finds out as he finds it."

He nodded. In the short time we'd been here, my father had already aged. Arabella was the apple of his eye. It would kill him if anything happened to her.

It would kill all of us.

I followed Nicco through the door marked 'private' and down the hall to Zander's office. Nicco went in first and then beckoned me inside.

"Matteo wants to talk to you," he said.

"*Matteo* can go fuck himself." Zander was nursing his broken nose with a bag of ice.

"Caitlin is missing," I said.

His eyes went wide. "You know Caitlin?"

"I… yes." I pulled a chair closer to him and sat down.

"I'm not sure I follow."

I looked to Nicco, and he nodded, silently giving me permission. "Last year, I met Caitlin when we were here in Providence. I had no idea she was one of your girls, or even knew you. She told me she worked at a diner called Stella's. We… we spent the night together."

I gauged Zander's reaction, but his stone-cold mask gave nothing away.

"It was one night. I went home to Verona and never saw her again… until a couple of weeks ago, when the hospital over in Pawtucket called Enzo. We were on our way to see you but detoured to the hospital where we found Caitlin…"

As I remembered what it was like to see her lying there, in that hospital bed, it took everything inside me not to pounce on him. But I had to keep myself in check if we were going to get the information we needed. Caitlin and my sister came first; they trumped my burning need for vengeance.

The bastard didn't even flinch.

"We took her back to Verona County with us," I went on. "Gave her a safe place to stay."

That got a reaction. Jealousy and anger blazed in his eyes. Yeah, the fucker didn't like the idea of someone else looking after his girl.

It sent a sick thrill of satisfaction through me. Especially knowing he would never get to lay a hand on her again.

"Earlier today, Caitlin and my sister went missing."

"What?" he spat.

"Now you can see why we suspected it was you."

"I didn't… I swear to you, Bellatoni, this wasn't my doing."

"Strangely, I believe you. But you need to tell us everything you know about Cait so we can try to piece together who might have taken them."

"I… fuck," he heaved a deep sigh. "I don't know what to

say. I found her on the streets about four years ago. She was cold and hungry and needed a place to stay."

"So you took her in?" It came out harsher than I intended, and I felt the weight of Nicco's stare burning into the side of my face.

"She was new to the area; I was a girl down at the club. It was a win-win."

Yeah, right.

"At first, she worked the floor, taking orders and serving drinks, that kind of thing. Until one night after closing I saw her fooling around backstage with a couple of my dancers."

My spine went rigid as I listened to him recall those early days with Caitlin. The day he'd discovered her love of dancing.

"She was good," he said. "Really fucking good. So I offered her a spot, told her she could make a decent wage dancing for me. But I quickly realized the error of my ways. Caitlin was a little too good. Men queued up for her and it drove me in-fucking-sane." He looked me dead in the eye as he said the words. "I almost killed a guy for touching her. I was completely bewitched by her. But she fought me at every turn, determined to keep things strictly professional between us."

"So you took what you wanted instead." My voice was low, deadly. Rage like I'd never known it coursing through my veins.

"Matt," Nicco hissed.

I forced myself to take a deep, calming breath. I could do this—I could do it for her.

"None of this is helping us," I said. "We need to know

about her life. Friends? Family? Did she ever talk about anyone important in her life? Or her past?"

"Never. And I never asked. Most of the girls who end up working for me are running from something."

Wasn't that the truth.

But it didn't help us.

"So there's nothing?"

Zander shrugged, but I caught the glimpse of regret in his eyes. "I can't think of anything."

My patience began to wane, frustration bleeding into my voice. "You've known her all this time and you can't think of anything that might help us?"

"I… Wait, there was something. I didn't think much of it at the time, but when Dominic Cabrioles and his men first visited the club, he took an immediate interest in Caitlin. Offered me a lot of cash for a private audience with her."

"I thought you said she didn't dance no more."

"She didn't, but business is business." He shrugged again, as if dealing in sins of the flesh was a normal occurrence.

And maybe it was for assholes like DiMarco, but I couldn't stand the thought of Caitlin being forced to dance to line his pockets.

Nicco stepped forward. "Did Cabrioles say anything else?"

"He backed off pretty quickly when I made it clear she belonged to me. But now that I think about it, he was unusually interested in her."

"I'll be back." Nicco got straight on his phone and strolled out of the room, sending in one of his guards to no doubt make sure I didn't overstep my orders.

"You love her?"

DiMarco's question caught me off guard.

"I… I care for her very much."

He gave me a small nod, but I still couldn't gauge where his head was at. This wasn't the sleazy, cocksure asshole I was used to. But then, he was tied to a chair with a broken nose and no hope of being released.

"You killed Shaun to find her."

"He took something from me," he quietly seethed. "He betrayed me."

"He protected her, and you had him murdered in cold blood."

"Tell me, Matteo. What lengths would you go to, to get her back?"

I rolled my lips together. He was right. There wasn't much I couldn't imagine doing if it meant having her back safe in my arms.

But I still had honor and integrity. I wanted her to stand at my side, not cower at my feet.

"We're not the same."

"Maybe. Maybe not. But it doesn't matter now."

"No?" My brow arched.

"I am many things, Matteo. A fool is not one of them. You think I don't know how this goes? You think I don't know the second you get the chance, you'll put a bullet between my eyes? I can see it written all over your face."

I stood, taking a couple of steps closer to him. The guard moved with me, ready to intervene. Looming down over Zander, I said, "I pity you. You had her. You had her and you let her slip through your fingers because you're not a man, DiMarco, you're a coward. And I hope you rot in hell." I spat at his feet, turned on my heel and walked out of there without looking back.

The second I exited the room, Nicco glanced over at me. "You good?" he asked, pocketing his cell phone.

"Unless you want me to end him, I suggest you don't ask me to go back in there." I stalked off down the hall, needing some fresh air and a strong drink.

ENZO FOUND me outside the back of the club. I'd grabbed a bottle of whisky off the shelf and took off in search of some quiet.

"I'm not sure that's gonna help, cous," he said, eyeing the bottle in my hand.

"Like I told Nic, it's either this or I go put a bullet in his head."

"DiMarco will get his, you know he will. But first we need to find the girls and figure out this thing with Lombardi."

"You think it's connected?"

"Yes, no... maybe," he let out a frustrated sigh. "I don't know. But you heard what he said, Cabrioles took a liking to Caitlin. Maybe they were watching her. Maybe they thought she was the way to DiMarco and when we swooped in and saved her, it got the wires all crossed."

"We were careful, E. We would have noticed if someone was watching her."

Wouldn't we?

"She came to us with no cell phone, no bank cards, nothing that was traceable."

"Maybe they were already watching us, getting ready to make their move, and it was sheer coincidence that our paths crossed when they did."

"Yeah, maybe." I took another swig from the bottle, but Enzo snatched it off me and threw it against the wall.

"Hey, that was good whisky." I watched it sluice down the wall.

"I know you're hurting, cous, but we need you sober. Caitlin and Bella need you sober, okay?"

"Fuck. *Fuck*!" I punched the brick, relishing in the bite of pain.

"Better?"

"Fuck you," I grunted, clutching my busted hand to my chest. It was a mess, but I barely felt it over the anger residing in me.

"Channel it into finding them." He gripped my shoulder. "Because we will find them, Matt. And when we do, they'll need you."

I nodded, too choked up to reply. If anything had happened to them... I couldn't bear it.

Bella was my sister. My little sister for fuck's sake. And Caitlin... she was my heart.

The door swung open revealing my father. "There you two are," he said. "Come on, Tommy's got something."

"About time," Enzo grumbled, nudging me forward.

We followed my father back into the club, congregating with the rest of our men near the bar.

"Tommy just called," Nicco said. "He ran Olivia Walsh through the system, and it pinged numerous hits." He scanned his cell phone. "Married to Darragh Walsh, they had one daughter, Erin Walsh. Born May twentieth, two thousand."

My brain was already doing the math when Nicco locked his eyes on me. "He managed to pull a photo of Olivia." Holding up his phone to me, he said, "Look like anyone we know?"

No. Fucking. Way.

It was Caitlin. Well, her eyes and red hair, at least. The woman in the photo was at least twenty years older.

"So wait a second," Enzo said. "You're saying Caitlin O'Donnell is really Erin Walsh?"

"It looks that way."

"Where's Olivia now?" I asked, my heart crashing against my chest.

"Well, that's where it gets interesting. Officially, she's divorced and has lived alone in New Haven for years."

"And unofficially?"

"Tommy found numerous police reports for breach of the peace and countless overdoses."

"The mom's a junkie?" Lucino asked.

"Looks like it."

"Any record of who bailed her out?"

"That's where things get really interesting." Nicco fixed his eyes on me again. "It looks like Olivia Walsh has had an on-off relationship with Massimo Lombardi for the best part of thirteen years."

"Lombardi?" I balked, the ground going from under me. "No. No way."

We'd all heard the stories about Massimo Lombardi's predilection for the seedier things in life. Drugs. Trafficking. Brothels. Lombardi's empire was built of the underbelly of society. He couldn't be connected so personally to Caitlin.

It made no sense.

Yet, I couldn't deny the photo of Olivia had been like looking at an older version of Caitlin.

Erin.

Whatever the hell she was called.

No wonder she'd been cagey about her past. Her mom's boyfriend was the lowest of the low. And definitely not the kind of guy we were looking to do business with.

Lucino let out a low whistle. "If the rumors about Lombardi and his preference for young girls are true, it makes sense why she ran."

My blood ran cold. Lombardi wasn't just immoral; he was sick and twisted and definitely the kind of man you wouldn't want your daughter or sister around.

"Bella." My knees buckled as I slumped against the counter.

"Shh, figlio mio." My father squeezed my shoulder. "We'll get her back. Both of them." There was a fierceness in his eyes I hadn't seen in a long time.

"Do we have any idea where he might have taken them?" Enzo asked, the silent consensus being that Lombardi had taken them.

It was the only lead we had, and despite not wanting to believe it, it made the most sense.

"We can assume Lombardi has been watching Caitlin for some time. Hence why he sent his men here, to scope out DiMarco."

"If she hadn't ended up in the hospital, it's likely he would have grabbed her before now."

"So you're saying we should be thankful DiMarco roughed her up?" Sarcasm clung to my every word.

"Matt, that's not what anyone is saying," Nicco said. "But Lucino has a point. We have to assume Zander changed their course of action."

"What do we do now? What's the plan?" Enzo said.

"Tommy is pulling up a list of possible locations. They took Bella, so I'm inclined to think there's a bigger picture here."

"You think they'll use her as leverage?"

"Most likely. She's one of our capo's daughters. Which makes her a strong bargaining chip."

"We can't negotiate with a man like Lombardi."

"No, but we need him to believe we're willing." Nicco began texting someone.

Just then my cell phone started ringing. I dug it out of my pocket and frowned.

"Who is it?" my father asked.

"It's an unknown number."

"Answer it on loudspeaker. Everyone quiet." Nicco gave me a nod, and I hit answer.

"Hello?"

"Mr. Bellatoni?"

"Yes. Who's this?"

"I believe I have something that belongs to you."

"Is she okay?" I choked out.

"She's fine. They both are. But their remaining so will depend on your actions over the next hour. I'm going to text you coordinates. You are to come with Niccolò and no one else."

"How do we know we can trust you?"

"You don't. One hour. The clock is ticking." He hung up, and a text message came straight through.

"Forward those to me," Nicco said, pulling out his cell. "Tommy, yeah, I'm about to forward you some coordinates. Pull everything you can find about the location. I also want to know everything you can find on Dominic Cabrioles."

"What are you thinking, Nicco?" My father's brows knitted.

"We need to know what we're walking into. We also need allies."

"Cabrioles will never betray his boss." Lucino huffed as if the idea was preposterous.

"Everyone has a price, Luc. We have less than an hour to find out Dominic's."

CHAPTER 27

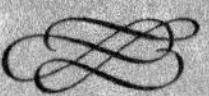

CAITLIN

"Please, let her go," I said for the twentieth time. After being dragged into this room and discovering that it wasn't Zander who had taken us at all, it was the man who had raised me for the best part of eight years, I'd been forced to sit here and talk.

Of course, Massimo Lombardi didn't talk in the conventional sense. He preferred to gloat. And for thirty minutes, I'd been made to sit here while he filled in the missing pieces about how he found me hiding in Providence.

I should have known she would sell me out. But she was my mother and I'd left her.

I'd left and never looked back.

That kind of guilt, it did something to you. Festered inside of you like poison. In hindsight, I should have used a burner phone or called from a pay phone. But she was my mom. The woman who had given birth to me. Part of me was just a scared child still, desperate for the attention and love of her mother.

And it had cost me dearly.

"So, you see, firefly." The nickname made me shudder. "This presented itself as an opportunity too good to miss."

Massimo sat back in his chair, steepling his fingers.

"You need to let her go," I said again, glancing at Arabella who was curled up on a worn leather couch. She sniffled and I mouthed, "Be strong."

"Let her go?" Massimo chuckled darkly. "And why, pray tell, would I do that? She is worth more to me than you."

Ouch.

His words cut deep, but he wasn't wrong.

"When the Marchetti find out what you've done, how do you think they'll react?"

He leaned forward, palms flat on the desk. There was an entire table between us, yet it still wasn't enough. Fear raced down my spine, the familiar bitter scent of his breath like a punch to the stomach.

My fingers curled into the arm of the chair, nails gouging the wood as I desperately tried to maintain some semblance of control. If I fell apart, Bella had no one.

And she was the important one here, the one who deserved to walk out of this alive.

I had to be strong—for her.

"I think, firefly." His lips twisted. "They'll give me whatever I desire."

"She's just a kid." My voice cracked. "She doesn't deserve this. I'll do whatever you want. Please just let her go."

Massimo's brow lifted with curiosity, and he dragged a hand down his face. "Was life that hard with me, no? I gave you and your momma everything. I made sure she had her fix, I made sure you had nice things. And all I asked in return was that you helped me keep my associates… happy."

My eyes shuttered, memories I'd fought hard to contain rushing to the surface.

When they opened again, I locked eyes with him, the man I'd spent four years running from, and inhaled a sharp breath.

"I was just a child and you made… you made me—"

"I remember it well, firefly. So young and supple and pretty."

Bile washed in my stomach at the affection in his tone, the longing.

"There have been others of course, but none as good as you."

Massimo Lombardi was a sick man. He treated his girls—his dancers and prostitutes—like dogs. Usually, he got them hooked on meth or crack, and then he made them do his bidding.

I guess I should have been grateful he'd never forced drugs on me. But I was special, he'd said. And besides, he had other leverage to use against me.

"Where is my mom, Massimo?" I changed tack.

"You know Liv." He waved his hand through the air. "She'll be out somewhere trying to score her next high."

She was alive.

Thank God, she was alive.

I'd always suspected that when I fled, she would fall

apart, or that Massimo would kill her. It's why eventually, I'd caved and called her. I'd needed to know she was safe. I'd needed to know she was still alive. When she stopped answering a couple of months ago, I feared the worst.

She's alive.

I hadn't realized how much I needed to know that until this moment. She was my family—the only family I had. No matter how hard things had been between us, I didn't wish her dead.

Massimo checked his wristwatch and tapped the table. "It's time."

"Time?" I cried. "Time for what?"

"Secure Erin," he ordered one of his men.

"No, *no!*" I yelled, leaping up to my feet. But a rough hand snaked around my neck and clamped down over my mouth. I could hear Bella crying out behind me and then everything went quiet.

Massimo lifted his cell phone to his ear and with his eyes locked on mine he said, "Mr. Bellatoni? I believe I have something that belongs to you."

Matteo.

My heart almost burst out of my chest. I didn't want this; I didn't ever want this.

Oh God.

What had I done?

"She's fine," Massimo said. "They both are. But they're remaining so will depend on your actions over the next hour. I'm going to text you coordinates. You are to come with Niccolò and no one else."

Another long pause while he listened.

"You don't. One hour. The clock is ticking." Massimo hung up, and then typed something out on a text message.

"It's done. Lock them back up until I say it's time."

"I-I don't understand," Bella said as we sat huddled in the small room again. It was dark and stuffy, the air heavy with fear.

"Who is he?"

"Massimo Lombardi was… is my mom's boyfriend."

"So he's like what, your stepdad?"

"I guess you could say that. Although they never married, and we didn't live together in the traditional sense." I wrung my hands in my lap, my stomach a tight ball of nerves.

"He's…"

"A monster." My eyes shuttered as eight years of bad memories flooded my mind.

"What happened?"

"You don't want to know," I breathed.

"This… this is what haunts you," Bella said.

"He's why I ran, yes."

"Tell me. I want to understand."

"Why?" I searched for her in the darkness, but Bella found me, her hand twining with mine.

"Because I think my brother loves you, Cait—I mean, Erin."

"You can call me Cait. I left Erin behind when I left New Haven. And don't you see, this is why I held back. Because I knew. Deep down, I knew I would never truly escape my past. But I never wanted to put you in harm's way, Bella. I never thought—"

"Shh." She shifted closer, laying her head on my arm. "We're your family now. And I know my brother and cousins will do whatever they need to do to get us back safely. Both of us."

It was the nicest thing she could have said to me, even if it was but a fantasy.

There was no happy ending for me in all of this. Now he'd found me again, Massimo would never give me up. And I wouldn't risk Bella or Matteo or any of their family getting hurt… for me.

Not anymore than they had been already.

"Can I ask you something?" she whispered, and I smiled. Bella had the innocence of youth. She might have been raised in the Marchetti family, but she was still young and idealistic.

"Sure," I sighed, too exhausted to argue.

"Do you love my brother?"

"I barely know him."

The lie wrapped around my heart like thorns, shredding me wide open. Because while I didn't know his favorite color, band, or food, I knew Matteo's soul. I knew his heart and his loyalty and devotion to his family.

I knew all the things that mattered.

The things about a person you could fall in love with.

"Your brother is a very easy person to love, Bella."

"That isn't really an answer," she mumbled.

"Well, it's all I have right now."

Silence enveloped us. This was always the worst part, the waiting. The calm before the inevitable storm. When

Massimo would demand I *performed* for his associates, there was always that moment before I went on where I would silently pray for someone to come and take me away.

Of course, no one ever came. And, like a puppet on strings, I was forced to dance at his will. I guess in some ways, I was lucky he never let any of them touch me. In those few minutes, I was able to completely detach myself and get lost in the music.

Dancing was my salvation then. But eventually, Zander stole that from me. Two men. Both obsessed with me in their own ways, using the thing I loved most in the world against me.

"Caitlin?" Bella's voice pulled me back to the moment.

"Yes?"

"I'm scared."

"Bella?" I whispered.

"Yeah?"

"I am too."

I DON'T KNOW how much time passed before anyone came back for us. We dozed in and out of sleep, too cold and uncomfortable and scared to really succumb to oblivion. My arm was stiff from Bella's weight, but I didn't have the heart to tell her to move. She needed me, and I would do everything I could to make her feel as safe as possible.

When the door handle finally rattled, part of me was relieved that this would all be over soon. I only hoped that

Bella, Matteo, and their family got to walk away without any casualties.

But I knew Massimo and although he was a monster, he didn't like unnecessary risk, and hurting Bella would rain down a whole heap of destruction on his empire.

Light poured into the room, and two men entered, dragging us to our feet.

"Caitlin," Bella shrieked as one guy carried her from the room, kicking and screaming.

"It'll be okay," I called after them. "It'll be okay, Bella."

The guy smirked at me, and I narrowed my eyes.

"What?" I snapped.

"I can see why Massimo was upset when he lost you." His eyes brazenly checked out my body. I had to swallow my repulsion. I knew men like this, and they didn't care to be emasculated.

"He didn't lose me, asshole. I left."

"Well, he found you now, and I think we both know he isn't going to let you go again."

My stomach sank.

Of course I knew that.

But it didn't make it any easier to hear.

He yanked me from the room, shoving me down the opposite hall, away from the office where I'd seen Massimo.

"Where are you taking me?" I said, fear bleeding into my voice.

"It's showtime, sweetheart," he chuckled darkly, shouldering open another door. This one led to a vast space, some kind of abandoned storage warehouse.

Bella was already tied to a chair, her big eyes pleading with me to do something.

"It's okay," I mouthed.

I had to believe it would all be okay.

Matteo and his family were smart. After all, you didn't get to be one of the biggest crime families in New England without some intelligence. So long as they got Bella out safe and unharmed, I could live with that.

I had to. Because I'd known all along there was no happy ending for me.

I just hadn't expected it to end like this.

CHAPTER 28

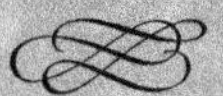

MATTEO

THE COORDINATES WERE FOR AN ABANDONED WAREHOUSE
on the state border separating Rhode Island and
Connecticut. Nicco and I rode in his Range Rover, tailed
by Lucino, Enzo, and my father. Stefan had remained at
the club with Zander and a couple of our guys. Another
SUV was trailing behind with the rest of our men in it.

Lombardi had requested that only Nicco and I show
up, but it didn't mean we would come unprepared.

"How are you holding up?" Nicco asked me.

"How do you think?"

Everything I thought about Caitlin was a lie.

It wasn't even her name, for fuck's sake. And yet, I'd
known—I'd known she was hiding something. I'd never
expected this though.

So much made sense now, even if nothing seemed to
make much sense at all.

"I'm sorry," he said.

"Yeah, me too." I stared out of the window, watching the scenery roll by. The GPS indicated we were almost there. There was nothing around for miles but a desolate stretch of land and a series of derelict warehouses.

"Lovely," I murmured as Nicco drove through the busted open security gates.

We pulled over at the first warehouse and the other two vehicles followed.

"Remember the plan," Nicco said, checking his pistol.

"You don't have to worry about me." I just wanted this over with.

We climbed out of the Range Rover and made our way back to my father's vehicle. He already had the window lowered.

"You good?" he asked. I nodded. "Save her, Son. Bring my daughter home."

"I will." The words were raw against my throat.

"Stay here," Nicco ordered. "We'll signal if we're in trouble."

Until Bella was in safe hands, we couldn't risk open gunfire. Not that we hoped it would come to that.

Lombardi was a monster, but he wasn't bloodthirsty. He ran New Haven with an iron fist through fear, not mindless killing. Besides, if he didn't honor his word, Uncle Al knew what to do.

"Jay, you're with us." Nicco beckoned for him to follow us back to the Range Rover. He'd joined us at Nicco's insistence. Bella knew Jay; if me and Nic couldn't get out of there, he could get her to safety.

"As soon as we negotiate Bella's release, you move.

Don't stop for anyone or anything. You get her to my car, and you drive."

"Got it, Mr. Marchetti."

"Please, it's Nicco." He gave Jay a sharp nod.

We climbed back in the Range Rover and Nicco put it into drive. "You'll wait outside the building. Once Lombardi gives us the green light, I'll text you."

"Got it. I still think we should consider placing two more men—"

"No. He'll be watching. We already risked enough by bringing two more cars."

But my father wouldn't stay behind, and we needed backup nearby, just in case things went south.

The coordinates led us to the furthest warehouse. There was a single black SUV parked outside, with one armed guard by the door.

"We need to be cool," Nicco said to me. "Follow my lead. No matter what happens in there, I need you to keep your head. Capisci?"

I nodded, too wound up to speak.

So much could go wrong. And my sister was in there. Caitlin too.

Her name isn't Caitlin.

I shut the little voice down. None of that mattered right now. All that mattered was getting them out in one piece.

The rest could wait.

"Okay," Nicco said, checking his gun. "Let's go."

Jay climbed out and opened Nicco's door. I rounded the hood and met them, and the three of us approached the armed guard together.

"Stop right there," the man called, his pistol trained right on Nicco.

Jay inched forward, ready to shield him, but Nicco threw out his arm and stepped forward. "Lombardi requested a meeting with us," he said calmly.

"He specified two of you."

"Jay is going to wait right out here. He's my cousin's bodyguard. She trusts him and I want someone she's familiar with waiting for her."

"You stay right there," the guy ordered, shifting his pistol to Jay.

"No problem, amico." Jay held up his hands and took a step back.

I didn't like the idea of leaving Jay alone with this asshole, but it wasn't like we had a choice. Lombardi held all the cards. Or at least, he thought he did.

"Wait for my signal," Nicco said to him, and Jay nodded, not taking his eyes off our less than friendly greeter.

"I need to check you for weapons."

"Hang on a—"

"Matt, it's fine."

Like hell it was.

But sure enough, Nicco let the guy pat him down and remove his gun.

"Your turn, sweetheart." He smirked.

I hesitated, but Nicco urged me to comply. "Fine," I hissed, unclipping it from its sheath and handing it over.

"Inside. Follow the hall."

"I don't like this," I said, following Nicco inside.

"Lombardi is protecting himself. He knows he's

playing with fire taking Bella. If I were him, I would have demanded the same."

"Or he's one very brave coglione," I murmured.

We walked the long hall in thick silence. My heart beat against my chest like a runaway train, blood pounding in my ears.

Eventually, we reached another door. Nicco opened it and stepped inside the large room.

"Ah, Mr. Marchetti, Mr. Bellatoni, you made it."

My eyes landed on Massimo Lombardi sitting in a chair, smoking a cigar. Over in the corner of the room, Bella and Caitlin were seated on a bench, their wrists bound and mouths duct taped. They were guarded by two guys.

Anger swelled inside me so rapidly, I struggled to catch my breath.

"Easy," Nicco whispered, keeping his eyes on Lombardi. "I don't appreciate your method of business, Mr. Lombardi."

"I needed to capture your attention. It was an opportunity too good to pass up. I'm sure you can appreciate that." Lombardi snapped his fingers, and two chairs were brought in for us. "Please, sit."

We did, the air rippling with tension. I surveyed the room again. Including the two men guarding the girls, I counted three more men. One standing directly behind Massimo, and two over by another door.

Dominic Cabrioles was nowhere to be seen.

I cast Nicco a sideways glance, but he didn't take his eyes off Lombardi.

"Now," Massimo said. "Let's discuss business."

"That's not how this works," Nicco said. "You came into my territory and kidnapped my cousin, and you want to talk business? You have some big balls, my friend."

Lombardi chuckled, darkly. "Excuse my brashness. Your cousin was but an incentive."

"That's my sister you're talking about," I growled.

"Matt," Nicco warned. "I'm sure Mr. Lombardi realizes what a mistake he made by dragging an innocent into this. I'm sure he wouldn't want to find the full wrath of the Family at his doorstep all because he didn't do the right thing when he had the chance."

Nicco was like another person, sitting there, issuing veiled threats to Lombardi. This wasn't my best friend, my cousin, the guy I'd grown up with. This was Niccolò Marchetti, the boss of the Marchetti crime family.

The Boss of Dominion.

Lombardi regarded him, narrowing his eyes slightly, no doubt trying to assess the young man seated before him.

"I'm sure you can understand, I didn't expect to get your attention without making a grand gesture as it were."

Grand gesture?

The guy was fucking delusional.

"Drago," he snapped his fingers. "Release the girl."

He dragged Bella up by her arm, and I was up and out of my seat, running to catch my sister as she stumbled forward. "Shh, Bella. Shh." I hugged her tightly, my eyes finding Caitlin over her shoulder.

Her gaze was full of apologies, regrets, and explanations. None of which I had time for right now, given the terrified girl clutching my sweater.

"I have someone waiting outside to return Arabella to our family," Nicco said.

"Fine, bring them in."

Nicco sent the text and seconds later, Jay appeared. Gently, I pulled the duct tape off Bella's mouth and cupped her face. "I need you to go with Jay, okay?"

"N-no, Matt, I want to stay with you. I want—"

"Shh, Bella. I need you to listen to me. Go with Jay and do whatever he says. I'll be right behind you, I promise."

I hated myself at that moment, but she needed to hear the words and I needed to say them, even if it was a promise I wasn't sure I could keep.

"I don't understand," she cried. "What about Caitlin? We need to—"

"Go," I nudged her into Jay's waiting arms. "I'll see you soon."

I dipped my head, silently indicating for him to take her. Her shrieks pierced the air but slowly tapered out as they moved further out of the room.

Seconds ticked by, each longer than the last. Until Nicco's cell phone eventually pinged, and he let out a long breath. "They're safe."

"Despite what you might think, Mr. Marchetti. I am no monster."

My eyes involuntarily flicked to Caitlin. I was sure she would have something to say about that, but I managed to swallow the words.

Bella was safe. Jay would be taking her far away from here and Lombardi's grip.

I could finally breathe a little easier.

Nicco wasted no time getting down to business. "You had your men approach Zander DiMarco, but I can't work out your true motivation. Was it only to get to Erin, or was it to make inroads into our territory?"

All while he spoke, I watched Caitlin, gauging her reaction. But she gave nothing away, her green eyes devoid of emotion.

Fuck, Tink, what did he do to you?

"I'll admit, I have searched a long time for Erin. It wasn't until a few months ago her mother finally confessed that she had the means to contact her." Lombardi sat back in his chair, crossing one ankle over his knee. "Of course, I didn't expect to find her under the protection of someone like DiMarco. But I quickly realized that I could use that to my advantage. For weeks, I watched that spineless creature obsess over her. It was pathetic really. But love is a man's only weakness, and I knew that in his own way, DiMarco loved my firefly."

My firefly.

He had a pet name for her.

I was going to puke.

Staring straight ahead, I tried to rein in the storm of emotions battering my insides.

"My plan was to use his feelings for Erin to leverage my organization's foothold in Providence. But then he almost killed her."

Lombardi's whole demeanor shifted. Gone was the amiable businessman, replaced with a deadly monster. His hand curved around the arm of the chair, gripping it so tightly the blood drained from his knuckles.

"I couldn't believe it when we lost her again. Gone, from right under our noses. Until we picked up security footage of you." He pinned me with a hard look. "Leaving the hospital with her."

Fuck.

All this time we were worried that Zander would discover the truth, but we had been worrying about the wrong person.

"You're not an easy bunch to track down," Lombardi shifted on his chair. "But nothing is impossible to find, you just have to know where to look. And I have always been intrigued by the Marchetti and their stronghold in Verona County."

"And here we are," Nicco said.

"Here we are indeed."

"What do you want, Lombardi?"

"I want what you have, Niccolò. Power. Legitimate business revenue. We both know you're going to put a bullet between DiMarco's eyes for trying to cross you." His eyes locked on mine again. "And for… hurting her. The way I see it, you'll need a new partner to run things in Providence and I want to be considered for the job."

"And what makes you think I would ever consider doing business with the man who kidnapped my cousin?"

"You're a reasonable man, Niccolò. I took a risk with Arabella, yes. But I needed to get your attention. Would you have considered sitting down with me otherwise?"

No, he wouldn't.

Because Massimo Lombardi was scum. His lack of morals and values made him a dangerous man to work with. And he knew it.

The faint smile touching his mouth told us as much.

"My reputation leaves little to be desired." I snorted at that, and he added, "Okay, very little to be desired, which is why I'm looking to clean things up. Times are changing and we have to change with them."

"What's in it for us?" Nicco asked.

I shot forward in my chair. "You cannot be serious," I shrieked. "He's a sleazeball. You can't trust him as far—"

"Matt." Nicco glared at me. "If you can't keep your opinion to yourself, you'll have to leave."

I slumped down with defeat, flicking my eyes to Caitlin again.

Erin. Her name is Erin.

She stared at me, but I didn't attempt to decipher any of what I saw there, dropping my gaze instead.

"One of my top guys, Dominic Cabrioles, knows a thing or two about business, especially running a successful string of clubs. We can provide security, a high caliber of girls, and investment. You help me clean up my reputation, and he'll make your family a lot of money. I can also take care of DiMarco."

"He's mine," I snarled.

"Easy there, Bellatoni. That kind of rage isn't healthy for a guy like you. But I can't blame you for wanting to defend Erin's honor." He glanced over at her. "She really is something special."

This asshole made my skin crawl and I wanted nothing more than to lunge for him and wipe that smirk off his face.

"It would seem we have much to discuss," Nicco said.

"I'm glad you think so." Lombardi exhaled a steady

breath, his eyes flicking to the door. "Once Dominic arrives, we can iron out the details."

"And what of… Erin?" Nicco asked.

"She'll remain under my protection, of course. I'm sure since discovering her true identity, you don't want her to remain with you?"

Me.

He was asking *me* that question.

"I…" Nicco shot me a hard look, and I choked out, "you're welcome to her. Whatever I thought we had, it's over."

"Excellent." Lombardi clapped his hands on his knees. "I think this relationship could be very lucrative for both of us."

"Indeed." Nicco nodded, while I sat there, numb.

CHAPTER 29

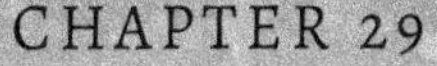

CAITLIN

It's over.

The words echoed through my skull, over and over.

Matteo couldn't even look at me. And I didn't blame him. Everything he thought he knew about me was a lie. I'd lied. I'd led him down a path that didn't exist, because the woman he fell for, the woman he met all those months ago, she didn't exist.

I was Erin Walsh. Daughter of an abusive drug addict and pawn in her boyfriend's sick games.

I'd spent most of high school doing Massimo's bidding, entertaining his friends. He'd drag me around New Haven, to bars and clubs and seedy back rooms, and have me *perform*. My life wasn't my own, my body wasn't my own.

One night, things had gotten out of control. One of his associates had tried to touch me. I'd managed to fight him off, but he'd roughed me up pretty bad.

I was sixteen. Ostracized by my classmates at school for being Liv Walsh's daughter and Massimo Lombardi's pet. That's what they'd called me. *His pet*. Teachers were too scared to report it to child protective services, and no one cared enough to ask me if I was okay.

I was all alone.

So I ran.

I had a small amount of cash saved up, so I used it to buy a bus ticket out of New Haven. I had nothing but the clothes on my back, some extra supplies crammed into a rucksack, and the instinct to survive.

For the first year, I'd moved from town to town, never staying in one place too long. I slept in store doorways, on park benches, and in shelters. Once I knew Lombardi's men weren't following me, I started staying put for longer. I'd bus tables, collect empties; anything to make a few bucks. It's surprising how little you can live off when you have to.

Then one day, right before my eighteenth birthday, Zander found me.

I knew his offer was probably too good to be true, but the sad fact was, I needed a steady job if I was ever going to get an apartment. And he wasn't concerned about my lack of social security number or ID.

The door opened, pulling me back to the present, and Dominic Cabrioles stepped inside. He smoothed his suit jacket and dipped his head. "My apologies," he said. "I was taking care of some things."

"Dom, join us," Massimo had someone bring in another chair. "We have much to discuss."

I risked glancing over at Matteo again. He seemed agitated, unlike Nicco, who was a picture of calm.

"The girl?" Dominic asked, sitting.

"Has been safely returned to them."

He gave Nicco a small nod, running a hand over his head.

He was new. Or at least, he hadn't been with Massimo when I'd known him. I'd never laid eyes on Dominic before that night at DiMarco's. Part of me wondered if Massimo knew how he'd acted that night or if it was all part of his ruse to test Zander. Either way, being in the same room as him again made my skin crawl.

"Do they understand why we had to take the girl as well?" he asked Massimo.

"Sì, they do. And hopefully we can all move forward and discuss business."

"I'll need to discuss this with my uncles," Nicco said. "I'm sure you can understand they will have concerns about aligning ourselves with the Lombardi, especially after you took Arabella."

"Of course, of course. We should sit down in a week, when tempers have cooled. Dominic, take Erin straight back to New Haven. I'm sure she's eager to be reacquainted with her momma. Take Carrick and Thiago with you. I'll follow with Drago, Grayson, and Miller."

"Very well. Gentleman." He addressed Nicco and Matteo. "We shall talk soon."

Nicco stood, clasping Dominic's hand. "To new allies."

My heart withered in my chest. They were going to let them take me. Just like that.

Deep down I'd known it would happen, but part of me clung to the hope that Matteo would fight for me.

You lied to him. What did you expect?

I stared at him, pleading with him to look at me. If this was the last time I ever saw him, I at least wanted to try to tell him everything I was feeling.

But he didn't glance my way. In fact, he very obviously, very purposefully avoided looking anywhere near my direction.

Defeat slammed into me, making me choke on a whimper. Luckily, it couldn't escape my duct taped lips. Neither could the yelp of pain as Dominic grabbed my arm and wrenched me to my feet.

"We meet again, Red." He smirked, and bile washed in my stomach.

I didn't take my eyes off Matteo, desperately hoping to get one final look at him.

Look at me. Please just look at me.

We finally reached the door and Matteo looked over, our eyes connecting for the briefest moment.

Then he was gone, and I was being led out of the building toward a black SUV with my heart in tatters and my pride in disarray.

"Mr. Cabrioles," one of the guards said.

"Get her in the trunk."

Trunk?

"Are you sure that's—"

"Do you have a problem following orders?" he growled.

"N-no, sir. We shall secure her immediately."

"See to it that you do."

Without a second glance at me, Dominic climbed in the SUV.

"Let's go, sweetheart." The guy snorted. "Guess you've got a long way to go to get back into the boss's good graces."

Another guy popped the trunk and I stared at the dark, small space before glancing back at the building.

"No one's coming to help you," the guy barked. "In you go."

Oh God.

He was right.

No one was coming to save me.

Least of all Matteo.

CURLED UP ON MY SIDE, I focused on the purr of the engine instead of the erratic beat of my heart. We'd been travelling for what felt like forever, but realistically, it couldn't have been more than thirty minutes. Every minute slower and more drawn out than the last.

My heart was broken. Shattered by the only guy who had the power to mend it.

But I'd expected nothing less. The Marchetti were criminals, yes. But they had a code. They had principles. Family was everything to them.

Once Matteo found out the truth about me, I'd known everything would change.

The things I'd done—the things I'd been forced to do at the hands of the man who had raised me for all those years. Like it or not, I was tainted. First by Massimo, and then by Zander.

Matteo needed a woman by his side who was strong, not one who had enough emotional baggage to fill a plane.

It didn't matter now; he'd let me go. He and Nicco weren't prepared to go to war for me, and I couldn't blame them.

I wasn't worth it, I knew that.

But I wasn't sure I could go back to this life, not after all I'd done to leave it behind. Once I'd seen my mom one last time, I would find a way to end it. Maybe I should have done that in the beginning. But I was young and naïve back then. I thought that maybe, just maybe, the universe had other plans for me.

I was all out of hope now.

Matteo had given me a glimpse of how good things could be. He'd shown me what it could feel like to be loved and adored and treated with respect. And it was everything.

But it wasn't my story.

Tears pricked the corners of my eyes, emotion balled in my throat. But I would not cry.

The SUV slowed to a stop, and I strained to listen. We couldn't already be back in New Haven, could we?

Fear snaked through me. Had I missed something? Had Massimo been lying when he ordered Dominic to bring me back to New Haven? Was that code for get rid of her?

Oh God. Was Dominic going to kill me?

I swallowed down the rush of bile up my throat. Doors

opened and slammed shut, heavy footsteps hitting the asphalt. I could just make out the rumble of voices, but they were too far away to decipher the conversation.

A heavy thud rocked the SUV and I screamed; the sound trapped behind my sealed lips. There was another thud and then eerie silence.

What the hell was going on?

The trunk popped open, light spilling inside. Dominic's face came into view, and he said, "Come on, we need to move if we're going to make the drop."

Drop?

He helped me out of the trunk, and I scanned our surroundings, my eyes almost bugging out of my head at the two dead bodies.

I stared up at his, my eyes wide with fear.

"I'm going to remove the tape. But you have to promise not to scream, okay?"

I nodded slowly, confusion saturating every cell in my body.

He tried to be gentle, but my lips smarted against the strong adhesive.

"W-what is—"

"Shh. I need you to be quiet, okay? We don't have long, and I need to deal with this… mess." He gently took my arm and led me around to the front passenger door. "Get in and wait for me."

Dominic opened the door and helped me inside, not offering to cut the restraints binding my wrists and ankles. Did he think I was a flight risk, or was I still a prisoner?

My head was spinning as I slumped against the cool leather seats.

"I'll be right back."

"W-wait," I said as he went to shut the door. "Why are you doing this?"

His eyes narrowed. "I'll explain everything soon."

I nodded, watching through the rearview as he rounded up the dead bodies of his men, and loaded them into the trunk.

When he came around to the driver's door, I caught the glint of his pistol as he climbed inside. "Who are you?" I breathed, my body trembling.

Dominic looked at me and gave me a strained smile. "A friend."

WE RODE IN SILENCE. Every time I went to ask a question, the words died on my lips. Exhaustion anchored me to the seat, my limbs heavy and sore.

It was the middle of the night, the rest of the world sleeping while Dominic Cabrioles was driving me to some undisclosed location.

When we eventually pulled off the highway and the car stopped, I twisted around to face him. "Where are we?"

"I need to make a call," he said, slipping from the SUV.

Glancing around, I tried to find a landmark or something, but it was futile. There was nothing but miles and miles of highway flanked by dense trees. We could have been anywhere.

Headlights flashed up ahead and my body went rigid. The vehicle slowed, making the same turn as us until a black SUV much like this one, slowed to a stop.

Dominic walked over to the driver's window, and it lowered. I couldn't see inside though. Fear skittered up and down my spine, making me shiver.

But then, the back door opened, and a figure climbed out. He stepped into the stream of moonlight and my heart almost burst out of my chest.

Matteo.

Matteo was here.

I tried to open the door only to realize I was still bound. Our eyes collided through the glass, and I saw it then. I saw what I hadn't been able to see back at the warehouse.

He cared.

Matteo cared.

With big sure strides, he approached the SUV and opened my door. "You're here," I choked out as he reached for me. "You came."

"Shh, I got you. I got you." Gingerly, he lifted me out of the SUV, lowering me to my feet. "Really, Cabrioles?" He hissed, noticing my restraints.

"What?" Dominic shrugged. "I couldn't trust that she wouldn't try to gut me like a fish. Fuck knows I deserved it for what I put her through." His eyes glittered with apology.

"I-I don't understand." Silent tears streaked down my cheeks.

Nicco appeared, dipping his head slightly toward me.

"Sorry for the theatrics. We needed Lombardi to believe everything was okay."

"Wait a minute," I swung my head between them. "All that back there... you were acting?"

Relief slammed into me. Matteo hadn't meant it; he hadn't meant any of it.

It had all been for show.

A wave of emotion crashed over me, and I swayed on my legs.

"Easy there," Matteo caught me.

I realized now; he would always catch me.

"Lombardi?" Dominic asked.

"He's secure. We need to get Cait... Erin—"

"No," I blurted out. "I'm not Erin, not anymore."

That girl was dead to me. Everything she was, everything she'd survived. I didn't want to shackle her past to my future. I couldn't.

Matteo's expression softened and he nodded with understanding. "We need to get Cait somewhere safe. We'll deal with DiMarco and Lombardi tomorrow."

"Very well. I'll lay low until I get the call." Dominic settled his hard gaze on me. "For what it's worth, I am sorry for how things went down at the club. I'm ambitious, but I'm no monster."

Matteo pulled me closer, and I drew strength from being in his arms. I still didn't understand all that had transpired to get us to this point, but one thing was certain, Dominic had betrayed Massimo to deliver me safely to Matteo and Nicco.

And for that I would always be grateful.

"Come on, let's get you somewhere warm," Matteo led me back to their SUV, climbing into the back with me.

"Are you hurt?" he asked, running his eyes over me.

"I'm okay."

"Cait, I am so sor—"

"Don't." I slid my finger against his lips. "Not yet. I know we need to talk. I know we both have things we need to explain, but right now, I just want to be here with you."

"I can do that." He slipped his arm around my shoulder and pulled me into his side. "I love you, Cait. I need you to know that. I think I've loved you since that night I saw you standing in that alley."

"Matt, I—"

"Don't. Not yet. I just needed you to know."

My eyes fluttered closed as I finally let myself relax. Matteo was here.

He came for me.

And he loved me.

I woke up in soft sheets in a bedroom I didn't recognize. It reminded me of my room at the cabin, but the décor was different, and it was smaller.

Sitting up, I ran a hand over my wild curls, trying to tame them. I could hardly remember getting here. But I remembered Matteo. The way he'd carried me to bed, whispering promises in my ear that had carried me off into a deep sleep.

Smiling to myself, I touched my lips. He'd kissed me. *That* I could remember.

Voices beyond the door caught my attention, and I pushed back the sheet and padded over to it. I was in a brand new, oversized Tinkerbell t-shirt.

I was desperate to go and find him, but I needed a girl's minute, so I went into the bathroom and cleaned up a little.

When I was done, I took a deep breath and went in search of the man who had saved me.

I found Matteo in the kitchen area, making a fresh pot of coffee. "Good morning," I said.

"Cait?" His head whipped around, his expression softening the minute he laid eyes on me. "You're awake." He smiled.

"I am. Sorry for crashing on you like that."

He abandoned the coffee, taking big strides until he was in front of me. "You have nothing to be sorry for, not a damn thing." He slid his hand into my hair and leaned down, touching his head to mine. "How are you feeling?"

"Weary. A little confused. But I'm okay."

I'm here with you. It's more than I could have ever asked for.

"You must have some questions." He searched my eyes.

"I do. But no more than you, I imagine."

"Go get comfortable and I'll make us both a mug of coffee."

"Okay." I went to walk away, but Matteo snagged my wrist, whirling me around to him. His hands cupped my face as he stared at me with a heady mix of relief and longing.

"I meant what I said last night. Every word. I love you, Caitlin. I'm in love with you."

"Matteo, I…"

He kissed me, stealing whatever words I'd been about to say. And the truth was, I didn't know. I had so much going around in my head, it was very confusing.

But the second his lips touched mine, everything quieted. My soul rejoicing at being reunited with its other half. I wound my arms around Matteo's neck, kissing him back with the same desperation and ferocity. Our tongues tangled, his hand drifting down my spine, forcing us closer.

But it wasn't enough. I needed all of him. More than that, I needed him to need all of me.

"Cait," he breathed, tearing his mouth from mine. Matteo inhaled a ragged breath, gazing down at me with such reverence I felt winded. "We should talk."

I nodded, not trusting myself to speak.

"Go. I'll be right there."

On shaky legs, I managed to get to the couch, and sat down. Matteo made quick work of making the coffee and joined me.

"Thank you." I accepted the mug from him, grateful for something to hold, to stop me from reaching for him. He was right, we needed to talk first. The rest, I hoped, would come later.

"What do you want to know?" I asked.

Matteo drew in a sharp breath and said, "Everything."

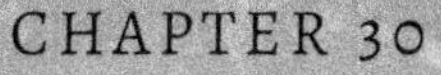

CHAPTER 30

MATTEO

Caitlin told me everything. She told me about her life growing up with Massimo. She told me about what he used to make her do, the way he'd make her dance and perform for his associates; sick men who got their kicks off watching a child dress up and play stripper. Then she told me how one day it went too far so she ran. Escaped Massimo, her junkie mom, and fucked up life and ran.

By the time she was done, I could barely contain my anger. My body trembled with rage as I stared at her, imagining what life had been like for her. How she'd escaped one monster, only to end up right in the arms of another.

It was almost too much to bear.

"Matt?" she whispered, blinking away the silent tears clinging to her lashes.

"Come here, Tink." I pulled her into my arms, needing to feel her.

Caitlin was safe. She was safe and she was here. Nothing else mattered.

"I thought… when you said all those things, I thought I'd lost you…" Her walls shattered and she cried into my chest, violent sobs wracking her body.

"Shh, I got you."

But it wasn't only her I was worried about. A vortex of anger spiraled inside me, sucking my soul dry. What Massimo and DiMarco had done to her… what she had survived.

Caitlin wasn't only strong; she was a fucking warrior, and she deserved so much more than the hand she'd been dealt.

"Gosh, look at me." She pulled away, drying her eyes on the back of her hand. "I'm a mess."

"You're beautiful." I pulled her hands away, using the pad of my thumb to swipe the remaining moisture away.

"What happened last night, Matt?" she asked.

"We thought DiMarco had taken you. But when we interrogated him, it became clear he didn't know what we were talking about. Nicco had asked our investigator to look into you—"

"He had?" Her eyes went wide.

"Yes. I wasn't happy about it, but I understood his motivations. I need you to know I trusted you, Cait. I have always trusted you."

"It's okay," she said. "I'm okay. I take it he found something?"

"Your mom… he managed to track her down after finding her number on your old cell phone records."

"That's how Massimo found me. He was watching me for a while."

"Yes. He saw an opportunity to use you as leverage against DiMarco. But that plan went to shit when Zander hurt you and we found you in the hospital."

I still couldn't believe how many things had fallen into place to lead us to this moment. It was fate that had brought Caitlin back into my life, there was no other explanation.

"When we talked to Zander, he mentioned that Cabrioles had taken a shine to you at the club, so Nicco reached out to him in hopes that we could use him in negotiations with Lombardi. Luck was on our side, because he jumped at the chance to remove Lombardi from power. Turns out, he's a very ambitious man who is keen to align himself with powerful players."

"You mean the Marchetti," she said, and a faint smile traced my lips.

"He agreed to double-cross his boss in exchange for control of DiMarco's empire."

"I… wow. I don't know what to say."

"You don't have to say anything, Tink. It's over. Cabrioles proved himself and I think he was telling you the truth. He isn't a bad guy, he's just a guy caught up with bad people."

"I'm so sorry, Matt. I never wanted to put you or your family in harm's way. But I'd been running for almost five years, and I knew if I told you—"

"Hey, hey." I ran my hand over her shoulder and squeezed gently. "It's okay. Arabella is safe. You're safe. Everything's going to be okay now."

Things could have ended very differently, I knew that. But they hadn't, and I wasn't about to punish Caitlin for something out of her control.

"Bella loves you," I said. "She's been blowing up my cell phone all morning desperate to see you."

"S-she has?"

I nodded. "But I thought you'd want space."

And I needed some time alone with you.

"I don't know what to say. Everything you've done for me; the fact that I'm sitting here now. I owe you my life."

I slid my palm along her cheek. "All I'm asking for is your heart."

"It's yours," she breathed, leaning into my touch. "It's been yours since that night eight months ago."

Cautiously, I leaned in, ghosting my lips over Caitlin's. Electricity sparked between us, the way it did whenever we were close. And I soaked it up, relished in the feel of her, her warmth and soft skin.

I loved this woman and I would spend my life showing her.

"What will happen to them?" Caitlin whispered against my lips. And I hated that these people were still between us. But she deserved closure. We both did.

Cupping her face, I stared her straight in the eyes as I said, "They die."

"Are you sure about this?" I asked Caitlin as we pulled up outside one of the Family's other cabins. This one wasn't used for family getaways or laying low though. This was where we disposed of our problems.

"I am." She gave me a weak smile. Neither of us were particularly looking forward to this, but we knew we needed to put the past behind us and move on.

Nicco, Enzo, and Luis were already waiting for us.

"Luis?" Caitlin leaped out of the car and straight into his arms. "Thank God you're okay."

"I'm sorry I failed you." He dipped his head in apology.

"Never," Caitlin said, squeezing his arm. "Tell him, Matt. Tell him it wasn't his fault."

"Luis knows," Nicco reassured her. "Are you ready, Cait?"

She nodded.

"You're looking good, cous." Enzo pulled me in for a hug, clapping me on the back. "How is she?"

"Good," I said quietly. "She's… good."

We'd spent two days off the grid at the other cabin. Two days sharing stories about our pasts and hopes for the future. Then I'd loved her, more times than I could count. I'd loved her not with words but my body.

We'd finally surfaced for air after Nicco called to inform me that everything was set.

"I'm happy for you, Matt."

"Thanks." I squeezed Enzo's shoulder before rejoining my woman. She stepped into my body with easy familiarity, as if she belonged there.

And she did. Without a shadow of a doubt, Caitlin belonged with me.

"Let's get this over with," I said, adrenaline coursing through my veins.

"It doesn't have to be you," Nicco said, grimly.

"Yes, it does." I needed to look them both in the eyes one last time.

"You should be aware that Lombardi is… a mess," Nicco told Cait, and I gauged her reaction.

She didn't even flinch.

"Good. I hope it hurt."

Enzo let out a low whistle as he followed us inside.

The cabin was cold, bare of furniture or décor. Fitting really for a man's last few hours on Earth before he was forced to atone for his sins.

Caitlin stuck close to me as we moved deeper into the cabin, down the hall to the last bedroom. Inside, Lombardi and DiMarco were each tied to a chair, their mouths taped and ankles bound.

Nicco was right, Lombardi was a mess. One of his eyes was swollen shut and his lip was busted open. He'd obviously put up a fight… and lost. And a sick sense of satisfaction went through me. He deserved more, so much more, but it would have to do.

"Wake them," I said. "I want to look them both in the eyes when I do it."

Caitlin tugged on my hand, and I glanced down at her. "Wait over by the door with E, okay?"

"No, I want to be at your side when you…" She inhaled a sharp breath.

"Okay," I said, withdrawing my pistol.

Luis roughly grabbed Lombardi's head and the fucker cracked his eyes open. The second he saw the gun in my hand, he began thrashing against his restraints. Luis moved to DiMarco next, slapping his face. He woke with a start, his eyes immediately finding Caitlin and filling with relief.

He'd made his peace with this. But it still didn't change the fact he'd hurt her.

"Caitlin, do you have anything you wish to say to them?" Nicco asked her.

"I…"

"It's okay," I said. "I'm right here. They can't hurt you anymore."

She stepped forward, steeling herself. "I will not let you define my future. After today, I won't even give you a second thought. But today, today I hope you rot in hell." Her eyes found mine and she nodded. "Do it."

Two gunshots rang out in the small room, reverberating inside me as I watched their lifeless bodies slump in the chair.

It was done.

And Caitlin was right.

Once we walked out of here, I would never spare them a second thought.

"CAIT!" Bella was on us the second we walked through the door, wrapping her slim arms around Caitlin's waist. "I'm so happy you're here."

"Hey, Bella." Cait hugged her back. "It's good to see you."

My sister jabbed me in my arm, and I frowned. "What the hell was that for?"

"That's for making me wait to see her. Do you have any idea how hard it's been?"

"Sorry, pulce. But I needed some time alone with her."

"Whatever." Bella rolled her eyes, lacing her arm through Cait's. "I'm just glad you're here now. Mama is making—"

"Sorry," Cait mouthed over her shoulder as I watched Bella drag her toward the kitchen. I chuckled, my heart fit to burst at the sight of two of the most important women in my life all wrapped up in each other.

"Son." My father came to greet me. "How is she?"

"Good, she's good."

"And you?"

"I'm getting there."

He gave me an understanding nod. "I'm eager to meet the woman who has captured your heart, figlio mio."

"You're not angry?"

"Arabella is safe. You have your woman at your side. And Cabrioles will make a better business partner than DiMarco ever did. Things seemed to work themselves out for the best." He clapped me on the shoulder. "Now come, let us eat. Your mama is cooking up a storm."

Why was I not surprised?

We found Caitlin, Bella, and Mom in the kitchen. Talking like old friends. Cait glanced up and smiled, and it was like a fist around my heart.

"I love you," I mouthed.

"I love you too." Her cheeks burned as Mom caught us.

"Oh, Michele, would you look at that." She clutched her chest. "Our Matteo is all grown up and in love."

"Okay, woman, let's not embarrass the boy." He got us

both a beer and handed me one. "It's nice to finally meet you, mia cara."

"You too, Mr. Bellatoni."

"Please, it's Michele. I can't be having my future daughter-in-law calling me Mr. Bellatoni, can I now?"

"Dibs on being bridesmaid."

Caitlin's eyes were the size of saucers as she gawked at my family.

"Welcome to the family," I said around a knowing smile as I approached her.

"They're very… welcoming." Caitlin buried her face in my shoulder, laughing nervously.

"Hey." I gently grabbed the back of her neck and steered her face to mine. "They might be joking, but I'm serious. I want that. One day, I want it all… with you."

"Matt," she let out a soft sigh, gazing up at me while my family continued planning our entire future around us.

"What do you say, Tink? Want to spend the rest of your life with me?"

"I… yes. Yes, I want it. So much."

"Good." I brushed my mouth against hers. "Because you're mine now, Caitlin. And I don't plan on ever letting you go."

EPILOGUE

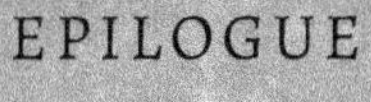

MATTEO

S OMETHING FLUTTERED OVER MY HIP BONE, STIRRING ME TO life. "What the—"

Holy shit.

I must have died and gone to heaven because Caitlin's mouth was on me, sucking me down like a popsicle she couldn't get enough of.

"This is one hell of a wakeup call." My hand slid into her hair as I thrust gently into her mouth, loving the way it felt.

"Good morning." She grinned before flattening her tongue against my shaft and licking from root to tip.

"Fuck, Cait," I breathed when she did some little tongue flick at the end.

"You like that?"

"I don't like that, I fucking love that. But I'd love you riding my dick even more." I pulled Cait up my body, and her legs fell to either side of my hips as she sat above me.

"Hi." She smiled again.

It was a sight I would never grow tired of. Her green eyes alight with love, laughter, and happiness. Over the last month, our relationship had only gotten stronger. Everyone loved her: my family, my friends, me. God, I loved her so fucking much. She was everything I'd ever wanted, and I couldn't wait for the rest of our lives together.

"Matt." Cait rolled her hips, teasing me.

"Ride me, Tink. Show me how much you want me." Grasping myself, I steadied one hand on her hip as she rose up on her knees slightly to work me inside her.

"Fuuuuck, that feels good."

"Move, I need you to move," she panted.

I gently thrust forward, finding the perfect pace while Caitlin circled her hips. She leaned down, kissing me. Hot, wet, dirty kisses that drove me wild.

"It's official," I murmured against her mouth. "You have permission to wake me up like this every morning."

"More..." she cried. "Harder."

Placing my feet flat on the bed, I really let her have it, fucking her faster, until our collective moans filled our apartment.

"Yes... *yes!*" Cait threw her head back, her thick red curls spilling down over her shoulders.

Sometimes I could hardly believe this woman was mine.

"Are you ready to come for me, Tink?" I sat up, sliding my hands under her arms and up over her shoulders, anchoring us together.

"Yes... God, *yes...*"

"Together." I kissed her, plunging my tongue deep into her mouth as I guided her up and down on me, over and over. "Clench for me, Cait," I urged, and she squeezed around me, milking me.

"Fuck… *fuck*!" The familiar tingling started at the bottom of my spine as I slipped a hand between us and rubbed her clit.

"Matt… I love you," she cried, falling over the edge. I buried my face in her neck as my own release slammed into me.

"I love you, so fucking much." Winding my hand into her hair, I gently tugged, forcing her to look at me.

"Hi."

"Hi."

"That was—"

"Incredible."

"It was." I smirked. "Give me five minutes and I might be good to go again."

"We have to pick Bella up soon."

"Ugh, that's today?" I flopped back on the bed, taking Caitlin with me. She rolled off me and ran her nose along my shoulder.

"We promised her. It's junior prom. She needs a dress."

"Junior prom," I grumbled. "She's sixteen."

"And you need to face up to the fact she's no longer a kid."

"She'll always be my kid sister."

"You're impossible," Cait muttered, pecking my lips. "I'm going to clean up and then make breakfast."

"I could always eat you." My brows waggled and she batted my chest.

"Behave."

"With you?" I captured her lips again. "'Never."

Caitlin finally untangled herself from my arms and climbed off the bed, smiling back at me. "I'm really happy, Matteo. I hope you know that."

She slipped out of our bedroom, and I stared up at the ceiling wondering how the hell I got so lucky.

Sure, we'd been through hell and back to get to this point. But she was worth it.

And I would spend my whole life showing her.

CAITLIN

"What about this one?" Bella darted from rack to rack, pulling out dresses. Pink ones and black ones, one with sleeves and strapless ones. Her excitement was infectious, and I couldn't help but get swept up in it.

"I could do your hair," I said, observing her latest favorite gown. "Something intricate and sexy."

"Sexy?" Matteo appeared out of nowhere. "I thought we agreed on innocent and demure?"

"No, you agreed to that. We overruled you and decided with sassy and sexy." I threw Bella a conspiratorial glance and she smothered a giggle.

"Something low cut and short," she added. "Like mid-thigh."

"What?" Matteo's eyes practically bugged out of his head. "No! No way is she wearing something mid-thigh with her… her breasts falling out all over the place."

"Did you just say… breasts?" Bella exploded with

laughter; so loud that we drew the attention of the store assistants.

"Is everything okay?" one of them called, and I smiled.

"We're fine, thank you. But I think we're ready to try on a few dresses."

Bella clapped. "I want to do this one, and the two we chose earlier."

"Good choice. Then we'll think about shoes and accessories."

"Accessories? Nobody said anything about accessories."

"God, Matt, you're such a drag." Bella followed the assistant to the dressing room while Matt and I took a seat on the plush velvet couch.

"It's nice that you're doing this with her."

"Let's be honest, Tink. I'm just here to pick up the bill."

"So dramatic," I rolled my eyes. "Bella looks up to you. She loves you and this is important to her."

"And I love you." He swooped in kissing me deeply.

"Matt, we're in public."

"What's the problem, Tink? Scared you can't control yourself around me?" He winked playfully.

I liked this side of Matteo. Oh who was I kidding? I liked all sides of him. The last month had been the best few weeks of my life.

I'd moved into Matteo's apartment immediately after everything happened. He'd offered to get me my own place, but I didn't want to waste another second without him.

We'd spent an entire week barely coming up for air. But

life had to keep moving. Matteo had responsibilities to his family, and I found a part-time job helping with children's dance classes at the VCTI where Arianne volunteered.

Nicco and Arianne had arranged for my mom to go into a drug treatment program and surprisingly she was doing well. Whether things would stay that way remained to be seen, but I could only hope she saw this was a real chance for change, now that she was away from Massimo. Things would never be the same between us, too much had happened. But it was a start.

Life was good.

Better than good, it was perfect.

And I thanked God every day that Matteo found me in that alley all those months ago and saved me.

"Okay you two, stop with the highly embarrassing displays of PDA," Bella called through the stall door. "I'm ready to show you the first dress."

"We can't wait," I said, elbowing Matteo in the ribs when he rolled his eyes.

"What do you think?" Bella stepped out and Matteo almost stumbled off the couch.

"Holy shit, pulce. Is that you?"

"Asshole," she muttered.

"I'm being serious, Bella. You look beautiful."

"I do?" She glanced down at herself, twirling slowly. "Caitlin, what do you think?"

"Matt is right, sweetheart. You look stunning."

"I want this one. I feel… like a princess. Connor is going to die."

"*Connor*. Who the hell is Connor?" Matteo stood up, frowning at his sister.

"Didn't Cait tell you? I have a date."

I jumped up, lacing my arm through Matteo's.

"Isn't that nice, Matt. She has a date." I dug my nails into his arm, and he stuttered, "Nice, yeah, real nice."

Bella snorted. "I already cleared it with Daddy, so you don't get to sabotage this for me." She stormed off toward the stall.

"A date?" He whirled on me.

"It's junior prom. Of course she has a date."

"Over my dead body."

"Maybe we can find a compromise." I pushed my body into his, running my hands up his chest.

"A compromise, you say. I'm listening."

"I'll go buy a set of that lingerie I caught you eyeing earlier, if you promise to play it cool about her date."

"The black and gold set with the suspender belt?" he whispered, eyes hooded with desire.

"And the crotchless panties."

"Fuck, Cait," he groaned, running a hand down his face. "You're killing me here."

"Do we have a deal?" I cocked my brow, waiting.

"Get it in the pink as well and I think we can come to an arrangement."

I smirked. "Men. So predictable."

He leaned in, brushing his lips along the shell of my ear. "You won't be saying that when you're bent over the back of the couch with my mouth on your pussy."

"Matt," I breathed, shivers skittering down my spine.

He stepped back, winking. "Don't start games you can't finish, Tink."

Bastard.

Bella appeared a second later, glancing between the two of us. "What's wrong with you?" she asked me. "Why are you all flushed like that?"

"Me? I'm fine."

Matteo caught my eye over her shoulder and shook his head with silent laughter.

"Your dress is beautiful," I tried to change the subject, ignoring the ache deep inside me.

"Are you sure you're okay?"

"It's hot," I said. "Don't you think it's hot in here?"

"I'm okay. Maybe you're coming down with something?"

"Maybe." I gave her a tight smile before suggesting we look for accessories. Bella was all too happy making a beeline for the rows and rows of purses.

"You okay there, Tink?" It was Matteo's turn to smirk.

"I'm fine," I said indignantly, brushing past him.

"We could always sneak off to a stall and I'll help you with your little problem."

"You're a bad, bad man, Matteo Bellatoni." Heat burned my cheeks, and he chuckled.

"Only for you, Tink. Only ever for you."

AFTER TORTURING Matteo with another couple hours of accessory shopping, we gave Bella a ride home and returned to our apartment to get ready for dinner with Arianne and Nicco, and Nora and Enzo.

We tried to get together as a group at least once a

week. It wasn't always easy, but family was important to all of them, and we tried our best to make it work.

"Wow, this place is—"

"Very exclusive." Matteo kissed my cheek, his hand pressed to the small of my back as he guided me to the front of the opulent looking building. He threw his truck keys to the valet and jabbed a finger in the young man's direction. "Look after her like she's your own."

"Y-yes, Mr. Bellatoni."

"Seriously, for a truck?" I rolled my eyes.

"She's not just any truck." He leaned closer. "If you play your cards right, she's the truck you might get lucky in on the drive home."

"Do you ever stop?" My lips curved.

"Never."

"Good evening," the maître d' greeted us.

"Hello, we're joining Mr. Marchetti," Matteo said.

"Ah yes, they are already at your table. This way please."

The restaurant was beautiful. It had a curved window with panoramic views of the river. Everything was gold and black, giving the whole place an elegant feel. And everyone was dressed to the nines, Verona's elite socializing.

It was world's away from anything I'd ever experienced, but I loved it.

"Caitlin." Arianne stood to greet us, pulling me in for a hug. "You look beautiful."

"Thank you, so do you."

"Cait." Nicco kissed my cheek.

"This place is amazing."

"Isn't it?" Arianne patted the seat beside her. "We don't come here often. Nicco doesn't like all the fuss. But since we're celebrating, I persuaded him."

"Celebrating?" Matteo said. "Nicco didn't mention we were celebrating." He sat on my other side, resting his hand on my knee. I loved that he always insisted on having some part of him touching some part of me.

"So… what are we celebrating?" Matteo prompted, but Arianne glanced over his shoulder.

"Oh look, here's Enzo and Nora."

The two of them joined us and we all did another round of hugs and compliments.

Nora picked up her menu and let out a low whistle. "I hope you brought your wallet, babe."

"Nicco invited us," Enzo grumbled. "I figured he'd pick up the tab."

"Classy, E, really classy." Matteo snorted, taking a long pull of his beer.

I was used to being with them in public by now. The constant stares and whispers. Matteo and his cousins were well-known around Verona County. Even more so since Antonio had stepped down.

He had made a surprising recovery and finally been released from hospital a couple of weeks ago. But health complications had deemed him unfit to continue his duties, so he'd officially handed Nicco full responsibility.

Matteo didn't go into much detail about it all, and I knew there would always be things he couldn't tell me, but I didn't resent him for it.

I loved and trusted him implicitly. His family were nothing like the monsters of my past. A past I rarely gave a second thought to now my life was full of people who genuinely cared.

"How is the job?" Nora asked me.

"It's great. The kids are just the sweetest, and Debra, the dance teacher, is talking about handing me more responsibility soon."

"That's amazing. I keep thinking that maybe college isn't for me, you know? I'm restless."

"E not keeping you satisfied, Nor?" Matteo chuckled, and Enzo flipped him off.

"Says the guy who didn't use his dick for eight months after he got ghosted by Caitlin."

"What?" I gawked at Matt, certain Enzo was busting his balls.

"It wasn't that bad, but it's absolutely not something we're discussing right now at dinner."

I smothered the laughter bubbling in my chest.

"Anyway, what's going on with you two?" Matteo changed the subject. "You said we're celebrating?"

Nicco took Arianne's hand in his and she nodded. "We have something to tell you," he said.

"We're pregnant." Arianne beamed.

"Oh my God, babe, that is… oh my God." Tears filled Nora's eyes. "What… how… tell us everything."

"Not everything, Boss. I don't need to hear your sex stories." Enzo smirked, adding, "Congratulations."

"It wasn't planned, so it was quite a shock," Ari said. "But we've taken some time to think about it and after everything that happened with Antonio, we've decided we want this." She gazed up at her husband as if he was the only man in the room.

"That's amazing news, congratulations." I hugged Arianne, emotion welling in my chest.

Matteo slipped his arm around my shoulder and pulled me into his side, dropping a kiss on my head. "One day," he whispered. "One day that'll be us."

I wanted it.

More than anything.

I wanted the big white wedding, and two or three little olive-skinned, dirty-blond haired babies running around. But we had all the time in the world, and I didn't want to rush a single second of it.

"Congratulations, guys. It's amazing news." Matteo lifted his beer in the air. "To baby Marchetti. May his—or her—life be filled with love, happiness, and super cool uncles."

"To baby Marchetti." We all toasted.

"Thank you," Nicco said. "You're the best friends a guy could have, and I'm lucky to call you family too." He lifted his drink in the air and smiled. "To family."

Matteo dropped his mouth to my ear again. "To family. My heart. My home. My everything. I love you, Caitlin."

With tears in my eyes, I smiled up at the man who had saved me in more ways than he would ever know.

"I love you, Matteo Bellatoni, and I can't wait to spend forever with you. No regrets?"

His lips brushed my cheek as he whispered. "No regrets."

PLAYLIST

Hard Sometimes – Ruel
Falling – Harry Styles
What A Time – Julia Michaels, Niall Horan
Champion – Elina
Deep End – Birdy
Falling Apart – Michael Schulte
Ghost of You – 5 Seconds of Summer
Dancing With Your Ghost – Sasha Alex Sloan
Us – James Bay
Remember That Night? – Sara Kays
I Don't Want to Watch the World End with Someone Else
– Clinton Kane
Iris – Natalie Taylor
Fix It to Break It – Clinton Kane
Hold Me While You Wait – Lewis Capaldi
Forever – Lewis Capaldi

AUTHOR'S NOTE

Ask any author and they'll tell you that writing has its ups and downs. I found myself writing Matteo and Caitlin's story during a period that has been physically and emotionally draining. That said, these characters were so easy to fall in love with and I hope I did their story of healing and second chances, justice.

As always, a huge thank you to my team for help getting this story to where it is now. To Andie, my editor-extraordinaire for always going above and beyond to meet my last-minute deadlines, and to Darlene and Athena for proofreading at the drop of a hat. To my promo team and my readers/spoiler groups – your enthusiasm and support for my characters and stories makes it all worthwhile. To Give Me Books for organizing yet another book promotion.

And finally, to the bloggers, reviewers, and bookstagrammers who continue to support me, without you I wouldn't get to do this, so a million times thank YOU!

It's goodbye to the Verona Legacy world for now... but who knows what the future holds!

Until next time,
L. A. xo

ABOUT THE AUTHOR

Angsty. Edgy. Addictive Romance

USA Today and Wall Street Journal bestselling author of mature young adult and new adult novels, L. A. is happiest writing the kind of books she loves to read: addictive stories full of teenage angst, tension, twists and turns.

Home is a small town in the middle of England where she currently juggles being a full-time writer with being a mother/referee to two little people. In her spare time (and when she's not camped out in front of the laptop) you'll most likely find L. A. immersed in a book, escaping the chaos that is life.

L. A. loves connecting with readers.

The best places to find her are:
www.lacotton.com

www.ingramcontent.com/pod-product-compliance
Lightning Source LLC
Chambersburg PA
CBHW070523220726
48294CB00019B/156